AURA

RYLD'S SHADOWS

ANGEL MARTINEZ &
BELLORA QUINN

Ryld's Shadows
ISBN # 978-1-83943-777-9
©Copyright Angel Martinez & Bellora Quinn 2022
Cover Art by Kelly Martin ©Copyright March 2022
Interior text design by Claire Siemaszkiewicz
Pride Publishing

RYLD'S SHADOWS

Dedication

For all the readers who asked for more AURA,
this is for you. We couldn't do this without you.

Chapter One

"I thought you guys were supposed to be more...buff."

"Buff?"

"Stacked."

Ryld looked at the man blankly.

"Bigger. Muscular."

"Oh. Yes. Most of the aelfe are, as you say, buff. My kind, the drow, are as tall, but usually lighter in frame."

The man took a sip of his beer. "So what happened to you? Did you miss the call when they were handin' out the tickets for the tall and ripped lottery?"

Ryld processed that for a moment. None of that made much sense. Nothing had happened to him, he'd missed no calls as far as he knew, and he wasn't sure what gambling had to do with anything. He wasn't sure how, but his best guess, given the previous question, was the man was asking why he looked different from other elves he must have met.

"Simple genetics. I was bred for certain characteristics. My coloring. My...ability with magic." Ryld took a sip of his own beer. "Those genetic traits also carry markers for a smaller height and build." *And madness.* But Ryld had already learned humans had a deep fear of madness, so he kept that to himself.

"Yeah, no shit. You can't be mor'n five and a half feet and a buck fifty, if that."

Ryld blinked again. Five and a half feet was an Imperial measurement, presumably of his height, which, while accurate, was terribly inefficient. Since they were discussing his size, the other observation should have been about his weight, but instead he spoke of money.

"I have more than a dollar and fifty cents with me. The drinks here are known to be expensive. I made sure I brought enough."

His drinking companion laughed. "Never mind. You're a funny one."

That was odd. Usually, he didn't understand human humor and they could be more uncomfortable with his presence than amused by it.

"It's time to go, Ryld."

Ryld looked up from the human he'd been studying into the face of someone who had exactly the elven characteristic the human had commented Ryld lacked. Tall and broad shouldered, with dark, ash-blond hair, and a countenance that made sure all but the most inebriated of bar patrons stayed well out of his way. Ryld sighed and set his drink down half finished.

He stood without argument and bid the human good night, as was their custom, and followed his minder outside. As he crossed the threshold, a small flicker of dark caught his eye, but he ignored it and kept moving.

"The establishment isn't closed for the evening yet," he pointed out as they walked down the row of vehicles in the parking lot.

Cress gave his own sigh. "No, but it will be very soon. We've been over this, Ryld. You don't have to stay until everyone else has gone, and they kick us out."

"But…there were still a few humans I hadn't spoken to."

"Nor do you need to speak to everyone in the place in one night."

"Oh. Did I transgress? Make a mistake?"

"I know what transgress means, and no, you didn't. They don't have a rule dictating how many people you should or should not speak to."

Ryld stopped. "How do they know then? How many is appropriate? Without a rule, how do they know?"

Cress stopped too and turned to look at him. Ryld managed to meet his eyes for a moment, then shifted his gaze to a spot over Cress' shoulder. Better to look at a point over the other person's shoulder than drop his eyes, he'd learned. A downward-cast gaze was viewed as subservient, rather than simply respectful.

"When there isn't a rule, they decide for themselves how many people they speak with, and who."

Ryld caught another flicker out of the corner of his eye and swallowed. "If there were a rule, it would be so much easier to know."

"I know, but that's how it is. Sometimes there are rules, and sometimes there aren't."

Cress spoke in a low, soothing tone. The one he used when he was being *extra* patient. When he wanted to avoid *a scene*. Ryld didn't want there to be a scene either. His head would ache for days after, and sometimes he couldn't even get out of bed if it had been particularly bad. It wasn't as if they hadn't had this conversation about rules before. There was no reason to get upset.

"Okay."

"Okay? Are you ready to go now?" Cress asked.

"Yes."

* * * *

"Another one, Brady. I don't have all night."

The bartender sighed when Hank thumped his fist on the bar. *That crack was already there. I know it was.*

"One *terabin* per customer. You know the rules."

"I'm not even close to drunk enough."

Shaking his head, the bartender put a glass of water in front of Hank. The water swayed. Maybe the bar swayed. A single *terabin* would've taken down a human and sent them to the ER. A second one would even put a troll on the floor. Hank was pretty sure he could manage another.

Brady put his hands on the bar and leaned in. "What's happened, Hank? This isn't like you."

Hank tried to answer, his short tusks getting in the way of his words. That hadn't happened since he was a teenager.

"What was that?"

"They fired me today. *Fired* me." Hank gave up trying to look menacing and put his head in his hands.

"Did you screw something up? Lose a decimal place or something?" What Brady knew about accounting probably wouldn't have filled half a jigger.

"No." Hank gulped a breath. "I did my job. I worked hard. But the new manager... She said I wasn't commensurate with the company image."

"Wait. Just 'cause of how you look? You could file a complaint?"

"Sure. Right. The pretty sylphs in the non-human rights office are gonna get right on that. Far as they're concerned, the only place I should be is locked up."

The bartender winced in an uncomfortable way and patted Hank's arm awkwardly. "Not like you're riding a varg down the street swinging a battle-axe. You're, you know, civilized. Still can't serve you another one."

A bitter smile curled Hank's mouth as he took the water and chugged half of it down. "Thanks, Brady. I feel so much better now. I'll... I guess I'll find something. Somewhere."

Out on the sidewalk, Hank breathed in the relatively fresh air. Poisoned with exhaust fumes and all the reek of too many humans in too small a space — still it was cooler and not the close, claustrophobic smell of the bar. He probably shouldn't have let Brady's racist comments go, but tonight he was too damn tired to deal with it, and Brady needed to count his lucky pebbles that Hank wasn't some thin-skinned goblin kid with a chip bigger than his head. *You're okay, Hank. You're one of the few good goblins. Not like those other filthy barbarians.* Pat the half-gobbo on the head and smile.

He wanted chilies, huge bags of them, wanted to drown in the capsaicin high they'd bring. But he had enough sense, even this drunk, to know he'd overdo it in his current state of mind and probably end up in the ER from a ghost pepper OD again.

Once was enough.

No. Go home. Get some sleep. Figure it out in the morning.

He'd manage. He always did.

It was just that this time he thought he *had* managed. Found a place for himself. Reached the spot where things could be routine, and he could be normal. Just another worker bee in the crowd.

The screech of tires on pavement yanked him out of his reverie and just about made him jump out of his skin. His reactions were muddled and slow, but the shot of adrenaline racing through him as he stared at the truck only inches away was almost enough to knock him sober.

The driver's door opened, and a tall elf got out. His face was full of haughty arrogance and disdain, as was usual for aelfe, but his words were even and neutral as he asked, "Are you all right?"

Before Hank could answer the passenger door opened, and another elf got out, this one a drow. "You are walking where vehicles are supposed to be driven."

"Get back in the truck, Ryld," the first elf said sternly.

"But, he's walking where vehicles are driven. That's against the rules."

"Get. In. The. Truck. Ryld."

"But…"

"Now!"

The drow cut his eyes away. He made some odd gestures but sat back down and closed his door. Even from behind the windshield Hank could pick out how unnaturally blue his eyes were. He'd only ever seen drow with red eyes or white.

"Are you all right?" the blond elf asked again.

Hank pulled in a slow breath, then two more. The rising nausea settled, and he leaned a hand against the lamppost on the corner. "Fine. I'm fine. You stopped in time."

The elf stared at him, maybe thinking Hank owed him a thank you for not ploughing over him. Finally, he gave a sharp nod. "Okay. Good."

That was it. He climbed back into the truck, shut the door, said something sharp to the drow and drove off.

Weird. That was...weird. Though maybe the *terabin* had made the whole interaction so strange. Maybe there hadn't been any blue-eyed drow insisting on road rules. Hank shook himself, hurried across the street and reached his apartment building without any further bizarre incidents.

He'd go to AURA in the morning. To job placement. He hated doing it since it always felt like such a failure. He should be able to find work on his own. Make his way without the help of bureaucratic agencies. But rent would be due soon. He *could* stop paying the utilities for a bit. He'd done it before.

No. That's going backward. Not going back to scraping by day to day. Just no. Go to placement. See what they can find. Job hunting while you have a job is always better.

* * * *

A human doctor had told Ryld that human and elven physiology was similar in many ways, but they had important differences in metabolism and biochemistry. In the years since the first Event had brought elvenkind into the human world, the lessons in those differences had been steep and painful. Many compounds that were medicine to humans were poison to elves, and vice versa.

Ryld added a small white tablet that same doctor had prescribed for him to the bowl of a mortar and crushed it with the smooth blunt end of the pestle until it was powder. He tipped the powder into a waiting mug of hot tea. Swallowing the tablet left a chalky bitter residue in his mouth so repellent he gagged the moment it touched his tongue. Putting it in his tea with a generous amount of honey helped disguise the bitter flavor.

Cress sat on his sofa, oilcloth in hand, cleaning a sharp curved blade. The light caught the bright edge and sparkled. Deadly. Dangerous. Beautiful. *Sharp sharp sharp.* Ryld closed his eyes, squeezing them tight for a moment while he took a gulp of the tea. It was hot and scalded his tongue, making him gasp, then choke and cough.

Cress sighed. He rested the tip of the blade on the edge of the table where a mark in the wood was etched from the same blade resting in the same spot many times. "Do you need help?"

Ryld shook his head, coughed again, then got his breath back. "No." He took another sip, careful this time. The honey helped but couldn't completely disguise the bitterness of the medication. A human medication. One not toxic to his kind. The human medical doctor had explained in great detail how it worked with human body chemistry in the brain to limit hallucinations and psychosis.

He had explained that he did not suffer from hallucinations, but the doctor asked, very nicely, if he would take the drug anyway. As an experiment. He did not remember what followed, but sometime later he found himself in the counseling chamber at AURA with no recollection how he got there or how long he had been there. Still, he had apparently agreed to take the medication because he was sent home with a bottle of the tablets.

Violet had been his minder then. She had been very kind to him but had been unable to stay with him after one of the creatures had nearly suffocated her.

"Ryld. Ryld…"

Ryld looked up, forcing himself to focus. Cress had that tone of voice that told him he'd called his name more times than he'd heard. His mug was empty. Had he drunk it all, or…? He glanced at the sink. No signs of splashed tea in the sink. He must have drunk it. He set the mug down carefully.

"Is it daylight yet?" Ryld asked.

Cress pointed with the blade at the window. The sky was still dark, but a shade that told him the sun was just below the horizon. *Time to sleep.*

"You have an appointment this afternoon. There are a few things I need to do that may take me longer than your appointment."

"Of course. I am able to get by on my own. I'll return here…"

Cress shook his head. "No. I'd like you to stay at AURA until I return."

Ryld cut his eyes away, forgetting not to look down. Flustered, he forced himself to look up again but couldn't speak when he met Cress' eyes. He shifted his gaze to the window. Not black. The softest gray outside. "I…I am able…"

"No. Stay at AURA until I return for you. Okay?"

The darkness that should be only outside the window crept along the edge, seeping in like a fine mist. Ryld licked his lips. "All right."

He agreed. He didn't want to agree. There were so many things he found fascinating here. So many things he didn't want to be pulled away from. Alone, he could do what he wished, without having to think of anyone lurking behind him, looming over his shoulder. He turned toward the hallway that led to his bedroom and stopped. *Social necessities.* "Good night."

"Good night, Ryld."

"It is morning, though," Ryld had to add before he went down the hall to his room.

* * * *

Hank couldn't remember getting through his apartment door the previous evening. Goddesses, that had been stupid. Wasting money on *terabin* that he was going to need for food. The evil stuff never made anyone feel *better* in any way, and he'd woken up on his living room floor with the headache to prove it.

Really stupid.

The shower helped a little. Forcing himself to eat his last piece of gouda on toast helped more. Starting the day with calcium-deficiency cramps would've been, as the humans here said, the icing on the cake.

He sat at his two-person kitchen table with his head in his hands, breathing slowly so he wouldn't start to cry. Wouldn't do anything but make his headache worse again. Still, it was all so frustrating. He'd been doing so well, getting good job reviews and even thinking about putting some money away each week.

If he'd known this would happen, he would've started saving months ago. If he'd had any warning, he could've stocked up on cheese and yogurt and bones. Now, he'd have to stop by AURA social services and go through the humiliation of getting government-funded Tums to keep functioning until he could afford good food again.

Of all the things Mum gave me, goblin calcium requirements was the thing that was least helpful after crossing over.

One last slow breath, and he managed to gather himself together enough to get dressed. Important to get there early or all the temp jobs would be gone. He reached for the dress shirts automatically, then stopped himself with a sigh. No one was going to hire a half-goblin, sight unseen, for an office job. More likely, it would be manual labor. *Henley, sturdy khakis and boots it is, then.*

Keys, wallet, sunglasses — since his eyes weren't up to dealing with the morning sun — and the *tek* stone from Mum on its leather thong around his neck for luck, he strode from his apartment, determined to make the best use of the day. Wallowing got you nowhere. A goblin did what a goblin had to do.

Some of his determination trickled away when he reached the AURA building and spotted the long line at placement. Nothing he could do about it though, so he took his place at the end of the queue behind a purple-haired sylph who gave him what she probably thought was a Very Forbidding Look.

"Just here for a job, ma'am," Hank murmured while his gaze wandered around the lobby. "Not for conversation or to bother pretty women."

She narrowed her eyes at him but turned back around and ignored him in favor of typing on her phone. Probably would get an office job right away. Maybe even reception in one of the departments in the AURA building. Wasn't there an elvish prince serving as the police captain now? They liked pretty things. Did police departments have receptionists?

Hank let his thoughts drift from tidbit to tidbit to keep himself from really thinking as the line moved slowly forward. Plenty of people got in line behind him as he waited, so at least he hadn't been the last to arrive and he was inside an air-conditioned building, out of the sun. There were positive notes to the day already.

Any happy thoughts he'd gathered died when he reached the front of the line.

"Name?" the pixie girl behind the front desk chirped.

"Hank Onyx-Wainwright." He signed in without being told. It had been a while, but he'd done this before. "Could I see Miss Ono?"

"Oh sweetie, sorry." The pixie batted absurdly long lashes at him. "Miss Ono retired last month. Mr. Oakfrond's free. You can go see him. Third door on the right."

Hank swallowed a sigh and headed down the hall to the offices. The kitsune job counselor, Miss Ono, had been his favorite. She'd believed in him and had helped him with the right classes and test prep to pass the CPA exam. She'd never pre-judged where his skills would lie. This new counselor, as Hank feared from the name, was an elf.

Not that he had anything against elves. Problem was, they so often had something against him. No, that wasn't fair either. Most drow and kolle had no problem with him, more or less, it was the aelfe who looked at him like something they needed to scrape off their shoes. There were a lot of aelfe in New York. When Hank turned the corner into the indicated office, he bit back another sigh. Of course Mr. Oakfrond was aelfe.

Oakfrond proved to be no exception to the usual *oh, you're a half-goblin* reaction. He glanced up from his computer with an expression that suggested he'd bitten down on a lemon slice and waved a hand to the metal folding chair in front of the desk. "Have you been actively looking for work?"

Hank leaned forward with his elbows on his knees, making himself smaller. "No, sir. I was employed until yesterday."

"Previous employer?"

"Tripartite Consulting."

"As janitorial staff?"

With a great deal of effort, Hank did *not* grind his teeth. "As a CPA, sir."

That got him a snort and a skeptical look. "Do you have something to prove that?"

"No, sir. But it's in the employment records."

Oakfrond didn't bother to check. He continued to train that hostile glare on Hank. "How long were you employed there?"

"Two and a half years, sir."

Elegant eyebrows of pale green crept up toward Oakfrond's hairline. "Did you hit someone? Is that why you were fired?"

"No, sir. New management..." *Was incredibly racist.* "They wanted a certain corporate culture. I wasn't a good fit."

"Have you worked construction?"

Any job. Take any job. This isn't the time to be picky. "It's been a few years, sir. When I first crossed over. But I have."

"Good." Oakfrond nodded, apparently satisfied that finally his prejudices had panned out. He handed Hank an index card with a name and address. "Report to the foreman tomorrow. Nine o'clock. Don't be late and don't start fights."

"Yes, sir." Hank folded the card and stuck it in his wallet as he fled the office.

At least he knew who *not* to see the next time he came in. He'd manage until a real job came up. It was fine. Miss Ono had asked once why he didn't go to the goblin community to look for work, and it was still tempting. But most goblins in this world regarded his lack of claws and his not-quite-the-right-shade-of-green skin with suspicion. Being half-human hadn't always been accepted back home, and it didn't seem to be much different here. No, Hank was on his own, without family or clan, and he couldn't think about that too much, or his determination not to cry was going to crumble. *I miss Mum and Dad so much...*

He took the elevator up to social services, took a number and sank into one of the chairs lined up by the back wall. Tums, then back home to rest and take stock. He thought he had enough food to last him until the end of the week, if he was careful. Otherwise, he might have to plan some restaurant dumpster diving. Not ideal, but he was going to make it through this.

I will.

Chapter Two

From the time he was a small child, Ryld could remember people staring at him. Some with curiosity, many with revulsion or fear, a very few with pity. All, he was certain, did not know or did not care that he recognized the nuances of the emotions that filled their eyes. What he hadn't known was why. His coloration was unusual, and he was smaller than any other drow he knew, save for perhaps some of the females. But he was still a drow just like any other, or so he'd believed.

For all that he had not understood why he garnered such interest from other children and adults alike, he had never been invited or encouraged to integrate into any social circles, nor was he the subject of an undue amount of cruelty. Not deliberate cruelty from those uninvolved in his upbringing at least.

Part of the drow maturation process involved a great deal of social positioning, cunning maneuvering and biting treachery. Actually, those carried into adulthood for the drow, just on a more devastating scale. Ryld had been excluded from all of it. If any dared to break from the ranks of agreed ostracism imposed on him, they were swiftly brought back in line by their peers with hissing whispers behind hands or sharp reprimands from adults. The isolation had driven him to despair.

In those years, he could not have conceived a time he would have preferred that isolation. Would never have dreamed he'd long *not* to be corralled and directed. Would not have believed for a moment that a series of casual touches and a hand on his arm guiding him would feel so unwelcome and intrusive. By the time he and Cress had exited the subway a few blocks from AURA, Ryld's skin was crawling and the shifting shadows at the edges of his vision had grown from small spiders to tiny lizards. He ignored them, as well as Cress' hand pulling him along, and the stares of the people they passed.

At least now he knew the stares were not because of the color of his skin and hair and eyes. The people who lived in this city were used to the strange and unusual. If he had to guess, probably the brightness of his choice of garments against the dusty gray of his skin made them glance his way. Or maybe just the way Cress dragged him along while he was trying to focus on a hundred other more interesting things calling his attention.

Humans had an endless variety of garments. Colors so vivid he could get lost in the dyed fabrics for hours. The textures were every bit as varied, and Ryld spent as much time as he was allowed collecting as many different types as he could. Today he wore a long shirt in a fabric so light it floated and clung with his movements. The fuchsia color almost made his eyes water if he looked at it too intently. The feel of it against his skin had made him want to wear nothing else, but

Cress had insisted he must wear trousers of some sort. In order not to ruin the feel of the shirt too badly, he had chosen dark, close-fitting trousers in a fabric that sucked to his lower half like a second skin and could stretch in every direction he moved. He was still not convinced they were named yoga pants because people wore them during the activity, rather than named after the way they stretched just like the people doing the activity itself.

Ryld noticed the way Cress lowered his shoulders and his posture went from leaning forward to more upright, the grip on his arm loosening fractionally as they entered the elevator that would bring them to the floor where Counseling was located. Did he relax because they were in a building filled with people capable of *dealing with* Ryld if there was *a scene*? Or was it because Cress knew he'd soon be rid of Ryld for an afternoon? *Probably both.*

When Cress first had taken the job as his minder, Ryld had been polite, but encouraged no familiarity. He had already made the mistake twice, believing his minder would become his friend. It was the third one, Thomas, who had told him being his minder was a job, and they were not going to be friends. He was glad Thomas had told him. Now that he knew the social structure, it was easier to stay within it, and he didn't have to try so hard not to make his minders uncomfortable.

Cress still had hold of his arm as they went through an archway into the reception area. He halted in the center of the room. Two corridors led in opposite directions from this room. The one on the right led to Counseling, but Ryld had learned they must wait until they were told to go down the hallway before doing so.

There were several people already waiting, some standing, some sitting in chairs, some chatting and some tapping on electronic devices. *So clever those devices.* He coveted them with an intensity rivaling his passion for brightly colored clothing. So far he had not been able to obtain one.

"Ryld. Ryld."

A loud snap of fingers directly in front of his face made him involuntarily bare his teeth, although he did manage not to snarl. He immediately stopped, forcing his lips closed and focusing on Cress. He had been told humans were unsettled by the pointiness of his eyeteeth for some reason. Not that there were many humans in the room. Were there any at all?

"Ryld! Pay attention. Stay here."

He stared at Cress, and Cress stared back until Ryld shifted his gaze away.

"Stay," he said again.

Cress walked away, and Ryld stood where he had been left. Sometimes when he was told to remain in a location it was acceptable for him to move as long as he stayed within a given parameter. However, Cress seemed particularly unsettled today, and Ryld thought it best to stay exactly where placed rather than call after his retreating back to ask where the arbitrary boundary might be.

* * * *

Generally, Hank tried to mind his own business when he was in the AURA building. Crossovers in various states of adjustment, employees doing all sorts of important or mysterious things, cops pelting down a hallway — none of these things were his business.

But it was hard to ignore the little guy in his fuchsia tunic. Impossible, actually, since even out of the corner of his eye, the color beat a tattoo against his *terabin* headache.

Not the little guy's fault. At first, Hank thought he was a kid, maybe a teenage drow, but when he turned his head... *No, definitely adult.* And the elf with him, his keeper, his prison guard, his...something, was being a complete asshole.

If someone had snapped their fingers in front of Hank's face like that? Well. He wasn't a violent person, but it would still have been tempting to bite a couple off.

Now Mr. Fuchsia just stood there, rooted to the spot, like he wasn't allowed to even take a seat or anything. Some instinct drew Hank up from his own chair despite his headache, and he approached slowly, not wanting to appear threatening.

"Um, hi." *Good. Great opening.* "Are you okay? Ryld, was it? Was that guy — do you need help?"

Large blue eyes blinked slowly at him. Not a human shade of blue, more like...cyan or something. From a distance they probably looked all one shade, no iris, no pupil, just a solid blue, but up close Hank could make out a faint darker ring of blue within the blue that suggested an iris, and an even darker point at their center.

"I am okay. Yes, my name is Ryld. I don't need any help. Thank you. Are you here for counseling?"

All right. Counseling. They wouldn't let anything bad happen to the little guy — to Ryld — and they'd know if someone was abusing him, right? Hank summoned up a smile. "No. Not today. I'm here to get some calcium supplements."

Ryld stared at him, unblinking now. He was so still it was almost eerie, then his hands twitched, just a little bit. "Are you an orc?" His blank face became more animated with the question.

Anger prickled at Hank's spine since he'd just about had all the racist crap he could take in twenty-four hours, but there was something so sincere, so open about the question that Hank wasn't at all sure Ryld knew what he was saying.

"Um. I'm half-goblin, if that's what you mean." He cleared his throat uncomfortably. "You really can't go around saying that to people. Someone might punch you."

This got him a slow blink. "I've offended you? The words 'I'm sorry' don't mean anything, I've been told, but other sources say it is customary to say the words to make amends. Is it okay for me to tell you I'm sorry, or would you like to hit me?"

There were other people in the room paying attention now. They were kind of hard to miss, standing in the middle of the reception area, and Hank heard a few titters.

He sent a quick glare toward those snickers and lowered his voice so only Ryld would hear. Something was up. Something that he'd seen in some humans, but he didn't know enough about. Just because the little guy was different was no reason to be rude, though. "It's good to hear *I'm sorry* when someone means it. And, no, I don't want to hit you. I just wanted you to know that other goblins and half-goblins might not be, um, understanding about it. *Orc* is a, well, it's a racist slur. It's not meant kindly."

"Oh…thank you. That's very helpful. I would like to be helpful in return. It's very unwise to walk where motor vehicles are supposed to be driven...if you didn't know that."

Hank gaped at him a moment before the memory came back of bright blue eyes in the passenger seat of a truck. He hadn't been a drunken illusion. Sort of a relief. "That was you last night. I was a little plastered." Then he realized that might be too slangy a term. "Drunk. I was drunk and wasn't being careful. But thank you, I'll be more careful."

A big smile, the first he'd seen on the drow, flashed across his face, then just as quickly disappeared. "If you get drunk often, you might need a minder. They can be helpful too. Sometimes." He laughed, a quick soft sound.

"Ryld."

They both looked at the elf who had just called his name. "Come."

"I have to go to counseling now," Ryld said, as if Hank couldn't already deduce that. "Good night."

He walked to the elf who was eyeing Hank suspiciously and, all right, the asshole wasn't being threatening, just high-handed. In a moment of contrariness, Hank smiled and called back, "Have a good day."

Then the receptionist from the social services side was calling his name, and he lost sight of the pair. *A minder.* Someone thought the little drow needed a minder. Hank shook his head as he went to have his mandatory talk with the nutritionist. Ryld had seemed like he was doing okay on his own.

* * * *

"Just choose one. They're all the same."

They are not all the same at all. One colorful box had a cartoon tiger, another a cartoon bird, another a cartoon frog, another a cartoon bear…none of them contained any of those animals. Mostly they contained grain and sugar. With those ingredients one would guess they all tasted the same, as Cress suggested, but that wasn't true. There was one that was nothing but tiny grains that were so hard and tasteless they were like chewing sand. Awful. He wanted to avoid making a mistake like that again. Food cost money, of which he had a finite amount. Wasting food would waste his money and then he would have neither.

Cress sighed.

Ryld reached for a box. This one had insects on it. He was almost certain it did not contain insects but he had to be sure. Not that all insects tasted bad. He showed Cress the box.

"This one has insects on it." There was an unnerving quaver in his voice.

"Bees. They make honey and the cereal contains honey. There are no bees in the box."

Ryld nodded. He put the box back on the shelf.

Cress sighed again. Louder.

Ryld chose another box. This one he had tried before. It was palatable, so he put it in the cart. The next aisle contained shelf after shelf of soft drinks. Ryld didn't like them. The carbonation tasted like poison, the ones with unnatural sweeteners tasted like death. Even so, he turned the cart down the aisle because he could not resist looking at the bottles. Rows and rows of jewel tones, shimmering black, glowing amber, orange the exact same shade as tiny poisonous frogs. Real ones, not like the cartoon frog on the cereal box. He had been assured none of the beverages were poison, not to humans or drow. He understood why someone with malevolent intent would make a poisoned drink look ordinary, but not why anyone would make an ordinary drink look poisonous.

The next aisle contained many small bottles of pills, bandages, sprays, ointments... There were no dried herbs hanging from the ceiling or crucibles bubbling or mysterious creatures gibbering in cages, but this was a place one could find healing all the same. He didn't need healing and knew it was acceptable to skip the aisle if it didn't contain anything he needed, but he turned and read the names on the labels. So many. So very many. How could anyone look at them all? His eyes caught and stopped on the words *calcium supplement*.

The orc — no, that was offensive. The half-goblin. Hank. He'd heard the receptionist call out that name, and the half-goblin had answered so that must be his name. Hank had said he was at AURA for calcium supplements. He picked up the bottle.

"Do you need those?" Cress asked.

"Yes." It was not a lie. He needed them because if he saw Hank again he could give them to him, and then they might have a conversation about them, and he could discover why Hank went to AURA for calcium supplements instead of the store. He put them in the cart without explaining any of that to Cress. It was so hard to explain anything to him. Cress wasn't unintelligent, Ryld knew that, but he was slow to understand complex connections such as why Ryld wanted the calcium supplements.

Once the bottle was in his cart he no longer had any interest in shopping for groceries and turned the cart toward the place where he could pay for his items, and they could be packed in the bags he'd brought to carry them home.

"Is that all you're getting?" Cress asked.

"Yes."

Cress put a hand on the side of the cart, making him stop. "Are you sure? You didn't get everything on your list."

"I'm sure." Ryld paused. "I don't feel well. I want to leave. Now." Not a lie. He didn't feel well, he felt excited.

Cress looked at him a moment longer, then let go of the cart. Ryld hurried to pay for the items, and they left the store.

Ryld had lived underground his entire life. He had seen above ground only a few times at night. Descending into a tunnel was the most natural thing in the world, and yet going down the stairs to board the subway made all the fine hairs on the back of his neck stand on end, a growl waited to rumble in his chest, and the shadows darted about with anticipation.

The powerful reek of the tunnels alone was enough to scrape along his nerves. The press of bodies and shouts and laughter of people competed with the head rattling noise of the trains. His senses were battered before they even reached the platform. His hands itched to cover his ears, and he desperately wanted to close his eyes, but that was dangerous. His heart was beating fast and hard as they boarded, and the deep breaths he took did not seem to help him get any air into his lungs.

"Keep it together, Ryld," Cress said firmly. "You're okay. Everything is fine."

"Hey, what's wrong with him?" a passenger asked.

"Nothing. He's fine," Cress said, grabbing Ryld's arm.

The grip was hard and unexpected, and Ryld pulled away without thinking. Cress took his arm again and pushed him forward. A woman in front of him unexpectedly stopped at the same time, and Ryld ran into her.

"Watch it!" she snapped.

Sound disappeared. There was nothing but the drumming in his ears. His vision was rapidly narrowing. Oh no. There was about to be *a scene*. It was his last coherent thought.

* * * *

For Ryld, losing control was not the bad part. He rarely remembered anything after crossing a certain point. The bad part came after. It was disorientating to be on the subway train one moment, with his bags of shopping, surrounded by people and loudness and foul air, Cress' sharp tone in his ear and hard hand shaking him. The next moment all was quiet and dark. There were no bags in his hand, no people and loud noise, no subway train.

His sight returned first. He was outside. He lay curled on his side, a damp piece of cardboard under him. The sun was down. He did not recognize anything around him. Sound returned next. A hum of traffic, people talking as they walked, music escaping the confines of a restaurant. The rest of his senses all turned on, the ache of cold seeping into his bones, small pains in his arms and larger ones in his body. The alleyway he lay in smelled of rot, garbage and urine.

Shadows moved in erratic darting dances at the corners of his vision. They had no form, no substance, just transparent shapes of darkness. That was good. Perhaps none of them had broken free this time. His stomach tightened and a sourness coated his tongue at the thought that he was probably wrong. At least he hoped that whatever havoc his beasts had caused had not caused anyone serious harm. The fact that he was alone was worrying.

He had escaped Cress' care, which meant Cress had either let him run because he had no choice, or Cress had become too injured to follow him. He hoped it was the former. The beasts were extremely difficult to kill, although kill wasn't the correct term because they were never really alive. Independent of him they were mindless and ruthless, viciously attacking anyone near them, bent on destruction and ruin. They could not be reasoned with, and weapons did not hurt them. Magic was the only thing that could destroy them.

Ryld pushed himself up to sitting. His clothing was dirty and damp. He hurt, but not so badly he thought anything was broken. His hands were dirty too, but only with grime, not blood. One of his shoes was missing. His foot was bleeding. With one thumb he touched the wound, then brought the blood up to touch above his heart, then the ground. Blood was a powerful offering and must not be wasted…the words came back to him from long ago. He believed blood was powerful. He had been bleeding when he'd made the offering that opened the sky and brought him from his home to this new world. He had wished to be free from his tormentors then, and here he was. *Should I wish for something now?*

He didn't always. Sometimes when his blood ran, he simply gave it freely. *What would I ask for?* He closed his eyes. He was lonely, but he knew better than to ask for companionship. Cress was a companion. He didn't hate Cress, but he would not have chosen to spend time with him. Sometimes Cress made him feel even lonelier, though how that could be when he was not alone he didn't understand. There was so much he didn't understand. He wouldn't want to understand everything, though. If he understood everything, there would be nothing left to explore. That would be intolerable. But…he did wish someone, anyone, could understand *him*. Yes. That was a good wish for the offering of blood. *I wish there was someone who could understand me.* He wiped the last trace of his blood onto the dirty pavement.

He stood. The dampness made him shiver with cold. He smelled of fear and the reeking alleyway. The street was not familiar, so he chose a direction. Time passed. He didn't know how long. Finally he saw buildings he knew. Home was still a long way to walk, but AURA was close. It would be safe to rest there.

He didn't have an appointment. He knew that, even if he didn't know the day. Counseling appointments happened when the sun was up. He did not have an emergency. At least he didn't think he had an emergency. He stood in the center of the lobby. If he didn't have an emergency, what should he say to the AURA officers?

He was still trying to decide when the elevator doors on the far wall opened and a small group came out, talking, laughing. Their smiles died and their laughter cut off when one of them saw him. An aelfe.

"Hello? Are you all right?"

"I don't have an emergency."

The aelfe, a blond one, offered a puzzled smile. "Okay. That's good to hear. But you don't look too good there, bud."

Ryld looked down at his clothes. "I am not clean, no."

"It's all right. I mean, it will be." The aelfe reached out a hand but didn't touch. "I'm Officer Flax. Did you want to come up to medical? Have someone check you over?"

"No, I don't want to." He paused. "But that's irresponsible. I don't know what happened to my minder."

That seemed to give the aelfe pause. The human officer behind him, who had been checking his phone, murmured something in Officer Flax's ear. The aelfe's eyes widened.

"Oh. Got it." His smile seemed a little strange when he turned back to Ryld. "What's your name, bud?"

Ryld blinked at him, though he should have given his name in return since the officer had. "Ryld."

"Good. That's good." Officer Flax swept a hand toward the elevators. "We're supposed to get you up to Counseling if we see you. People have been looking for you, you know. Lysander probably knows what happened to your...minder."

He was speaking slowly, more carefully than he had a moment before. It was always a strange thing to see — how just because a person didn't understand him, they assumed he wouldn't understand them. At least he wasn't afraid, or hostile. The human next to him, however, he was suddenly afraid.

"I don't have a counseling appointment. I was underground. The subway...the...the shadows..." The beasts weren't really shadows. A shadow was just the absence of light, but when he tried to explain what they really were, it just created confusion. "Did they hurt anyone?"

Officer Flax spoke softly, moving to his side as if to herd him toward the elevators. "Not that I've heard, bud. It's okay. You're here now. And Lysander's expecting you even though you don't have an appointment. He's kinda worried."

Ryld sighed. "Lysander is very kind. He can't help. Not really."

The human officer took a step toward Ryld, but Officer Flax held a hand up to stop him. "There's lots of ways to help, you know. They've got showers up there and stuff."

Ryld would rather go home, but he already knew they were unlikely to let him go there alone now. His head ached terribly, and he just wanted to get out of the light. He stared toward the elevator. Waiting, patience, delaying what he wanted were not things he did very well, but he knew it was what people expected of him. It was polite.

"He's bleeding. He should go to medical," the siren officer with them said in a sharp, too loud tone that made Ryld wince.

"Doesn't have to if he doesn't want." Officer Flax was definitely herding now, slowly, toward the elevators even as they all turned to look at the trail of bloody footprints on the shining tiles. "Doesn't look too bad, right?"

No one was grabbing him. That was good. Ryld thought if he started moving, maybe no one would. With a tiny sigh, he limped toward the elevator and only Officer Flax came with him, waving the others off as he punched the correct number for Counseling.

Lysander was waiting for them when the doors opened, so one of the officers must have called him. Phones were useful. Ryld found himself wanting one again.

"Goodness, there you are!" Lysander's tail waved madly behind him, something Ryld had come to associate with strong emotions in fauns. "Cress called in. He's a little banged up, but fine. Come in, come in. Would you like a shower and some clean clothes from the box? The nymphs brought all sorts of new things for the collection yesterday."

Ryld looked down at himself. There had been times he had thought clothing ruined and had been surprised after they were washed, but he didn't think this time the lovely fuchsia shirt would be salvageable.

"I need to go into the dark."

"Of course, dear. Once you're cleaned up, let's get you settled in one of the cave environments. We can turn the lights all the way off if you need." Now Lysander was herding, gently, though it made sense since the sooner they moved the sooner Ryld could escape the light.

More patience. More waiting. He must be polite, but he didn't think he could bear it. He had made his arms stay loose at his sides while he walked here, but now he gave into the tension and curled them to his chest. "Now. Please."

"Ungrateful brat."

Lysander and Flax were the only ones near. They hadn't spoken the words.

"Filthy."

He turned, looking for the one who spoke, but couldn't see her.

"Ryld," Lysander spoke even more softly now. "That's fine. If you'd rather have the dark first, that's absolutely fine. Can I have one of the night-adapted medics come look at your foot while you rest?"

He nodded. He should speak, so people would understand him, but they wouldn't really anyway, and he couldn't make himself. Instead he stared at Lysander, willing him to make the darkness appear now, before it was too late.

"Come on, hon. This way," Lysander whispered, and with a hand barely on his arm, guided, got them moving, his little hoofs tapping on the tiles, then silent when they reached the carpeted hallway to Counseling.

He knew where the caves were. He had appointments there sometimes. They weren't far. But it felt far. So many steps until they were finally there, and Lysander turned the lights off as he'd promised. Lysander kept his promises.

Chapter Three

Flax stood in the elevator lobby after they'd gone. Just stood there. Shivering. *Gods*, that kid gave him the willies. It wasn't that he was different. Neurodivergent, the humans said. Okay, maybe that was part of it, since Flax didn't have any training, any knowledge of how best to approach someone like Ryld. No, it was the rumors. The whispers. Everyone in the building had heard about him by now. The kid—fine, not a kid, but damn it, he was even smaller than Kai—they'd found in the Appalachians, living in a cave. The monsters he could summon. Rumors of giant spiders.

He shivered harder. Nothing freaked him out like giant spiders. *Big bad hunter, yeah, that's me, but the giant spiders back home were nasty, nasty beasties.*

He shook himself one last time and called down to dispatch. "Hey, Molly? Has anyone been dispatched to check for monsters in the subways?"

"Negative, Officer Wolfheart. Director Hiltas went himself and gave the all clear."

"Oh, um, okay, thanks."

Still, he stood staring at the entrance to Counseling, trying to calm his racing heart, wondering how close he'd been to pushing the little drow into summoning monsters. This was what happened when *kalesi* were separated. *Makes an elf all jumpy.* Sage needed to get done with his stint at the Academy. Ash needed to come off night shift in medical so they could actually sleep together again.

The elevator doors slid open behind him, and he spun, knives out.

"Whoa, whoa, Flaxy-boy!" Sin stood there with his medical bag and both hands raised. "It's just me! Not looking for a fight!"

"Gods…" Flax sheathed his knives and ran both hands over his face. "Sorry, sorry. I need to get home."

"I'll say. I'd say go get yourself some, but I just passed Ash in the treatment rooms." Sin edged around him carefully. "You take it easy. Maybe get a beer and put your feet up."

Flax tried to laugh it off, but he held the elevator door so it wouldn't close before he could escape the lobby. Escape the building. Behind him, Sin muttered, "Damn freaky elves, the whole bunch of 'em."

"Some of us more than others," Flax muttered. He let the elevator doors close but instead of going down to the lobby he pushed the floor for medical. Ash might be busy, but he might be able to spare a moment.

He did *not* rush through the doors to medical like a child running up the steps in the dark. Nope. Not at all. Once there, his heart already started to calm, though. Kellen was on the front desk—friendly, kind-hearted Kellen—and the place had the normal sounds going on of a medical department at the end of the day. People gathering lunch bags, saying goodnight. People typing up chart notes. Nothing bad here. Nope.

"My hunter? Is all well?"

At least he didn't jump out of his skin when Ash appeared at his elbow. He did turn and fling himself into Ash's arms, though. "I'm okay. I'm... I needed to see you."

Ash gave a soft laugh, interrupted by a more concerned sound. "What has distressed you? I would ask what has frightened you, but my Flax knows no fear."

"It was that strange little drow. Ryld. He was... I took him up to Counseling."

"That is good to hear." Ash set him back to search his face. "That he is found."

"Yeah. I feel ridiculous reacting like this. But I got a little skittish around him. I—" Flax cut off as the doors to medical slammed open, and an elf limped through.

Cress? Isn't that his name? He leaned against the intake counter, head on his arms. "They were huge. They told me, but I didn't... They were huge."

"I should see to this." Ash patted Flax's chest and let him go to approach the patient.

Flax wasn't going anywhere, though. He needed to hear this.

"Let's get you into bay two," Kellen said. "How bad is the injury and what happened?"

"It bit me, I think," Cress said as he started limping toward bay two. Ash followed to help Kellen with the intake, and Flax silently trailed after them both.

"What happened exactly?" Kellen asked again while he pulled supplies from a cabinet.

"You know about the drow fre...uh, the drow? He lost his shit again. That's what happened. On a packed subway, he freaked out and suddenly people are screaming and bleeding, being slashed to ribbons." Cress shook his head. "They looked like some kind of demented baboons, or deformed dogs. Three of them. I had to go after them to protect the humans and by the time backup came, the drow was gone."

While he talked, Kellen silently went about setting out gauze and antiseptic and got him to lower his pants. "Were there a lot of injuries?"

Cress snorted. "Tons. Mostly minor, but you know what happens when people panic. They run everywhere. Trample each other. The human police came, and human emergency services. But what's a human going to do against that kind of magic? I had all I could do just to keep them relatively contained." He hissed as Kellen started to clean the slashes on his leg.

"That's it. I'm done. I can't take any more of this shit."

"This happens often?" Ash asked.

Cress shook his head. "Not this bad, but...it's constant. He's never *not* surrounded by this...like, fog of dark magic. It's always seeping out of him. Even humans that don't have a drop of magic in them can sense it and look at him sideways. You'd think it would at least get better when he's asleep, right? I mean, how can anyone keep that up? But no, it gets even worse. He goes to sleep and the whole apartment drops to freezing cold, or heats up like a furnace, and if there's any light in the room at all the shadows crawl on the walls. Creepy as fuck. I'm so done with this job."

Flax leaned against the doorframe, out of the way and as silent as he could make himself. He narrowed his eyes toward the end. Okay, the kid had freaked him out, too. Something was wrong. Wasn't controlled about his magic. But to call him a freak? To accuse him of constantly radiating dark magic? He didn't have a lot of sympathy for someone who just quit when a job got hard, and maybe that colored his thinking, but he wondered how much of this little speech was to make Cress look better and the little drow guy look evil.

"Did AURA enforcement get there to kill the creatures?" Flax did his best to keep the ice from his voice. From the admonishing glance Ash shot him, he'd failed.

"They got there." Cress snorted. "Lot of good they did. Things were gone by that time."

"Gone?"

"Yeah. Soon as that little *sulitek* stops freaking out, they poof. Like they were never there." At the silence in the room, Cress glanced up. "What?"

Flax shook his head and walked away. The racial insult had been particularly vile, and Cress knew it. Made Flax like him even less. In the morning, he'd have a talk with Kai. Not that he'd probably be bringing Mr. High and Mighty anything he didn't know, but just in case. It would help to get a more objective picture of things as well.

Poor kid was gonna need a new babysitter, too.

* * * *

It hadn't been a bad day. Hank had stayed until dark at the construction site helping to clean up debris and secure tools. The humans had kept most of their comments to themselves and only some of them eyed him coldly. Most of them just seemed happy to have someone strong to haul things from one place to another. That was fine. He carried, hauled and shoveled all day.

Not work he wanted to do forever, but physical labor was fine for now. Hank didn't have to think or to worry. Just do.

He walked quickly toward the subway station that would take him home. The site was in one of those neighborhoods humans sometimes called *transitional*. Still a lot of crime in the area with lots of new, pricier construction starting. Humans were strange like that. They let communities fall apart, blamed the people living there, then displaced those people to start over instead of making it better.

He'd adapted to living in their world, but humans were still weird.

"*Kach, orc-tza!*" a voice called behind him in lowland goblin.

Hank quickened his pace. The station was in sight, half a block away. If he ignored the taunt and kept walking, he could make it.

A young goblin stepped out of an alley to block his path, swinging a chain and grinning nastily. "Maybe the orc don't understand goblin, Pej. Growin' up with human stink on him an' all."

"Maybe he don't," the first voice answered, and Hank turned to see another youngster close behind him, smacking a baseball bat against his hand. "Don't mean we can ignore him walkin' here."

"I don't want trouble, little brothers," Hank said in goblin, hands held wide in a gesture of non-aggression. "Just want to get home."

Four more goblin teenagers, variously armed, had joined them.

The one with the bat, presumably the leader, hawked at his feet and continued in English. "We aren't your brothers, *orc*. Not your cousins or your neighbors. You don't belong here and you got some balls walking down our street."

Hank knew it didn't matter what he said, but he blurted out, "It's the only way to my subway stop."

Chain-kid smacked his weapon against the sidewalk and threw his head back to let out an ululating goblin war cry. The others took it up, and Hank dropped into a defensive crouch. He didn't want to hurt them. Kids. They were kids.

Bat-kid swung first, aiming for Hank's head. Hank brought an arm up, the blow jolting him all the way to his shoulder. The other kids attacked as if they shared one brain, swinging chains, tire irons and two-by-fours. With a weapon of his own, Hank could have defended himself relatively well. Barehanded, he just did the best he could, trying to keep the blows off his head and ripping weapons out of their hands when he got hold of them.

At least one kid got a two-by-four to the face, though by that time, the brawl had deteriorated far enough that Hank wasn't sure if he'd done it or one of the kid's compatriots had missed.

By the time police sirens wailed up the street, Hank was on his knees with his arms over his head, too dizzy and pummeled to keep fighting. Great. He was going to end up unemployed and in jail for hitting juveniles. The downward slide was just going to keep right on going.

Someone was yelling, "Weapons down, boys! AURA enforcement!" as he slid into the dark.

* * * *

Beeps. Soft voice. Too bright lights. Hank reasoned he was either in Medical at the AURA building or in a human hospital somewhere in the city. No, no, he definitely smelled yeti along with elf and human. AURA, then.

44

He tried to move a leg. An arm. *Ow. So much ow. Goddesses.*

"Oh, hey. Are you waking up for us?"

Hank turned his head, which didn't like that movement one bit, to find a handsome smile attached to a handsome face beside his bed. There were horns and wings... Right. Incubus medic. Hank had seen him for minor things before. *What's his name?* Nope. Asking too much from his head again.

He probably should've asked. Instead, he blurted out, "Are the kids okay?"

One black eyebrow climbed as the incubus said, "You've gotta be kidding, right? Those fucking punks beat you into the pavement and you wanna know if *they're* okay?"

"They're just kids," Hank whispered.

"I get it. Goblin instincts about kids." The incubus checked vitals and shone a light into Hank's eyes, which his head *really* didn't like. "But it's still weird. Anyway, yeah, the little shits will be fine. One's got a broken nose. Another's got a broken wrist. Some bruises and crap. Nothing serious."

"Hey, Sin!" a voice called from the doorway. "You were supposed to call me when he woke up."

The incubus, Sin, rolled his eyes. "He *just* woke up, Officer Ants In His Too Tight Pants. Lemme do my job first."

The AURA officer, an aelfe, swaggered into the room and took a seat in one of the plastic chairs. "My pants are not too tight."

"Oh well. They must just get tighter around me, then." Sin adjusted an IV and gave Hank a wink before he sobered again. "Sir, can you tell me your name?"

"Hank Onyx-Wainwright."

"Excellent. So far, so good. Any idea where you are?"

"AURA Medical department, I think."

"Perfect. Not gonna ask if you know what happened since we kinda covered that." Sin waved a hand to the officer. "He's all yours, Flaxy. No thumbscrews in the patient rooms, please."

The officer, who really had every right to be angry, shook his head and laughed. "You're ridiculous. Go away so I can chat with your patient."

Sin raised the head of the bed and handed Hank the call button. "You press that if he starts to annoy you. Or even if you just want to watch me throw him out."

A smile would've been appropriate, but Hank's face hurt too much. The officer moved his chair closer when Sin left and pulled out a tablet to take notes.

"Morning, Mr. Onyx-Wainwright. I just—"

"Hank. Please. Just Hank, Officer."

"All right. Well, you can call me Flax, then. Just a few quick questions, and I'll let you rest. What were you doing on that street after business hours? It's nowhere near the address on your ID."

"Going home from a job site." Hank took a breath. That didn't hurt too much. "Temporary. Through job placement."

"All right. Easy to verify." Flax tapped away on his device. "Have you been unemployed long?"

"No. Just this week." *I really don't want to go through all that again.*

The officer just nodded. "The goblin kids said you threatened them. Wanna tell me your side of it?"

"I knew it wasn't a great neighborhood." Hank hitched himself up farther to take the pressure off a sore spot on his back. "I should've left with everyone else, but I wanted to be helpful."

"Being in a bad place doesn't make you guilty of anything, Hank," Officer Flax said gently.

"I tried to walk fast. Tried to pretend I didn't hear them when they shouted. I guess me being on their street was threatening enough." Hank sighed. *Oh, yes. That hurts.* "Half-goblins…where some of them are from, half-goblins are drow foot soldiers."

"Maybe. Did you threaten them?"

"No. I told them I was trying to get home. Shouldn't have called them little brothers. Just made it worse, I guess."

"Who swung first, Hank?"

"The kid with the bat, I think. Probably. It's all a little hazy now."

Officer Flax stood and offered a smile. "All right. That's all for now. I'll be back if we have more questions."

It would've been nice to say something amusing or witty to that. Hank was too tired and just closed his eyes to shut out the light. At least it wasn't a prison medical facility, and the floaty feeling told him there were pain meds going into his system. Goblins healed quickly, but he'd take all the help he could get right then.

* * * *

The weekly department heads meeting wasn't something Kai liked to miss. He *wanted* to know what was happening in the rest of the building. Often, the activities of other departments affected his own. Anything could, and often did, affect the Research department.

This week though, the residual feel of physically manifested psychic beasts had stayed with him to the point where he was distracted and on edge. Tenzin patted his knee under the table, which both helped to ground him and made him think wicked thoughts about that hand sliding higher...

Sweet Mother, what had Tirola from Accounting been talking about? No, no, that was fine. Val was talking about the recent goblin gang fiasco.

"I don't think Judiciary will come down on Mr. Onyx-Wainwright hard," Savannah, the head of Legal, offered. "I've suggested community service since his record is squeaky clean. Honestly, up until this week, he's been a textbook, model crossover citizen."

"Good to hear." Val gave a firm nod. "Other than the goblin incident, we're where we always are. Short-staffed and searching for recruits."

"Aren't we all?" Lysander sighed, shuffling his papers. His normal cheerful façade had cracks in it today, and Kai had to wonder about *that*, too. "I've just lost the last minder we hired for Ryld. I'm sure that's my fault. Temperament-wise, he probably wasn't the best choice. But I thought a warrior would be at least a *safer* choice. Ryld's last relapse was too much for the minder, though, and if a single bad moment serves to drive him off, he was never as brave as he claimed."

Kai snorted. "They rarely are." Then gestured to Val. "Present company excepted, naturally."

"Naturally," Val said at his driest. The department heads all stared at the table a moment, deep in their own thoughts, until Val said, "I wonder, though..."

Kai waited and finally prompted him with a wry smile, "What does the great and mighty Captain Hartgrove wonder?"

"Tenzin, you have a patient downstairs with a hell of a lot of defensive wounds. A large patient who probably could've done a hell of a lot more damage than he did. Lysander, you have need of someone patient, strong and, one hopes, kind. Savannah, you're suggesting community service for Mr. Onyx-Wainwright. I think all this comes together rather fortuitously."

"Where is Ryld now, Lysander?" Kai leaned around Tenzin to see the head of Counseling.

"He's in one of the cave environments. There are physical symptoms after an episode, and he needs the dark and the quiet."

Kai stood, the need to be *doing* vibrating through his bones. "I'd like to talk to both the half-goblin and to Ryld before we assign another minder."

Val shot him a dark frown. "Kai, that's not your decision."

Kai waved a hand, hoping the gesture didn't appear dismissive. "Hmm. I claim rights as a drow mage in this instance. No one in this room can feel what Ryld does. Not as I can."

"It's fine, Val." Lysander's smile almost looked cheerful again. "I'll welcome an outside consult in this case."

Good, good. Kai gave everyone nods and stalked out. Maybe the half-goblin would be the right person. Maybe the situation was unsustainable. Maybe... Well, it wasn't Ryld's fault. Of that, he was quite certain.

He debated with himself who he should talk to first, but there wasn't much point discussing the placement with the half-goblin if Ryld was too unstable. That decided, he found half a dozen trivial things that needed to be done, dithering, delaying, before making his way to Counseling. Although, the area Ryld was currently housed in would more accurately be called psychiatric treatment. It wasn't that he didn't like Ryld, or that he found him unsettling. No. Seeing Ryld was simply a reminder of exactly how twisted and cruel his own people could be.

Not every drow lived and breathed manipulation or was arrogance-driven to conquer every other people within their reach, but enough fit exactly that description that it was hard sometimes to argue the prejudices held against his own kind.

He set his thoughts aside as he entered the artificially created cave. He'd entered one exactly like it thousands of times before being taken from his world. He knew it was exact, or as near to as possible, because he had designed it when Counseling had requested specifics for a drow living space and he'd modeled it after his own bower back home.

The interior was dark, but not complete blackness. A soft cool glow came from a lantern on one wall. Ryld sat cross-legged on a low platform covered in furs. His eyes were closed, and his face peaceful.

The light from the lantern cast his silvery hair and light gray skin in shades of blue that complemented the color of his eyes when he opened them to regard Kai.

"Kai Hiltas. Director of Research." Ryld spoke softly.

"Correct." Kai put a palm to his chest and offered a polite bow before he sank to the floor in a position mirroring Ryld's. In drow, he continued, "How do you fare, little brother?"

Ryld tilted his head, as if considering. "Lysander says I no longer have to take the medicine the humans made, since it doesn't work for me. The shadows are small today. I didn't mean to hurt anyone, before."

"I know." Kai laced his fingers together as he regarded Ryld steadily. "Everyone will be well. The humans. The aelfe who accompanied you. Although, he is a coward and has decided not to return. A few shadows frightened him. Such are the Dawn People."

Ryld nodded, as if he'd expected the news. He leaned forward, lifting a hand and letting it hover hesitantly over Kai's arm, then drawing it back. "It's not the shadows that frighten them." There was a great deal of sadness in those words, no matter that they were simply spoken.

"What frightens them, then, little brother?" Kai asked as gently as he possibly could.

"I do. They made me too well. I try not to be a monster, but they all feel it. They stare. They move away. They don't know why, but they do."

Kai shook his head. "They fear what they can never understand. I have known monsters. Many of them. True monsters blend with their environments. Fool you into thinking that they speak fair and true words until it is far too late, and the blade is already sunk in your back. True monsters…well, they are not you."

"The monsters made me. What else can I be? Kai Hiltas, you look like the monsters too, but you aren't one. Even you find it difficult to look at me and hide your thoughts."

"I *try* my best not to be a monster." Kai snorted. "I'm not certain everyone in this building has always agreed I'm not. And I can't tell you that you are ordinary. That would be a lie. And I can't tell you that I'm not angry with the monsters who made you. That, too, would be a lie, since I know they made you for their own selfish gains. You are *powerful*. So powerful. And all drow are raised to fear power, to some extent. Some things, one can't leave behind."

"I too thought I could leave the fear behind. It followed me here, though. The fear, the whispers, the names, the shadows…they all followed me here. *Sulitek*. They think I don't know what that means."

"Hmm. Yes. Those things followed us, too. A drow mage of any sort must be evil, you see. I heard much of that before I carved a place here." Kai spread his hands. "But we are drow. We are adaptable. We absorb knowledge. We learn. Though you are right. In some ways, switching worlds has only changed the places where we encounter fear. As a drow queen's seeker, I was at least physically insulated by warriors and battle mages. Here, I have faced armies of undead, a stone mage, a mad drow intent on building a mage's tower. So many things I never thought to. Ones learns. One adapts. Are you aware of your shadows when they manifest? Do you see their shapes?"

"I am aware of the shadows always. They are always with me. I keep them down." He made a motion with his hand, thumb toward the floor, like he was squashing a bug. "But sometimes they get too big, and they get away."

No one has trained you, child. You're right to think that frightens me, but it also makes me, oh, so very angry. "When they get away, do you know their shape, then? Or are they truly away?"

Those large blue eyes so unusual for a drow blinked at him. "All shapes. Any shape. Monsters. They want to be monsters, so they have claws and teeth to rend and destroy. That's all they ever want to do."

Kai nodded, though his thoughts spun and spun. "They were designed as weapons. The monsters, the true monsters, designed you as a weapon. So careful in construction. So careless with what happened after." He shifted onto his knees, preparing to rise. "Counseling would like to give you a new minder. Someone they hope is braver and kinder than the aelfe.

He would be a half-goblin, if he agrees. Would you do well with someone like that, do you think?"

"If you call them an orc, they might punch you."

The smile slipped out of Kai's control. The youngster was absurdly charming in his way. "That is absolutely correct. Also, it would be rude. But I think you would be polite."

"I am polite. Except when I'm not. But that's an accident. I know goblins. Some are kind. Some are cruel. Just like drow."

"A fair point." Kai tipped his head in acknowledgment. "Would you like to meet him before you decide?"

That did not get the expected reaction. Ryld looked visibly upset. "I have to decide?"

"Not if you don't wish to, no." *Oh dear. That was quite the misstep.* "If you'd rather have Lysander make the decision, that would be acceptable to everyone, I'm sure."

Ryld went very still, and Kai was about to ask if he'd made another misstep, but apparently Ryld was just thinking it over before answering, "Lysander is very kind. But he doesn't understand all the time. Deciding is…hard. But yes. I will decide."

"Very good." Kai rose and bowed again, falling back into old habits. "I will let them know. Thank you for speaking with me, little brother. I'm sure I'll see you again soon."

Kai had taken only a few steps when Ryld said so softly he wasn't sure if he meant Kai to hear, "I wish you could be my minder, Kai Hiltas."

Chapter Four

Hank's room was situated in such a way that he could see the nursing station through the open door if he raised the head of his bed. Maybe all the rooms had a nursing station view. He didn't have any way to know. The meds were making his brain wander.

His view that afternoon included a huge, white-furred being — Tenzin. Every crossover knew Tenzin from their time in assimilation. Lots of initial medical workups. Lots of checkups to see if they were thriving. Tenzin was especially soothing for the newly arrived.

A drow stood with Tenzin. A sharp-dressed drow in an expensive charcoal-gray suit and subtly floral red and cream tie. Interesting. Maybe he was an advocate or someone else in Legal. Maybe he was in public relations, though that would be unexpected. Maybe…

Those thoughts cut off abruptly when Tenzin straightened the drow's tie, smoothed a stray wisp of frost-white hair back, and kissed the drow's forehead. *Oh. Oooohh.* That *drow*. The infamous Kai Hiltas. Everyone also knew *him*. By name, anyway.

He was…shorter than Hank had expected. Though everyone looked small next to Tenzin. *That's nice. That he comes to see his husband. Nothing unusual there.*

Hank's brain stopped its meandering again when Hiltas strode down the corridor. And kept striding. To Hank's room.

"Great. What now?" Hank murmured as anxious thoughts invaded the med haze.

"Afternoon," Hiltas began briskly before he even cleared the doorway. "I'm glad to see you're awake."

"Mr. Hiltas. Um, hi?"

A crooked smile twitched at the drow's mouth. "Kai is fine, please. Especially if I'm to call you Hank, as Tenzin instructs."

"That's fine, sir. Am I in trouble?"

"A certain amount, as I understand it." Kai pulled over the doctor's rolling stool and took a seat. Maybe so he wouldn't be shorter than Hank on the raised bed. "But nothing insurmountable. Legal states that you'll be asked to do community service rather than jail time for brawling on the street. Good news, yes?"

"Yes, sir. That's very good news." Inwardly, Hank cringed. Community service might mean he wouldn't have time to work. *Oh well. One thing at a time.*

"I have a proposal. One that would fulfill your community service, since it truly is a service to the community at large, but would come with a small stipend, as well." Kai's smile showed teeth now. "Ah, I have your attention."

"What…would it be, sir?"

"If you don't stop calling me *sir*, I may change my mind." Kai huffed a breath and looked off into the distance, maybe gathering words. That couldn't be good. "There is a young drow. He is a bit different from most drow. The way he processes information. Reacts in social situations. Also, he has powers that get away from him in—distressing circumstances. They can be dangerous."

Hank considered this. Something about it all sounded familiar. "All right."

"He needs someone with him. Someone who can act as a buffer against these situations. Who can perhaps anticipate and prevent some of them. Someone who can protect bystanders if it comes to that. Do you have any magic?"

"Just the usual amount." Hank shrugged. "I can shield some. Do some wind strikes. Nothing big or fancy."

"That will do, I think. For a start. His name is Ryld and he—"

"Ryld?" Hank sat up farther before he remembered that was a bad idea. "I know Ryld."

"You...?" Kai blinked at him. "You do? And how is this?"

"We met the other night. Then we talked in the lobby while he was waiting for an appointment."

More blinking. "I see. And how did you find Ryld?"

Hank shrugged, though he knew perfectly well how he'd felt that day. Protective. Amused. "I thought he was fine. I don't know him well, of course. But he was nice to me. Didn't care much for his minder."

That smile crept up again. "*That* one is no longer employed here. Would you like to think about it? What I'm asking, I'll be frank, could become dangerous."

"To help Ryld? Sure. I don't have a problem with that." How dangerous could the little guy be?

"Good. As soon as you're on your feet, I'll take you to him."

With that, Kai put the rolling stool back in its place and swept out. Probably the weirdest job interview Hank had ever experienced.

* * * *

The darkness and familiarity of the cave was comforting, at first. The dark gray walls, mostly bare room, and lack of distractions allowed Ryld to stay calm. Outside, he had worries and responsibilities. The price he must pay for all the delights the outside offered. Staying in the cave for longer than a few days started to have the opposite effect from the initial comfort. Ryld knew this from experience and this time was no different. It was time to go home.

There was one obstacle yet before he could do so. He must have a new minder. Lysander said he would come today. Then Ryld must decide. This had caused him no end of worry, and the shadows slinking in the undergrowth of the small forest were the size of house cats. If they got much bigger, he might have to retreat to the cave.

Ryld took a deep breath and closed his eyes. No. He didn't want another *scene*. He wanted to go home, wanted to touch his things, wanted to go for a walk and see all the lights and color and people. If this new minder was like Cress…or worse, he would need to be responsible and choose.

The first voice to reach him through the trees wasn't Lysander's, though. The sharp, precise tones belonged to no one in Counseling. A glimpse of white hair through the trees. *Kai.*

A small part of Ryld was disappointed when he spotted someone with Kai. He knew, of course, that Kai was the head of his own department and terribly important. The thought that he would be Ryld's new minder had been childish. He knew that.

Oh. But the person with Kai…

"Hi, Ryld." Hank gave him a little wave from behind Kai's shoulder. "How're you doing?"

"I-I'm…" It was custom to give a brief answer to the effect that there wasn't anything wrong. Except it was also not polite to lie. "…better." It was as if finding the right word had a sort of power of its own to make it true. Ryld relaxed. "Were you hit by a vehicle?"

Hank chuckled, a deep, warm sound. "No, no, I took your advice and stayed out of the road. But some goblin kids didn't like that I was walking on their street. So I guess you could say I was hit by a pack of goblin kids. Though I'm better, too."

Ryld smiled. "Good. Are you here for Counseling?"

"Hank is here at my request." Kai had stepped to the side, so they had clear sight of each other while he observed their conversation like a crow waiting for prey to emerge. "Remember that we spoke of someone who might be appropriate as your new minder. A half-goblin. That is Hank."

When Ryld only stared, Kai went on with a little flourish toward Hank. "Would you like Hank to be your new minder, Ryld?"

Ryld stood. The shadows swirled around him, invisible fingers brushing through his silvery hair. "You said I could decide?"

"Yes. You can decide, or you can leave it to Lysander if you prefer."

"How long?"

"How long?"

"How long before I have to decide?"

Kai tilted his head, looking more corvid by the moment. "You may take as long as you need to, Ryld. But I'm told that your return home hinges upon your decision."

Ryld made a small motion with his hands, then clenched them to make them stop and be still.

"That hardly seems fair," Hank put in. "He has to choose me now or stay when he clearly wants to go."

Ryld brought a hand up and pointed forcefully at Hank. "Yes! Those words." He put his hand back down quickly. Pointing at people was impolite.

He expected Kai to be annoyed. Important people were often annoyed with him. Instead, Kai clasped his hands behind his back and rocked from heel to toe. "Well, then. I am open to suggestions."

Hank scratched at his head, mussing the already shaggy, thick hair. It was a red brown. Not a goblin color. "I dunno. I think…and I don't mean any offense, sir."

"Go ahead. Call me that one more time." Kai flashed sharp teeth in a parody of a smile.

"Sorry. Habit. Um, but I kinda think the whole minder thing is, well, it's a little shitty."

Kai rolled a hand in a *go on* motion.

"Would it be okay…I mean, I know Counseling won't let Ryld go home by himself. But I could go as a…as a companion? A helper? Just until Ryld can decide on someone official again."

"Yes!" Ryld shouted the word. He winced and put a hand over his mouth. Shouting wasn't polite. Shouting drew attention. Shouting would make people stare disapprovingly. He waited, but neither Kai nor Hank told him to be quiet.

Slowly he removed his hand and spoke the word again, quietly. "Yes. That is what I decide. I would like Hank to be my...companion."

"A reasonable choice, little brother," Kai said in drow, then switched back to the human language. "Very good. I'll have a car come round since Hank should pack some things before heading to your apartment. Too much traveling for tired people otherwise." Kai tapped a forefinger against his teeth. "One moment, though."

He vanished through the trees, so quick and graceful he might not have been there, and Ryld suffered a rise in anxious thoughts again. Had he changed his mind?

He was back in a moment, though, holding a paper-wrapped packet out to Ryld. "You should have two shoes for going home."

Ryld accepted the package and bowed his head. "Thank you, Kai Hiltas."

* * * *

The world outside of the AURA building had not changed, but it seemed much larger all the same. For a time, when he had first been ripped from his world and found himself on a forested mountain, Ryld had been alone. Truly alone. For the first time ever. It had been terrifying and exciting in equal measure. He didn't know for how long he was alone on the mountain. Long enough to have found a shallow depression that could barely be called a cave and make it his home. Long enough for the seasons to change from cold to warm to cold again. Long enough he had thought perhaps the drow ritual leaders were wrong about what became of a person after death, and perhaps the world he'd found himself in was the afterlife.

Then the strange people had come. Humans. He didn't know that was what they were at the time. They had been kind, coaxed him with their strange words and food to come down from the mountain into the valley where a lot more humans lived. He'd started to learn their language and he'd learned their fear of the great spiders that had come to their home. One day the humans all gathered and built a large fire in a pit and made mounds of food. They'd laughed, shouted, danced and played music that had hurt Ryld's ears, then stars started to explode in the night sky and Ryld had fled. The shadows that got away from him were huge. He had heard screams...and sometime later he was taken to another wondrous place and met Lysander. He learned he was not in the afterlife and learned many other things. This new wondrous place would be his new home.

Hank had a home too. The building he lived in reminded Ryld more of a hive. Many, many small rooms behind locked doors. They weren't all Hank's rooms, of course. They were shared by many, many people.

The building Ryld lived in was smaller, but the rooms were larger. "My minders have all lived in the other bedroom in my apartment. Would it be...is it acceptable for a companion to stay in the same room my minders used?"

Hank didn't sigh. Didn't make a face. He considered the question. "I'd say yes. It's your apartment, right? So, you can tell me what space I can use."

"Hank."

Hank looked up from the bag he was packing.

"Are you unhappy? This is your home. I wouldn't be happy if I had to leave my home."

"Oh." Hank looked around the room as if seeing it for the first time. "Things haven't gone the way I'd planned. That did make me unhappy. But the apartment's just a place to sleep. To come back to after work. It's never been *home*? Not really. So I'm not unhappy about leaving for a bit."

"It's a shithole," Ryld said. He shifted on his feet uncertainly. "That's what a place you don't want to live in but have to stay at is called, isn't it?"

Hank let out one of his soft, warm laughs. They reminded Ryld of the fuzzy fabric humans sometimes used for blankets. "I guess it is kind of a shithole. I *have* lived in worse places, when I was first trying to make my own way here. But yeah. Kind of a shithole."

Ryld smiled. He was sure the sharpness of his teeth was showing and made an effort to smile with his lips closed. He liked Hank's laugh. He didn't entirely understand what had made him laugh, but unlike most times when he didn't understand laughter, Hank's laugh felt good.

Once Hank had gathered all the things he thought he might need, they left the apartment. The driver helped Hank put his belongings in the back of the car and then they were off.

It was different having a companion already. Hank didn't watch him constantly, for one thing. He hadn't grabbed him or directed him once. He hadn't reminded him of everything he needed to do. He was just there beside him. He told Hank, "I'm glad you won't have to stay in your shithole tonight."

"You know what? Me too." Hank's smile had to work around his tusks, but it was still a smile. "And it'll be nice not being alone."

Yes. It will.

By the time they arrived at the building Ryld lived in, he was thinking of food. "Are you hungry?"

"I am. What do you usually do for dinner?"

"I eat food. Most things. Sometimes a food looks good but tastes bad. And sometimes it looks like poison but isn't. What type of food do you like?"

"I'll eat just about anything. Half-goblin, half-human, I get all the omnivorous stuff going on. I really like cheese, though."

Ryld nodded. "They each have their own names and taste different, but are all still cheese," he recited, then smiled at Hank. "Like a family."

"The cheese family is a large one." Hank said it seriously, though his eyes sparkled. He took his bags from the car and swept one of them toward the building. "Lead on. I like your building better than mine already."

"It's not a shithole," Ryld agreed. "I have cheese. A few kinds. Maybe they're cousins." He led the way into the lobby, slowing as they passed the rows of mailboxes. Hank didn't remind him to check his box for mail. He reached the elevator doors and decided he would get the mail tomorrow.

Hank looked around at everything with interest rather than growing annoyed that the elevator didn't come more quickly. When Ryld opened the door to his apartment, his new companion stopped in the threshold. "Wow. This is…wow. This is really nice."

"It's much better than the cave I lived in," Ryld agreed. "If it's too hot, or too cold, you press these buttons." He showed Hank the thermostat on the wall. "This space is all one room, but you can tell by the items where the kitchen is, the table to eat on and the sofa and chairs over there for relaxing. Down here are the bedrooms and bathroom." He led Hank to the first bedroom and opened the door.

The room was neat and tidy. A bed, dresser, nightstands. None of the items Cress had brought with him remained. "This was the room Cress stayed in, but I don't see anything that belongs to him here now."

"Okay. Good. If I find anything, we'll ask Lysander where to send it." Hank put his bags down and took something from around his neck that he placed on the nightstand. "There we are. Now I can sleep here."

Ryld shifted on his feet, staring at the nightstand.

"Ryld?"

"It's rude to ask about personal things. But not always."

"Oh. Yeah, I guess. I think it's okay to ask as long as you let it go if the person doesn't want to tell you." He picked the object up again to show it to Ryld. It was a stone, gray patterned with green and gold, with a hole. The stone was strung on a leather cord. "It's a *tek* stone. From my mother. I don't know if goblins in other worlds even have them. It's to keep your child safe."

"Oh. How does it work?"

"The parent pushes some of their shielding into the stone. But mostly, the ritual's about love." Creases had appeared at the corners of Hank's golden eyes, a sheen on them of water gathering. "A parent's love for their child. To keep them safe. I tell myself... I tell myself I can still feel her in the stone. I don't know. It's probably my imagination."

"You miss her. I'm sorry."

"Thank you." Hank wiped at his eyes. "I do. I miss them both. I don't know why it's hitting me so hard tonight."

Ryld lifted his hand. Very slowly he placed it on Hank's arm. Touch was a strange and dangerous thing. Mostly, he didn't like it when someone touched him. But sometimes he ached with the need for touch. Some touches, even uninvited, had been comforting, lifting him from despair. Logically he knew that the type of touch, the person doing the touching, and the circumstances around it were all factors in how the sensation made him feel. Still, it was confusing to try to anticipate how other people might react when he touched them, no matter what his intention might be.

"You are in a strange place, with a strange person. Sometimes that can bring emotions to the surface when we don't expect them."

Hank covered Ryld's hand and gave a little squeeze as he drew in a deep, shuddering breath. "You're right. Sure that's part of it. Probably still a little tired, too. Dinner. Let's go see what we can round up."

Relief was one of the feelings Ryld liked best. So far Hank had made him feel relieved several times in the few brief encounters they'd had. He hadn't recoiled from his touch. Surely a good thing in someone who was a companion.

Chapter Five

Kai had left his office door open at the end of the day, so the conversation at his admin's desk drifted through to him.

"Please tell me he's not still working, Mindy." Tenzin's voice had that tired note in it. The one Quinn described as being *so sick of your shit, Kai.*

"I don't think so. He swore he was done." The volume of Mindy's voice changed, more than likely as she swiveled in her seat to peer into his office.

"I still hear typing."

"You want me to go in and dump him out of his chair?"

Tenzin heaved a sigh. "No, thank you, Mindy. I think I'll manage."

"I'm not working," Kai blurted out when Tenzin entered his office. "It's personal correspondence that I'd hoped to finish before you came up. I am... struggling."

Tenzin's forbidding glower softened as he picked Kai up, settled in the oversized desk chair, and set Kai in his lap. "Oh? What could you possibly be struggling with?"

Kai allowed himself a snuggle and a nuzzle at the thick white fur of Tenzin's shoulder before he answered. "An email to Lady Jessamine in Pacific Elvenhome."

"But you're in regular contact with her. Why would you...?" Tenzin leaned forward to read the screen. "I see. It's about Ryld. And you've gone a bit old school Kai here and there. If you're searching for advice, why not ask the drow queen who also lives there?"

"*No.*" Kai spat the word out short and sharp. He cringed. "Apologies, beloved. But Ryld is a drow construct. Something a drow queen would find far too intriguing and *far* too tempting. No, I'm not putting him back in the hands of drow royalty when he's managed to escape them here."

"All right." Tenzin's eyes flicked back and forth over the lines. "Kai. Any statement that starts off *Of course the drow*...is going to sound high-handed to an aelfe."

"Excellent. Good catch." Kai twisted so he could type from within Tenzin's arms.

"The hope is that Lady Jessamine, or one of her court, will have run across these..." Tenzin leaned in to read again. "*Physical manifestations of natural psychic power* before."

"That's the hope, yes." Kai added his auto-signature to the bottom of the email and sent it. "Pacific Elvenhome is so much more stable and civilized than the Minnesota one where Val and I lived. We were almost all male. The few female residents were artisans and artists, not leaders. I believe that lack created the poisonously volatile atmosphere there."

"I'm sure it contributed, love." Tenzin kissed the top of his head, his warmth soothing much of the tension from Kai's back. "Though there are grad students writing papers now on all of the things wrong with that initial Elvenhome attempt."

Kai snorted. "Well, I hope they're actually asking the people who lived through it. These children who don't understand primary source research."

"Shut the computer down, my angel. Let's go home."

"Couldn't we…?" Kai wriggled around to wrap his arms around Tenzin's neck.

"I am *not* having sex in your office. Especially since Mindy is right *there*." Tenzin stood with Kai still in his arms. "Home. Dinner. Then we'll see. You're not thinking about skipping meals, are you?"

"No. I had lunch." Kai reared back at his husband's skeptical expression. "I did! On my mother's bones!"

"Mindy?" Tenzin raised his voice. "Did he eat today?"

"He stole some fries from my lunch," Mindy called back.

Kai squinted at her as Tenzin carried him out of the office. "Traitor."

"Not gonna start lying for you, Mr. H. Not to the big guy."

"Home. Dinner," Tenzin repeated. "And you're not to touch a keyboard this evening."

Only a small part of Kai managed to be annoyed at that. The rest of him was already thinking of all the other things he *would* be touching,

* * * *

Settling into his new community service/job was more challenging than Hank had anticipated. Not that Ryld was difficult or demanding. Quite the opposite. But it was hard to know how to be useful. A service came to clean once a week, so he didn't have to do that. He popped down to the corner store for a few things Ryld didn't have, like bagels and peanut butter. He'd done the dishes. Unpacked his bags. Ryld had come out of his room for breakfast and vanished back in there again.

I guess he'll need me eventually, but what am I supposed to do until then?

Pacing was out of the question, too. Ryld had said something about work, and Hank didn't want to disturb him. Though Hank couldn't help being desperately curious about what kind of work it could be.

He wandered into the hallway to hang his jacket in the closet and as he turned to close the door, red lettering caught his eye on the hall table. *Don't pry. No, you're here to help. That's not prying.*

With a sinking feeling, Hank picked up the stack of mail and began sorting through it. *Overdue. Second Notice. Past Due.* "Well, crud."

Here was another thing he could be mad at that Cress guy for. Just letting things get worse and worse under his nose. Hank took the pile of bills with him and knocked on Ryld's open bedroom door.

"Hi. Um…" He stopped, mouth hanging open. A corner of Ryld's larger bedroom housed a drafting table where Ryld sat drawing a beautiful scene of leaves and colorful birds. No, not a scene, a repeated pattern in lovely greens and yellows.

Ryld swiveled around on the stool, his eyes were wide, and his shoulders had lifted about half an inch. Hank was about to apologize for startling him when Ryld smiled.

"Hank." He looked down again at the drawing then back up. "The leaves remind me of Lysander." His gaze dropped to the envelopes in Hank's hand and his smile disappeared. One sharp-pointed canine tooth snagged on his lower lip and worried at it for a moment before he went still.

"I don't want to upset you," Hank said as gently as he could. "But these things are easy to let get away from you. Ryld…this is what I do. What I did before I lost my job. Do you want help? Getting this all sorted out and taken care of?"

The tension in Ryld's body came down a notch or two to be replaced by confusion. No, wait. Not confusion. Curiosity. Ryld's expressions were subtle, they took some time to read, but Hank was already getting used to the nuances.

"Your job was to pay bills?"

Hank nodded. "Part of it, yes. I was an accountant and worked for a firm that had a lot of clients. Some of those clients needed us just to keep track of things." He wasn't going to get into cash flow management and zero balance accounts. "And some of them needed us to pay the bills so they would have time to do other things."

Ryld took a single breath then stood up quickly. "I would like to hire you to pay my bills." Before Hank has a chance to say anything, Ryld opened the drawer on the bedside table and extracted a wad of cash rolled into a ball. "Is this enough?"

"Oh, um…" So many things were wrong with this scenario. Hank took a deep breath and decided to start with what he hoped was the easiest part. "I'm already being paid to help you. It would be really unethical for me to take more money for doing what I'm supposed to do."

"Ethics are…very arbitrary." Ryld paused. "But some seem universal. Kindness. Fairness. Those two are basic. You are being kind, but I want to be fair."

"And I appreciate that. But it would be unfair of me to take more than what I should." Hank's brain itched to move on to the issue of that large roll of cash, but he wasn't going to rush Ryld.

Ryld nodded and dropped the money back into the drawer. "It would be easier if a bill only needed to be paid once, but they are never once, and the amounts change." He lifted his hand and his fingers fluttered for a moment. "Money has so many forms. Some is kept here. Other money is kept in accounts. It's hard to remember them all. I very much would like to not have to pay bills."

"I'm afraid as long as you live with humans, bills happen. Well, in a nice place with humans, anyway. But I can help make things easier to keep track of. And make sure that all the bills are up to date." Hank nodded toward the drawer. "Do you usually have lots of cash in your apartment?"

Ryld looked at the still open drawer and shrugged. "I—the money in the accounts… I can't remember how much, and where it's kept. The amount never stays the same. If I can't remember, I spend too much and then have to spend more because I spent too much." He pointed to the roll of notes. "If this is here, I can spend as much of it as I want. If it's gone, I have no more to spend. It's easier."

Hank took a seat in a nearby chair, so he wasn't looming. "You'd be surprised at how many people have these same problems. And you've hit on the idea of budgeting funds on your own, a little unconventionally, but that's okay. I can help you with all of this." He lifted his chin to point at Ryld's drafting table. "What kind of work do you do? It's very beautiful."

Instead of returning to the table, Ryld moved to the closet and opened the door to reveal a stuffed to overflowing interior. He stood for a moment before selecting a shirt and bringing it to Hank and laying it in his hands.

"Look," he said. He traced one finger over the subtle curve of texture. "The wind blows across sand and makes ripples like these. I draw the ripples in the sand because I find them beautiful. Someone takes my drawings and puts the ripples of sand in cloth, and someone else makes the cloth into something to wear."

"Wow." Hank held the shirt up to see the design better and, yes, ripples in sand. He could almost feel the wind blow through his hair. This explained the nice apartment. Somewhere in the back of his head, he'd thought it was AURA-subsidized and now he felt ashamed. Ryld had earned this place by making gorgeous things human designers coveted. "This is amazing. You're very talented."

Ryld shrugged, then stopped mid-motion. "Thank you."

Hank wasn't only learning his expressions, he was also learning to pick up on speech cues. When Ryld was curious, he was animated, excited, almost childlike in a way. When he was trying to understand, or make someone else understand, his tone was flatter, but still held a certain amount of emotion. Some things, though, sounded very flat, and Hank guessed he was saying them by rote.

"Would you like to keep the shirt? I have a lot of shirts," Ryld said, gesturing vaguely toward the closet.

Hank gave him a wry smile. "I appreciate the offer. Don't think it would fit me, though."

Ryld nodded. "Yes. You are big. Is that why you're not afraid to stay with me?"

"I..." Hank smoothed the shirt on his lap just to give himself a moment. "No, I don't think that's it. Cress was big. And I'm pretty sure he was afraid even if he acted all bossy and intimidating. I'm not a warrior, Ryld. My mom was. Taught me a few things, but I'm not naturally a fighter. And they told me about your shadows, just so you don't think it's because I don't know."

He took a breath and looked up into blue-on-blue eyes. "I like talking to you, Ryld. I'm, well, I'm comfortable with you. So I'm not afraid."

A slow blink, then, "I'm glad. I like talking to you, too. I hope I never make you afraid. Cress lied. He was afraid. Always. He thought if he could make me afraid too then he wouldn't be afraid anymore. But that doesn't work."

"It doesn't. That's how bullies think, though. I could see he was a bully by the way he talked to you." Hank rose and handed the shirt back, absurdly pleased when Ryld's fingers brushed his and lingered. "He's gone. No more need to deal with Cress. And you know, if something happens, with the shadows, and I do get scared, I'll always be more scared *for* you than of you."

Ryld nodded and returned to his desk. Skepticism. That was what the expression was. Well, there wasn't much Hank could do to prove it to him. Time would tell.

* * * *

Needful Things wasn't as scary as the title implied. Why the owners had thought naming a thrift store for a horror novel was a good idea baffled Hank, but it was just a nice, regular little thrift store inside. The usual back wall of knick-knacks. The usual corner reserved for books and CDs. The normal center racks of used and vintage clothes.

Good place to pick up a toaster, maybe. Ryld's is a little glitchy.

It was a beautiful summer afternoon — not a scorcher, not too sunny — so they'd walked the several blocks rather than taking the subway. The walk seemed to do Ryld a world of good, his attention pulled here and there constantly, so for Hank it was more of a stroll. Very relaxing.

Ryld headed straight for the clothes, which, now that Hank knew what he did for a living, wasn't surprising at all.

"Ryld! Oh my goodness, it's so good to see you. You haven't been in for so long I was starting to worry." A human woman approached Ryld, stopping more than arm's length away.

"Miranda Gern. Hello. I had…some trouble. I'm better now so I've come back."

"I see that. Where is tall and scowly?"

There was a long pause, then Ryld answered, "Cress is no longer my minder."

"Ah, I see." The woman, Miranda, looked at Hank. "Is this your new minder?"

"No," Ryld said firmly enough it made Miranda look at him again, startled. "This is Hank. He's my companion," Ryld continued in a more reasonable tone.

The woman looked Hank up and down appraisingly, with a smile that maybe was just a little too enthusiastic. "Well. Oh, my. Hello, Hank."

Hank gave her an awkward wave, wondering if he should say something about what the arrangement actually was. But he couldn't think of a good way without sounding even more awkward. "Hello, Ms. Gern."

"Please, call me Miranda. Have you been Ryld's...companion, long?"

"Not long." Hank shook his head, even though it was completely unnecessary. "Just after tall and scowly left."

She gave him a big smile. "Ah. Well, good riddance. Let me know if there's anything I can help you with. Ryld, there are some new items that came in a couple days ago on that rack over there."

Hank touched Ryld's shoulder lightly and pointed when he had the little guy's attention. "I'll be over in electronics if you need me."

There was a pause, and Ryld gave him the look Hank was starting to think of as *processing*. Then Ryld smiled. "Okay."

Hank made his way over to the corner to search for any likely appliances while Ryld headed for another clothing rack. He kept half his attention on Ryld.

Perhaps three minutes had gone past when Miranda approached him from the opposite side. "Hello again."

Her voice was still pleasant, but pitched low, confidential.

"Er, hello."

"I don't mean to pry — well, no, that's not true. I am prying. But Ryld is… I like him. You see? He's brought several of his minders in with him, but never a *companion*. Are you…?" She left the question hanging.

Hank stared at her a moment, trying not to be mortified. "Oh. Ah. No. Not that. The concept of *minder* really bothered Ryld. And from how his last one acted, I completely get it. So I'm here to be, well, more company for him than someone trying to keep him in line. Someone to help him when he needs help."

"Oh." She sounded disappointed. "Well, I suppose that's a step in the right direction anyway. I do wish…" She waved a hand. "Well, never mind. Maybe a companion is what he needs."

"I hope so, ma'am. I'll do my best." Hank gave her a polite smile, also doing his best to ignore the weird flutters in his stomach from her suggesting that he might be something more to Ryld. *No. Talk about unethical. And you're in no place in your life right now to be anyone's boyfriend. Lover. Whatever.*

In the five years since his disastrous crossing over — falling from a great height and nearly drowning in Lake Michigan with three broken ribs — he really hadn't sought out a *relationship* with anyone. There were the curious, of course. One-night stands who were usually disappointed that he wasn't a ferocious savage in bed. But he'd been too busy, too focused on becoming what this world needed him to be to entertain…

It hit Hank suddenly that he didn't even have any real *friends*. Wow. He was a sad, sad person.

Back home, at least he'd had the excuse of isolation, living on the mountain with Mom and Dad. Mom had taken on mercenary work after she and Dad had married, so she was away from home for long stretches. Dad was an herbalist and always busy. They did have neighbors, though. Families scattered across the hillsides. The village in the valley wasn't far, and they'd made regular trips down for supplies.

He'd made friends. He'd had the occasional lover, both human and goblin. Tended not to last long since the parents never approved of their sons and daughters seeing a half-breed.

But he'd never been so alone until he'd come to this city of eighteen million people. Something ironic in that, he supposed.

Miranda pulled him from his reflection by saying, "Oh my, that's certainly a look he's put together."

Ryld had found a wide-brimmed sun hat with large pink and yellow flowers attached to the band, oversized pink sunglasses with crystals all around the frames, and a long velvet coat in a shade Hank believed was called eggplant. The get-up should have made him look absurd, but somehow on his slender frame he carried it off.

He knew the smile blossoming on his own face probably looked goofy as heck, but he didn't stop it. "It really is. Does he buy a lot here?"

"Yes. Off and on. He used to buy a lot of things and go home with bags of stuff. Now he's more selective."

"Good thing. You should see his closet."

"I bet. If you bring him to the garment district, you better bring a cart, unless you want to work those muscles."

"Hank." Ryld wandered over to them. "Did you find any needful things?"

"Right. We were talking, and I got distracted." He pointed to the silver four-slice toaster on the shelf and asked Miranda, "Can I plug that in and see how it's working?"

"Absolutely."

A short while later, they left *Needful Things* with the toaster and Ryld's newest outfit. Ryld kept running his fingers over the plackets of the coat and holding out his arms to look at the color, or maybe he was admiring the faint paisley pattern. A few odd looks came their way, but Ryld seemed oblivious to any of them.

"Do you like to go to bars?" Ryld asked.

"Oh, sometimes." Hank stepped around a tiny elderly human and her shopping cart. "Though the last time, it was because I was feeling down and drank something stupid."

Ryld looked so earnest when he asked, "Was it the liquid pickles come in? It smells like it would be good, but it isn't. Not at all."

"Ah, that's true. Pickle juice isn't great. But it wouldn't get me blind drunk. No, I had a glass of *terabin*. Very bad idea. That's when I nearly walked in front of the truck you were in."

"Oh. Yes. If it makes you walk where people are driving, it's very bad." Ryld paused. "I sometimes go to bars. The drinks are more expensive than if you buy them at the liquor store, but people don't like to talk as much in the liquor store."

"Good observation. Right, bars are more of a social thing than really for good booze."

"There are as many types of beer as there are types of cheese. More families. Would you like to go out tonight?"

"Sure? I'm off the pain meds now, so it should be fine. You can show me where you usually go."

* * * *

Hank wasn't sure what he had been expecting. Whatever it was, this was not it. The bar was at the end of an alley, crowded with a mixed-age group of locals both human, and not. It wasn't exactly a dive bar, but definitely not upscale either. A faint haze of smoke hung near the ceiling despite the *no smoking* signs.

Ryld strode inside to the bar. He still wore the coat and sunglasses but had left the hat at home.

"Ryld, how's it going?"

"Good. Can I have a beer please? You choose. This is Hank. *Terabin* is a bad idea. Hank, this is Deshun. He makes all the drinks here."

"Hey." Hank gave the barman a wave as he looked over the taps. "I'll have the stout you have on draught. Haven't had anything from that new pixie brewery yet."

"Good choice." He gave Hank a once-over only slightly more discreet than Miranda had earlier. "Cress not with you tonight?" he asked Ryld once he'd deposited their beers in front of them.

"No. Cress isn't coming back."

The little crease line between Deshun's brows smoothed out. "Well, I'm sure someone will miss him." He sniffed and shifted his attention to Hank. "New in town?"

Hank took a sip. *Not bad at all.* Not as heavy as some of the human stouts. "No, I've been living a little farther uptown. Been here about five years now."

"You the reason Cress is gone?"

"No." Hank allowed a little smile. "He did that all on his own. He quit. Wish I could take credit."

"I'm going to talk to people," Ryld said.

Ryld promptly wove his way into the crowd with this pronouncement, leaving Hank at the bar.

"I was hoping you were going to tell me you broke his pretty nose for him and sent him packing, or at least that he was fired. Piece of work, that one. I really hope you aren't cut from the same cloth." The words were said lightly, casually, but could almost have been a threat if Hank chose to take them that way. Maybe he was meant to, he wasn't sure.

Far safer to take them as teasing, though. He snorted and took another sip. "The Mother Goddesses forbid. I certainly felt like punching him, the way he talked to Ryld, but it's bad form to start brawls in the middle of an AURA lobby. No, Ryld requested no more *minders*. I'm just here to be helpful."

Deshun gave a small grunt that sounded neutral. "Ryld's a little different, but he's a good dude. The servers love him. He tips really well, but they'd like him anyway. We watch out for him in here."

"That's good to know. And I think he's a good person too."

Deshun leaned an arm on the bar, getting closer. "Just wanted to make sure you knew it. I'm not putting up with any of that shit Cress tried to pull. Don't be tryin' to use him like bait."

Hank stopped with his beer halfway to his lips. He set it back down. "Bait?"

Deshun nodded. "It's none of my business who hooks up with who, but Cress telling some horndog that's been panting after Ryld all night that he could maybe make a three-way happen later if he was nice...that's just wrong."

"Fucking shale and scree." The mild curse didn't come anywhere near the volcanic rumbling in Hank's blood. That utter *bastard*. "I really should've punched him, and he really should've been fired. Did Ryld...? Did he understand that this was happening?"

Deshun seemed to consider this. "Ryld asked me once about human and crossover sex. Most awkward convo of my life, and I've been tendin' bar for ten years. Thing is, he already knew all about the physical stuff. It was more the cues he was fuzzy on. So I explained flirting. I don't know how much he understood, but I know he understood why that fuck boy elf was disappearing for a while and coming back later for him."

"I'm starting to see why literally nobody liked him." Hank couldn't help glancing toward Ryld where he chatted away with several patrons, making sure he was safe.

Did Ryld ever hook up? Was it any of his business? Well, yeah, it was, because what if Ryld got upset and there was an incident... Stones. Could he be in the apartment while Ryld was, ah...? He was going to have to be if it happened, and his stomach was churning just thinking about it. Because...because he was concerned. That's all. *Right. You keep on lying to yourself.*

Watching Ryld move through the room, stopping here and there to talk, was a bit like tracking a butterfly. One would think he'd be hard to keep tabs on, given his smaller stature, but the purple coat and pink glasses helped him stand out. By the time the bar was getting ready to close, Ryld had talked to nearly every person in it as far as Hank could tell. If he was interested in anyone he talked to for more than conversation, though, *that* Hank couldn't determine.

"Hank, they will be closing soon," Ryld said when he came back to where Hank was sitting at the bar.

"I hear." Hank chuckled as Deshun bellowed out last call. "Are you ready to go?"

"Yes. Are you ready to go?"

The way he said it, he seemed to be testing the words out. It was a small thing but told him Ryld wasn't used to the usual back-and-forth of a normal friendship. For that matter, Hank was out of practice, too. "Yes. Let's go."

Outside a drizzle was coming down. It was late enough and the weather unpleasant enough to make the streets fairly empty. Ryld seemed all talked out and walked by Hank's side without trying to look everywhere at once. Hank was about to ask if he'd enjoyed the night when a loud angry shout followed by the clang of something metal being dropped or thrown cut him off. The noise came from another alley between two buildings, and as they pulled level with it, Hank spotted two people fighting.

"Hey!" he shouted.

"Fuck off!" one of the men yelled back. It was dark, but Hank's night vision was good enough to see he had something in his hand, probably a knife.

The other man threw a trash can lid at the one with the knife. "Help!"

Humans in New York had always told Hank not to get involved. Keep walking. None of your business. He hadn't been raised that way, though, and that desperate plea wasn't something he could just walk away from. *Well, fuck.*

"Ryld, stay here, please," he murmured before jogging into the alley. "Put the knife down, buddy. Don't want things to get ugly."

The man turned and charged him, slashing with the knife. Hank blocked the downward motion, knocking his arm aside with one hand while planting the other in the center of the attacker's chest. The motions were automatic and effective, and the way the man crumpled so easily let Hank know he was dealing with an amateur. Just a mugger, not someone trained in combat. Still, the weapon couldn't be taken lightly.

When the man fell he didn't drop the knife, and Hank kicked at his hand to get it away.

"Hank!" Ryld's warning gave him just enough time to bring an arm up almost without thinking as the one that had screamed for help tried to bash him over the head with the metal lid. He too now wielded a knife in his other hand.

"Give me your fuckin' wallet!"

"You've got to be kidding me."

"Give it!" the man snarled. The snarl turned to a surprised shout of pain, and he went down as one knee buckled. Hank was as surprised as his would-be attacker because as far as he could see nothing had hit the back of the guy's knee. He didn't have time to ponder it as the other man was getting back up. Then he saw Ryld at the end of the alley where Hank had left him.

He had his arms up, his hands clutched into tight fists pressed to his chest. His lips were pulled back from clenched teeth, his eyes wide and staring, and more concerning a deep shade of black that made them look like pits in his head.

"Holy Mother," Hank whispered. He caught the next blow, pulled the man close and turned him toward Ryld and the gathering shadows. "Run. Run now. Both of you. If you don't want to die, *run*!"

All their posturing and belligerence evaporated in the face of Ryld's otherworldly transformation. They stood frozen for a precious second before pelting down the alley in the opposite direction while Hank threw a quick shield up between them and Ryld. Hopefully between anything else, but he couldn't tell in the dark alley what were shadows and what were...*shadows*.

Ryld's whole body was rigid and still. In the sudden quiet Hank could hear his harsh breathing. He waited another moment, braced, but when nothing came at him he called, "Ryld?"

No answer, no movement. He risked a step, then another. "Ryld, can you answer?"

Still no answer, but the harsh whistling breath paused, and he could see Ryld's throat work as he swallowed. Nothing attacked him either, so he closed the distance between them.

"Hey," Hank spoke gently, crouching down so he could look up into Ryld's face. "We're okay. I'm fine. Those jerks are gone. Danger's past, though there wasn't much, really. Couple of idiots."

No response, so Hank kept talking. He knew what he said probably didn't matter as much at this point as just keeping a calm, soft tone. The drizzle kept coming down. Hank wasn't sure how much time passed, several minutes perhaps, before Ryld made a soft sound of his own. His eyes closed, and he swayed on his feet. Hank wasn't sure if that was a good sign or things were about to get worse until Ryld opened his eyes again. Back to their usual shade of blue on blue.

"Ryld?"

Ryld exhaled, his shoulders slumping, and his arms finally dropping to his sides. "Hank." He looked down where Hank was crouched, then glanced left and right. His worried expression relaxed. The drizzle had picked up to a light rain, and his hair was plastered down to his head, the color more a silvery gray when wet.

"Hi. Welcome back." Hank rose and offered a hand in case Ryld wanted support. "How are you doing? Okay to walk the rest of the way home? I mean, I could carry you, but I wouldn't without asking."

Ryld looked around again. "Home? Where...where are they?" He suddenly focused on Hank, reaching out and running his hands over his arms and chest lightly. "You're not hurt? I didn't hurt you?"

"You didn't hurt anyone, far's I can tell." Hank's breath hitched once as Ryld's fingers skimmed over him. *Oh no. We're not reacting like some idiot teenage goblin. Nope.* "The guys in the alley ran away. Whatever manifested, I don't think it was big or anything. I didn't actually see it."

Ryld sagged, and Hank automatically reached out to put his hands under his elbows, steadying him.

"I thought... I felt one get away. Are you sure it wasn't more? I've never been able to stop them once they start to get away."

"Can't say for sure." Hank planted his feet as Ryld leaned into him. "One of them, I think, went after trash-can-lid guy. Maybe bit his leg, but it couldn't have been hard since he ran away fast enough. Do we, um, need to call someone? Does the shadow that got away need to be tracked?"

Ryld shook his head. "It was small. The small ones fade away once I'm…back. Not enough time for them to grow and become more…solid. More real. It's very wet out here."

"Heh. Yeah. It is. Think we can go home now?"

"Yes."

They started to walk and were almost back to the apartment building when Ryld said, "I'm glad the shadow bit the other man, and not you."

"Can't say I'm sorry about that either." Hank also wasn't sorry that Ryld continued to lean against him as they walked into the building.

Chapter Six

"So, you'll be down in Counseling, but not in counseling?" Mindy's words had taken on a sharply pointed tone.

"Do *not* start with me." Kai shook a finger at her.

"Fine. But you missed your last appointment." She held up both hands when he growled. "You're supposed to be going. You promised Tenzin. I haven't ratted you out yet."

"I'll reschedule. I *will*," he insisted when she raised an eyebrow at him. "But this afternoon I have to meet with Lysander about someone else."

"All right, Mr. H. But I'm gonna call down there and have them give me your next appointment time."

"That's a violation of privacy, Mindy." Kai sniffed as he swept past her desk.

"It's not!" she called after him. "I have all your appointments!"

Mindy was right, of course. He couldn't start neglecting things again. Lunch. Work hours. Doctor and counseling appointments, which Tenzin insisted on. He said that Kai carried around a lot of unresolved trauma which fed his self-destructive tendencies. Perhaps. But the most important part was keeping his promises to his husband, so he didn't go down the dark path of relationship destruction again.

Lysander was waiting in the deciduous forest room of Counseling, sitting on a rock, swinging his feet.

"Hello, Kai! I'm glad you're here first." Lysander's tail wagged behind him in an erratic way that indicated some anxious thoughts. "Hank is very much against the way we'd conducted meetings previously, meeting with the minder separately. He's insisting Ryld be here while, in Hank's words, he's being talked about."

"Ah. Well, I have no objections." Kai brushed off a bit of rock needlessly before he took a seat. It wasn't as if the forest were actually dirty. "I take it Hank has become somewhat protective of young Ryld."

"It sounds that way. Yes." Lysander hopped off his rock and trotted over to the doors as they opened. Somehow, he'd heard people approaching. Drow ears were good, but nothing like faun. "Ryld, Hank! Come on in. We're just going to chat for a bit. Does anyone need anything? Water? Tea?"

It didn't escape Kai's notice that Hank looked to Ryld first. Didn't answer for him or talk over him. They both declined the offer, but the whole interaction was subtly different than it would have been if Hank had considered himself the one in charge.

"You seem well, both of you," Lysander noted.

Ryld started to say something, then paused, as if anticipating having a response spoken for him, then continued. "Yes. I'm well. The shadows are quiet. Hank likes cheese, and beer, and I like cheese and beer as well. He is good at paying bills and finding toasters."

"Toaster finding's a learned skill." Hank gave Ryld a smile when he said it. "We're settling into things. There was a small incident the other night, but I'm sure you know about that since I called it into AURA enforcement. Not that they'll find the jerks, but doesn't hurt to file a report, right?"

"The honesty and efficiency of your reporting is appreciated." Kai gave him a nod. He meant it and hoped no one would mistake seriousness for sarcasm. "Ryld, how did you feel afterward?"

Ryld took his time answering. "I was afraid, but the shadows didn't hurt Hank, and I was glad." He paused, considering. A note of defiance entered his tone as he said, "And glad they bit the other man who tried to hurt Hank."

"That's understandable." Lysander's smile held a world of kindness, and Kai felt an odd twinge. If he'd attempted that sort of expression, people would have run screaming. "Though remember that our ultimate goal is to keep the shadows from hurting any people. Let's not lose sight of that."

Ryld didn't respond to that, so Lysander asked Hank, "You're helping with the finances? How is that going?"

"Really well. I'd worried that things were in worse shape, but honestly, it didn't take more than an afternoon to get things straightened out." Hank spread his hands in a self-deprecating gesture. "It felt good to dig back into numbers again. Anyway, I've helped Ryld set up auto-payments for his utilities, consolidated some of the accounts and figured out an amount he's comfortable with as weekly spending money so there's not too much actual cash lying around."

"That's excellent news…"

"They had knives," Ryld said. They all looked at him, and Ryld shifted and looked away. "They had knives," he repeated. "And Hank had nothing. Why shouldn't the shadows hurt them if they had knives, and Hank had nothing?"

"Ah, little brother. It is an excellent question," Kai responded in drow before switching back to English. "What you speak of are weapons. Weapons can be for attack or defense. The men had knives. Hank had the training his mother gave him. That, too, is a weapon. But weapons are something we must be able to control. To use precisely. Perhaps if you knew your shadows would *only* bite the man with the knife, I would agree. However, and please say if I'm wrong, you were not in control of your weapon, and the shadows could well have injured Hank, too."

Ryld's mouth was set in a mulish line, but he didn't argue the fact. Instead he said, "If Hank hadn't been with me, all of the shadows would have gotten away from me. Hank was there, and only a small one got free. Why?"

"Ryld, no one's sure how you do what you do," Lysander began. "I'm not sure anyone—"

Kai held up a hand to cut him off. "It is another excellent question. I've read all of the material Counseling has on your shadows, Ryld. While I won't say I understand completely how they happen—I have no such power myself—they appear directly tied to your feelings at the time. How upset you were, how afraid you were, how much you yourself felt not in control, all of these seem to contribute to how large, how many, and how dangerous the shadows are."

Everyone was staring at him. Ryld only blinked, so Kai went on. "I believe — again, please tell me if I'm wrong — that Hank makes you feel safer. That with Hank there, trying to protect you, some part of you felt less panicked. Do you think that's possible?"

"I don't know," Ryld said, after another long pause.

"I don't either," Kai admitted more gently. "Despite people saying I think I know everything, I most certainly do not. No good scientist does. But it's something I'd like you to think about."

The other possibility wasn't one he'd bring up in front of others, because if *that* possibility was entirely wrong, Kai would embarrass them all by mentioning it.

The rest of the session revolved around more mundane matters, everyday things, and assurances they were both settling into their routines. As they were wrapping things up, Ryld brought up one more concern.

"Hank says he cannot take my money when he pays the bills for me because he already is paid to help. Paying the bills is…a lot more help. When you have two jobs, shouldn't each job pay you separately?"

"We'll make a bureaucrat of you yet." Kai flashed him a sharp-toothed smile. "I agree. Hank has already shown that he's much more involved, more actively committed to his job. I will send a proposal to Human Resources —"

"Kai, dear, as much as I love to watch you take charge of things…" Lysander patted his arm. "That really isn't your place unless you decide to fund Ryld's companion out of Research's budget."

"Ah. Apologies. Dual funding?"

"I won't object."

"Good." Kai speared a flummoxed-looking Hank with a narrow-eyed look. "You, young half-goblin, are getting a raise, since you're doing more than one job at a time."

Ryld's smile practically lit the room, the first Kai had seen from him since they'd arrived.

Counseling was supposed to be helpful. Sometimes Ryld felt better after seeing Lysander, and sometimes he felt worse. He wasn't sure how helpful counseling really was, but today was one of the times he left feeling better. Kai Hiltas being there was a nice surprise, and his explanation about having control over one's weapons felt like a veil had been lifted on a mystery he'd never fully been able to articulate. The shadows were not the only creatures out of control. Ryld himself was a weapon, and he too was out of control. This information felt very important.

On top of that, he liked the way Hank talked. He didn't sound like any of his minders. He didn't feel like his private life was being discussed as if he weren't there. It was more like…talking with a friend.

They got in the elevator, and Hank pushed the button. The idea that Hank was a friend felt like electricity. Exciting and dangerous. *Never assume.*

The doors closed, and the elevator started to go down. The strange tickly feeling in his stomach didn't subside. He chewed his bottom lip, then made himself stop. "Hank." He sucked in a breath. "Can a companion also be a friend?"

Hank's face was serious—eyebrows drawn together, mouth drawn down, but Ryld thought it might be a thinking face and not an unhappy one. "I think so. If you read human novels, sometimes the rich ladies in them have companions and they're obviously friends. At least it seems to work best that way."

The electric feeling in his bones felt like it was making him vibrate. "Would you like to be my friend?"

Hank's mouth turned up in a crooked smile, and he reached over to give Ryld's hand a squeeze. "I would. The world is a lot less weird and awful if you have a friend."

The electricity zinged around inside him, but it didn't hurt. It felt warm and good. "I want to be your friend, too."

"Well, good. That makes being friends a lot easier."

Ryld liked the way Hank looked right now. His smile. And usually he didn't like anyone to hold his hands, but he liked the feel of Hank's hand around his. The elevator door opened on the lobby. People were in front of the door, waiting to get on. He almost blurted out to someone, anyone, that Hank was now his friend, but the words died. Cress was standing with the people. He was not afraid of Cress, but he hadn't seen him since they were on the subway. It was jarring to see him now and Ryld froze.

Hank's smile had vanished, replaced by a look of rage Ryld had never witnessed before. He surged out of the elevator and pushed a shocked Cress back, out of the crowd.

"You! You mud-fucking excuse for an aelfe. You've got a lot of nerve showing your face here."

Cress' face couldn't seem to choose an expression. Shock, confusion, and anger all mixed up there before settling on anger. "What's your problem, orc?"

"You, elf-boy. You take a job. You're entrusted with someone's safety. Someone's well-being. And you use him as *bait* so you can get yourself off? You *abandon* him when he most needs you? Selfish, unethical *coward*."

The shock of suddenly seeing Cress was not nearly as shocking as the sudden change in Hank. He had been smiling one second and now he was shouting. At Cress. If Cress would just go away, then maybe Hank wouldn't shout anymore. He didn't know how to make Cress go away though. Kai Hiltas had said it was wrong to have a weapon out of control, but the shadows were already stirring in corners, sliding down the dark paneled walls.

Cress' head jerked to one side and his nostrils flared. He brought his attention to Ryld and narrowed his eyes. "You better stop it, right now."

Hank shot a quick glance back at Ryld, and maybe there was more concern there than rage, but he turned back to Cress and punched him in the stomach so hard that the elf folded over and dropped to his knees. "That's for Ryld, you creep."

He hurried back to Ryld at the elevator, his voice softer as he said, "I'm sorry. I didn't mean to upset you. Seeing him just made me so furious."

Ryld blinked several times. That was better. The anger was still there, and Hank was trying to hide it, but not the same way as trying to hide that he was angry with Ryld. "You didn't upset me." Not a lie. He didn't like Hank shouting but it was Cress' fault he'd shouted.

They started to walk toward the doors. Cress got up before they made it outside. Ryld watched him warily, but he didn't charge after them. He did shout though.

"You better watch your back, orc! That fucking *sulitek* should be locked up or put down."

Ryld stopped. Hank halted jerkily too, or he might have collided with him. "I used to believe that was my name. Because I knew no other until I was grown," Ryld told Cress. "You can't hurt me with your words, or your hands or your looks. If you had lived with the drow, they would call your insults childlike. Also, I kept all the mean things people told me about you secret because it's impolite to tell. They don't like you, though. Not any of them. You should know that."

It wasn't nice to say that, but he didn't want Hank to hit Cress again, so he touched Hank's arm and made for the doors.

Hank's smile was back, the crooked one that looked like it might snag on his right tusk. "That was very brave. A lot braver than sucker-punching the jerk."

"You are my friend, Hank. That's brave enough."

Hank made a sound between a hum and a chuckle before he touched Ryld's hand again. He didn't grab it or yank on it, just waited until Ryld had twined their fingers together for the walk back home.

* * * *

My Esteemed Friend

Kai knew it was ridiculous to feel a rush of pride at being addressed that way by an elven queen. Hard-wiring couldn't be helped, he supposed. All things considered, though, it was lovely that Lady Jessamine had replied so quickly. They'd had no tech to speak of in the Minnesota Elvenhome where Kai had been placed after crossing over years ago. Landline telephones. Very few televisions. Certainly no Netflix. Most of the elves there had claimed to despise human inventions. It hadn't helped the oppressive atmosphere one bit.

Pacific Elvenhome was much more progressive and had embraced technology with enthusiasm. Lady Jessamine's emails sometimes even stated at the bottom that she had sent them on her phone. It was a lovely change.

I hope I find you and your darling husband well. Work continues apace on the new grove. While we can't rush the infusing of power into ancient trees, the grove is already a place of peace and healing.

News of your young friend is, as ever, fascinating. Physical manifestations are not unheard of, but I needn't tell you that. On my home plane, some drow battle mages had this power and through means both fair and foul, some of our mages learned something of its workings. None in my recollection have been as powerful as your young friend, but I have two mages here, both of whom survived the Great War on my plane, a conflict we all otherwise wish to forget.

Since it is a matter of harnessing this power rather than learning to use it, I wonder if my mages might be of some use to you in training Ryld?

We are far apart and yet but a thought away in this world. Please keep me updated and let me know if there is anything I might do to assist.

Fond regards,
Lady Jessamine

Kai did not heave a happy sigh when he finished the email. He didn't. The world of queens and courts were so far behind him now and a little friendly flattery had never turned his head. Still. It was nice to have someone interested, someone who wanted to help.

Certainly not the first time Lady Jessamine had offered her assistance either to AURA or to Kai personally. While AURA had been reeling from the lich queen incident — so many dead, so much damage both physical and emotional — Lady Jessamine had donated funds for repairs and had convinced the kolle to send structural mages to ensure the AURA building wouldn't collapse. Kai had admired the feat of diplomacy even then, prior to being in contact with the aelfe queen himself, since the kolle were reclusive and generally unwilling to leave their homes.

Then when Kai had been on the verge of pulling all his hair out trying to procure government funding for the server farm Research so desperately needed, Lady Jessamine had come to the rescue again, throwing her considerable personality and the weight of her title behind the effort. She had moved bureaucratic mountains, and for that, he would be eternally grateful.

"Lady Jessamine says she might have mages with knowledge of Ryld's manifestations," he called through to the kitchen where Tenzin was making something that smelled heavenly.

"Does she? That's good news, love. Maybe you should set up a conference call."

"That's an excellent thought." Kai made a note on his phone, excitement thrumming through him. The thrill of discovery, of process, of...oh, something *new*. It would sustain him through a very great deal.

Belatedly, he shut down his tablet and hurried into the kitchen to see if his husband needed help with dinner. He'd most likely be in the way, but it was best to ask.

"I take it your experiment with pairing Hank and Ryld is going well?"

"It is, dearest. From the moment I heard about Hank…" Honesty. One must be honest. "Er, eavesdropped on a conversation between officers about Hank, where they were shaking their heads over his physique and his restraint with those goblin young, I wondered if he would be a better choice."

"Mm, I agree. A much better choice. Although…" Tenzin shook his head and said, "I'm probably worried over nothing."

"What, Tenzi?" Kai hitched himself up onto one of the kitchen stools, alarms sounding in his brain. "What worries you?"

Tenzin lifted a lid and stirred its contents, seeming to gather his thoughts. "Culturally they would be better suited than the aelfe or humans that were Ryld's previous minders, but I do wonder how much Hank knows of Ryld's past." He set the spoon down in the holder and shook his head again. "I've read Ryld's file, a very thick file. It's like reading a horror novel." He glanced over at Kai, concern etched on his brow. "Do you think Hank has an understanding of his… I hesitate to even call it his upbringing."

Kai winced. He couldn't help that either and it was difficult not to squirm on his chair. "Tenzi…much of my past would also be considered a horror novel. Have you…? That is, would you want all the details? I would tell you everything. I simply thought that perhaps you didn't want to know."

Tenzin took his hand. "Beloved, in that you are correct. I don't need or want to know anything you don't wish to share. But you are very different from Ryld. You have control of your magic. The circumstances of your birth were quite different. I don't know if that matters to anyone or not, but it seems unfair that Hank might not fully understand. That sounds horrible of me, doesn't it? Like I'm judging Ryld. It isn't that. But Ryld *is* dangerous."

Kai thought back to how Hank had looked at Ryld. How patient he had been. How…kind wasn't even the right word. *Understanding.* "I'm not sure it would make a great deal of difference to Hank to know. Except perhaps to make him angry with Ryld's creators and his captors. However, as they say, knowledge is power. Perhaps it's best to arm him with all we can."

Tenzin gathered him close and let him simply snuggle into his fur until Kai stopped shaking. Hank wasn't the only one with instinctive understandings.

* * * *

Hank greeted Ryld's declaration that he wanted to stay in and watch a movie with enormous relief. Not that he minded going out, but he didn't do it often and he was drained from the day's excitement. From the, well, all the excitements of the past couple of weeks.

Fine. He was tired. He hoped he could stay awake for a movie, but if he couldn't, he didn't have to go anywhere.

"What kind of movie do you want?" Hank asked as he brought up the channel options. "Any idea?"

"I've watched movies about elephants, bears, snakes, dingoes… I liked the one about weasels the best. They're very fast."

"They're cute little guys." Hank scrolled through some of the documentaries. "Here's one about gray whales? How about that?"

"Yes. Do you like popcorn?"

"Yes, please." Hank shot him a grin. "That'll make it like a proper movie night."

Watching Ryld make food was an interesting process. If what he was making contained more than three ingredients, he checked the recipe. He set dials on the stove with surgical precision and measured everything to the exact drop. Popcorn, however, was only two ingredients to make, so no checking necessary. Either that, or Ryld just remembered the measurements he'd used from the last time.

Soon they had a huge plastic bowl filled with buttery popcorn, and then Ryld surprised him.

"This is very good on popcorn." He held up a small jar of cayenne pepper. "Goblins like hot things sometimes. Do you like this?"

It was hard not to shout, *fuck yes*, but Hank managed a mostly calm, "Yes. Very much." He didn't even drool noticeably.

Once they were on the couch with the bowl between them Hank hit play and got comfortable. A few minutes in and Hank's eyelids were already starting to droop.

"Sometimes this doesn't seem real," Ryld said.

"Hmm?" Hank dragged himself back to the waking world. "What doesn't seem real?"

"This." Ryld gestured with a hand that seemed to encompass the room in general. "This world. All of the things in it. All of the people. Maybe I am sitting somewhere else, watching this world like we're watching the whales."

"I think we all feel like that some days. The…well, they call it dislocation. But, yeah, I've had that feeling, too. That I'll go to sleep in this world and wake up back home, because it had to be a weird dream."

"I would be...it would make me unhappy, if you were no longer a part of this dream, if this is a dream."

Ryld reached his hand out slowly and put his hand in Hank's. "I'm glad you're my friend, Hank."

"I'm glad you're my friend too, Ryld." It was becoming a common refrain. Ryld didn't seem to be doing it for confirmation, or at least not only for confirmation.

"Friends sometimes have sex."

Well. Now I'm awake. "Um, sure." Hank knew he should be pulling back. Fast. That he should be saying no. A firm and swift no. But there was a hopeful wariness in Ryld's eyes, and he couldn't seem to get himself to move or let go of Ryld's hand. "Sometimes that's true."

It wasn't that he wasn't attracted. Entirely the opposite. He found Ryld achingly beautiful, his lovely sharp features, his astounding blue eyes and silver hair, the slender grace of him. So beautiful Hank had to look away sometimes. But sex could complicate friendships and it sure as hell could complicate work relationships.

"Ryld, I... I don't want us to... I don't want sex to change anything."

"What would it change?"

"You might... I don't know. Sometimes people feel differently afterward. Sometimes things don't work. Feelings get hurt. I'm supposed to be here to look out for you. What if...what if people find out and think I'm taking advantage of you?" *What if you see me naked and you hate what you see? Goddess.*

"I understand. Sometimes I hurt people's feelings with no sex involved at all."

"Ryld. I'm more concerned with *your* feelings. Mine are pretty hard to hurt." Hank lifted Ryld's hand running his thumb along the back, tracing the delicate veins there. "I'm not suave or talented in bed or even terribly comfortable sometimes. It…I can't just jump in bed with someone."

"No. That would be dangerous. I've made you uncomfortable. I'm sorry."

This. This is what I'm afraid of. Hurting your feelings. "Don't be sorry. Please. There are…" Hank moved the bowl of popcorn to the coffee table just as the documentary got to the part about whale sex. *Wow. Is that really…?* Hank deliberately turned away from the screen. "Well, there are lots of other nice things besides sex. Things that sometimes lead up to it but don't have to."

He lifted an arm in invitation. "Here. How about a snuggle for now?"

Ryld didn't exactly jump in his arms. More like inched over, just close enough so the outsides of their thighs touched. He felt stiff as he leaned back against Hank's arm.

"We don't have to…"

"No. I want to snuggle. If that's okay?"

"Sure. I invited you after all."

Ryld relaxed ever so slightly. His eyes were on the TV. After a few moments he said, "I will get better at snuggling. I like your arm around me."

"Everything takes practice." Hank forced himself to relax completely since his tension would no doubt telegraph to Ryld. "Pretend I'm another part of the sofa. You can lean on me or lie against me, however you're comfortable."

Ryld squirmed closer. He still felt stiff, but after a little while, bit by bit, he leaned more against Hank's side. The whales were into their calving season before Ryld spoke again.

"Since your jobs are to be my companion, and to do accounting, it's much more believable that I would be taking advantage of you."

"Heh. I guess you have a point." Hank turned his head to kiss the top of Ryld's head. It was an automatic gesture, and he hoped he hadn't misstepped. "I don't feel taken advantage of."

Apparently either the kiss or his words were the right thing because the last bit of tension slipped away from Ryld and he laid his head on Hank's shoulder.

"Is it all right if we keep this private?"

"Of course." Hank watched the baby whale cavort around mom. *Aww.* How could something so big still be so cute? "If there's ever anything you don't want me to tell, please say. If it's not something I think would put you in danger, I won't tell anyone. Not even Mr. Hiltas' cat."

Watching TV with Ryld nestled up against him felt more right than any physical contact Hank had ever experienced. He swore he was just going to enjoy it for a bit, but he was so comfortable that by the time the whales started to migrate, he fell asleep.

Chapter Seven

"The researchers are still uncertain how this section of woodlands became a swamp, but it seems to have stopped growing." Ryld looked over a railing into what used to be a small pond and now was a boggy area that stretched all the way from The Pond in the lower southeast corner of Central Park almost all the way to Wollman Rink and the Central Park Zoo. "They have renamed it a nature sanctuary. It's now both a nature sanctuary and protected boggle habitat."

"Really?" Hank leaned over the railing too to stare down into the water. "I didn't realize boggles lived in Central Park. That's... I guess I shouldn't be surprised at something like that, but it makes me happy somehow."

They walked a bit farther, and Ryld felt a strange, unsettled hollowness inside when Hank didn't take his hand. It hadn't been a good day. Counseling often made him feel better. Today, it had not. He knew Hank was trying to cheer him up with a walk in the park, which was nice of Hank.

"So, Ryld, bud, what happened up there today?" Hank walked slowly with his hands in his pockets. "We were having a nice chat. Mr. Hiltas mentions the place out west and *poof*. It wasn't a nice chat anymore, and I got worried."

"Kai Hiltas is much different than other drow, but he is still drow."

"True. How does that apply to the question though?"

Ryld drew a shape in the air with his finger, connecting invisible dots. "Always moving the game pieces. It's our nature." He paused. "I'm not sure I want to be a game piece."

"He's definitely a canny one, and I'd never say that I knew everything he's thinking." Hank withdrew a hand from his pocket and offered it to Ryld. "I get not wanting to be used in someone's games. Especially when it's someone as smart as Mr. Hiltas. But I do think his game in this case is trying to get as much help for you as he can."

Ryld slipped his hand into Hank's and instantly felt better. "I like my home here. I like that there are many humans, and not only elves. I like you. And you are here."

"I like you, too." Hank gave him one of those half-smiles before his expression became serious again. "So, Mr. Hiltas was talking about a trip. Not a move. When you go somewhere for a short time — to see something new or to learn something new — and then when you're done, you come back home. No one's saying you need to change your home. Or not come back. Or — and he should've said this, shame on him — that I couldn't go with you."

"Yes. It's helpful to have that information."

They continued to walk on the path and after a few moments Hank asked, "Does having that information change your mind?"

Ryld hesitated. "No. Change is hard. I'm told it's not just me that finds it hard. But other people don't have the shadows. It's a great distance away. It will take a long time. It's almost certain that just in travelling there might be *a scene*."

"Okay." Hank lifted Ryld's hand and kissed the backs of his fingers, just a quick gesture, but a welcome one. "I don't want it to sound like I'm trying to change your mind, but I do want to make sure you have all the information. They can't risk putting you on a bus or, goddesses forbid, an airplane, but they do have humans here who make portals. We could step right through, from here to there. No travel time at all."

Ryld kept his eyes ahead on the trail but glanced at Hank from the corner of his eye. "Yes. I was brought here from the mountains using a portal. I'm not allowed near one ever again. That's what the officer in charge of monitoring Events that day said. Kai Hiltas told me one of the shadow creatures destroyed an entire room full of expensive equipment before he was able to banish it. He didn't say the equipment was expensive, but that's the only sort they have."

"Oops. But he still wants to help you." Hank chuckled softly. "He really isn't like other drow. Anyway—if he's suggested a trip, he'll have thought of a way. I don't think his brain stops even when he's sleeping."

"That's correct, the cerebral cortex continues to function during sleep in mammals," Ryld confirmed. Hank smiled in that way he did when he found something amusing, and Ryld smiled back at him. "That was a joke. Even though it's true."

"An excellent one." Hank turned them down the path toward a more wooded area, probably seeking shade for both of them.

Ryld was glad for the shade, and that Hank was so thoughtful. The heat of the day didn't bother him as much as the brightness. Sunglasses helped, but staying out of the sun was optimal. Another smaller path ended in an area with a bench. A huge weeping willow cast ample shade and almost hid the bench from view. Ryld walked through the long hanging fronds.

"It's like a green cave."

"Nice and dim." Hank took his sunglasses off, tucked them in his shirt pocket, and tugged Ryld gently toward the bench. "Let's sit down a second. Just enjoy the shade."

Ryld sat and pushed his own glasses up onto his head. Hank still held his hand and was absently tracing circles over Ryld's knuckles with his thumb. It was very peaceful, enough that his early stress over the idea of travelling seemed like it had happened a long time ago.

"Hank?"

"Hm?"

"Do your tusks hinder kissing?"

Hank gave him a sidelong look. "Not entirely. Whoever's kissing me has to be a little careful, of course. And I can't do those wide-open-mouthed, face-devouring kisses humans do."

Ryld looked at him, horrified at the thought. He made a mental note to re-research human mating practices. "Devouring a face doesn't seem productive."

"Sorry. That was figurative. They don't really eat each other's faces. They're just really big, wet, sloppy kisses and you know what? Even those sound kinda gross." He added hastily, "Not that I think humans are gross."

"Would it be *taking advantage* if I kissed you? Without any face devouring."

Hank's face creased into his thinking expression, and he chewed on his upper lip with one tusk. "It wouldn't be taking advantage, no. Though it's good to ask first." More creasing as Hank watched the willow leaves sway gently. "Yes. I think I'd like that."

This is very exciting. Ryld lifted both hands and gently touched his fingers to Hank's cheeks. He pressed his lips to Hank's, and his tusks weren't in the way at all.

Hank pulled in a sharp breath through his nose, and Ryld wondered if he'd done something wrong. Then his eyes closed, and his hands came up to cup the back of Ryld's head, his lips pressing softly, searchingly against Ryld's.

Ryld's instincts had suggested kissing Hank would be nice, but his instincts had been woefully inaccurate. Kissing Hank was so much better than nice. It was nearly overwhelming. So different from any other kiss he'd had. There was nothing hard or punishing in it. Just softness and a tingle of heat. A swirl of different feelings rushed through him in a mess of confusion, so much of it he was afraid he really would be overwhelmed. He pulled back and had to close his eyes tight and breathe deeply.

"Ryld?"

Hank's voice sounded strange. Deeper. Something in it he hadn't heard before from Hank. Whatever it was didn't help the confused feelings go away. He shook his head and held up a hand, breathed in again and let it out slowly. After a moment or two the feeling of being on the edge of something started to fade, and he was both relieved and sorry. He opened his eyes and looked at Hank as he licked his lips. The taste of Hank's lips still lingering on his own was almost enough to set him off again.

"I've never felt a kiss like that. You're right. The tusks don't get in the way at all."

"You approached them just right." Hank's hands slid down his arms to take his hands gently. "And that was wonderful."

It was wonderful. Hank was wonderful too. He felt like that was some sort of discovery, but it couldn't be because he'd known that for some time. Still, it was hard to hold in the feeling that made him want to tell everyone he knew that Hank was wonderful. Besides, it was much nicer to sit in the shade and talk.

The sun had sunk much lower on the horizon by the time they decided to walk back to the subway and head home.

"Would you like to watch another movie tonight?" Ryld asked, thinking that if they watched another movie, maybe they could sit on the couch and practice cuddling. "You can choose this time."

Hank laughed. "And maybe this time I can stay awake. Sure. We'll see what's on when we get there. I'm sure we can find something we both like."

"There is a show about how many different things are made. If you like to know how things are made."

Ryld's skin prickled a warning, and Hank suddenly flew backward, landing hard on the ground. They had just reached the main path where they had turned off earlier.

"Hank!" Ryld turned to go to him and was only able to take three steps before hitting a solid, invisible surface.

"Keep him there while I take care of the orc."

"You should not call him that!" Ryld shouted as he pushed against the wall.

On the path, Hank was gathering himself to his feet. Cress stalked toward him, knives out. Another elf, one with no knives, held his hands apart, blue magic crackling from his fingertips.

"Cress, you stupid, mushroom-brained flatworm," Hank growled.

The growl did not seem to frighten Cress. He pointed a knife at Hank and snarled back, "It's your fault. I don't know what you told them, but I've been blackballed from the agency. What the fuck am I supposed to do for a job in this idiotic world?"

"Not my problem, elf-boy." Hank had circled around so he could see both elves. "Should've thought of that before you bullied someone you were supposed to be watching out for."

Cress screamed something in elvish that Ryld couldn't understand and charged, both knives held low. The knives whispered through the air in their own language, probably saying terrible things. The first one Hank caught on his forearm, low on the blade. The second didn't hit him since he seized Cress' wrist. They grappled, shoes sliding on the path as they pushed against each other.

Ryld pushed too. He put both hands against the barrier preventing him from going forward, but it didn't move. He tried to find an edge, but it was as if a glass bowl had been overturned above him. He hit it with his fist as he watched Hank and Cress struggle against each other. Both elf and half-goblin were tall, but Hank was bigger, stronger. But Cress had knives.

He kicked and hit the wall holding him. Then Cress pulled instead of pushing and kicked the side of Hank's knee. There was a terrible crunch and Hank's leg collapsed. He lost his grip on the one knife, and Cress drove it into Hank's shoulder.

Ryld's breath rasped in his throat as he yelled, "No!" The shadows at his feet were shifting, but he didn't pay them any attention. Blood bloomed in bright crimson on Hank's shirt and Ryld threw himself against the shield holding him. "No, nonono…"

Hank grabbed Cress' ankle and yanked his leg out from under him. Cress landed hard and sent a vicious kick at Hank's side. Cress' other knife came a hair's breadth from slicing Hank's face.

"Get away from him!" Ryld screamed. The voice didn't sound like his own. He'd never felt so filled with rage.

The knife was still in Hank's shoulder. The bloodstain widened and widened on his shirt. He got hold of Cress again and managed to hold onto his knife arm while smashing his forehead into Cress' nose. Now they were both bleeding. Cress still had two uninjured arms, though, and he smashed Hank's head against the pavement.

Ryld's vision narrowed, shadows blotting out everything around him. A wordless scream rose from his chest, then wind gusted all around him as the circle holding him shattered and black beasts as large as wolves streamed outward. Darkness, everything was darkness. He struggled against it for a moment longer, but it was no use. The shadows broke their chains and would do what they were made to do.

* * * *

"All units in the South Central Park vicinity, please respond."

Flax snatched up the radio handset, keeping one eye on the street as he drove. "Officer Wolfheart. West Fifty-seventh, approaching Seventh Avenue."

The dispatcher's soothing voice came back immediately, "Officer Wolfheart, proceed to disturbance, west of the Boggle Habitat. Possible spell beast attack, multiple injuries reported. Meet Officers Kensington and Aello on scene."

Flax signed off and switched his siren and lights on, weaving through the early evening traffic as fast as he could. He didn't have far to go and soon screeched up to the curb by the park to race off on foot. A reasonable person would think that *west of the Boggle Habitat* would be too vague to find the disturbance, but Flax knew better. An officer just had to head in the opposite direction of people running away and follow the screams.

As possible alleged disturbances went, the screams were in the moderate range on Flax's *How Bad Is This One* meter. Didn't mean he ran any slower.

As he barreled around a bend in the path, he spotted what had upset the parkgoers and it was all kinds of weird.

One elf, violet haired, young aelfe, lay on the ground staring wide-eyed at the sky. There was blood on his throat. Hard to tell if he was breathing from a distance. Elf number two, blond, young aelfe, was trying to crawl away into the bushes, knife clutched in one hand. What Flax had mistaken for red pants at first were actually legs covered in blood.

Half-goblin, and Flax recognized Hank immediately, also on his back, possibly unconscious. Flax was willing to bet the knife sticking out of his shoulder matched the one in crawling-away elf's hand. Crouched beside Hank... Well, that's where the weird went over the top. Ryld hunkered there, clutching Hank's hand, but his eyes were pits of black, and Flax had to wonder how aware he was of his surroundings. Pacing around the pair, back and forth in a protective circle, were four...what?

Flax had never seen anything like them. Wolves. Big ones. But their outlines were blurred, shifting, bits and pieces drifting off and coming back together and they were just the outlines of wolves. Made of blackness. These had to be the shadow beasts Flax had heard so much about.

"Dispatch, I'm on scene. Is Medical on the way?"

"Should be reaching you now, Officer Wolfheart."

Sure enough, the thud of large wings became audible over the residue of screams. Hal the griffin and his medevac team with... Flax squinted in the gathering dusk. Yep. Kai was riding on Parnassus' back, and Flax had never thought the day would come when he'd be relieved to see the nosy drow.

He jogged over to meet them, taking a wide arc around the circling wolves. "Hal! I haven't had time to assess anyone yet, but I don't want anyone trying to go near those shadow beasts. Injured elf there—" He pointed toward the bushes. "And there."

"I have eyes, Wolfheart," Hal snapped at him, but Hal rarely spoke gently in an emergency. "Sin, you take the one still moving. Feza, the one on his back."

Incubus and tengu glided toward their assignments while Flax turned to Kai. "Hey. Um. You know how to deal with these shadow thingies, right? Please say yes."

"Your faith in me is touching," Kai began at his driest, though his expression was too concerned for it to be biting sarcasm. "I can, yes. But it takes considerable energy to deal with one, and there are four." His white eyes narrowed. "And they are behaving in a most peculiar way."

"Are they? They're protecting Ryld, right? I don't know what happened here, but since Cress is involved, I've got a really fucking good guess. The shadows usually go after whatever's freaking Ryld out?"

"They do, indeed. However, in the past, they've simply gone on to independent rampages instead of setting up a security cordon."

"Huh. Okay." Flax rolled his shoulders and cracked his neck. Matt and Aello had set themselves on the path to either side of the site, warning parkgoers away. The medics were doing their thing. "What do you need from me?"

Kai set his suit jacket and tie, both neatly folded, on a nearby rock. "If you would keep them from tearing me to pieces, that would be much appreciated. Once I begin to banish them, they may turn on me."

"What works best? Fire strikes? 'Cause they're shadows?"

"Normally, I would say yes. But we're in a park, Wolfheart. Unless you have someone to act as fire suppression, I would suggest wind."

"Hey! I'm very precise! But okay, I get your point. No setting the park on fire." Flax cracked his knuckles and followed in Kai's wake as he approached the circling shadows. He hoped this wouldn't take long.

Hank looked bad, and the medics really needed to be able to reach him soon.

For a moment, Kai just stared at them, tracking their movements, but Flax nearly lost his balance when the drow suddenly pulled power up from the earth. Huge honking piles of it. The snarl was probably concentration instead of anger, the growing ball of black mage lightning creating eerie shadows on Kai's face. *Drow are scary. Even the ones you know won't hurt you.*

Kai drew his arm back and hurled the crackling ball at the nearest shadow wolf. It hit center mass, sending up sparks of black and green. The shadow condensed, its mass hurtling around in a shrieking whirlwind before it collapsed, the last of it dissipating on the ground in bits of tattered black fog.

While Flax didn't want Kai to be right, of course he *was*, and the remaining three shadows stopped their pacing and turned toward him, not quite snarling, but instead creating a bone-aching hum in the air around them. Maybe if the process required less power, Kai could've taken them all on his own, but he needed time to gather that much magic into his hands. He struck a second one with mage lightning before the remaining two leaped at him.

"No drow dessert for you!" Flax shouted as he sent off one wind strike after another. The blasts didn't knock the shadow wolves aside. No, that would be too easy. They did make it harder for the wolves to hold their shapes, though, and gave Kai room to scramble aside, both hands on the ground to pull power as fast as possible.

Flax had to stop and recharge, too, damn it. The wolves immediately reformed and leaped at Kai together. With a bat-shrill scream, Kai loosed a successful strike on the right-hand one, its whirlwind dissolution knocking him back as the final wolf fastened its jaws around his forearm.

How a shadow could have teeth, Flax couldn't imagine, but there they were, tearing at Kai's arm.

Just a little fire strike. Just to distract it. Flax hurled the fireball and hit the shadow wolf on its shadowy ass. It was enough to make the shadow whirl toward him and gave Kai the precious second he needed to banish it back into unformed shadow.

In a bone-weary, rasping voice, Kai called over, "What did I say about fire?"

"You're welcome very much, your high drowsiness," Flax yelled back with a snort.

Kai pointed with his uninjured arm to a nearby bush, happily blazing away.

"Oh, um. Right. Sorry." Good thing the Boggle Habitat was nearby. Flax pulled water from the marsh and doused the flames before they could spread. "Hal, we're clear! If you've got a medic free, I need a couple over here!"

A couple of the human medics who had ridden in with their winged colleagues rushed over. One of them tried to see to Kai, but he waved her off and sent her to help with Hank. Kai staggered up from the grass and managed the three steps to Ryld before crashing to his knees again.

"Ryld?" Kai spoke softly in drow for a bit. Flax didn't understand much more than *it's over*. Then Kai switched back. "Ryld? I need you to come back, please. Hank is badly hurt. You must let them take him to Medical."

The only response Kai received was a low growl that was infinitely more real and less creepy than the sounds the shadow beasts had made. Flax saw no sign of Ryld in the dark pits of his eyes.

"If he doesn't come back soon, can we restrain him long enough to get Hank help?" Flax asked quietly.

Ryld snarled in their direction, and Kai shot Flax an absolutely withering look. The shadows in the pockets of trees and brush all around them started to shift in odd and ominous ways, lumps of darkness trying to take on form and shake the tethers.

"Well shit, I didn't know he could reform them."

"He does not *reform* them," Kai hissed at him. "He forms new ones. Constantly. It's all a matter of degrees." He patted the ground in front of Ryld, trying to take his attention away from Flax. "We will do no such thing. There will be no restraints. Ryld knows that Hank needs assistance if he's to survive this."

"I hope he understands that. I really do," Flax murmured. The big guy didn't look good. There was a lot of blood on him, on the ground, on Ryld.

Kai switched back to drow. Flax didn't catch the words, but the tone told him enough. Soothing, then pleading.

Ryld stared at him. In the gloom it looked like his eye sockets weren't just black but empty. Flax suppressed a shudder. Whatever Kai was saying to him must have penetrated somehow. The expression of madness and rage faded. Ryld closed his eyes, sagging against Hank, pressing his forehead to his uninjured shoulder.

"Is he…?" Flax started to ask.

Kai waved the medic forward with urgency. "Let him alone for now." And to the medic, "I want him kept with Hank. Do *not*, no matter what the circumstances, separate them."

Chapter Eight

The dark stone walls and faint blue light of the cave were incongruent with the hospital bed. Still, it was a relief to have Hank here with him. The hours spent in the blazing white light of the medical ward while the doctors had worked to close the wounds Hank had received and make sure the blood they gave him wasn't going to kill him were torture. Ryld had lost track of the time. How long since Hank had been hurt, how long in medical, how long since they had moved them both into the cave?

Hank had been awake, briefly. He'd spoken to him, but Ryld couldn't seem to say more than a word or two. He slept in tiny micro-naps, jerking awake to make sure Hank was still there, that he was safe, from others and from him. Lysander coaxed him to eat. He drank a little but couldn't stomach the thought of food.

He sat cross-legged on the fur-covered pallet, his head level with the side of Hank's bed. It took a tremendous amount of effort not to snarl and hiss at the medtechs that came to tend Hank.

A rustle of cloth came from the cave entrance. Kai Hiltas slipped in on silent feet, his jacket draped over his shoulders. He sank onto one of the stone protrusions that served as chairs in the cave, cradling his heavily bandaged right arm in his lap.

"Little brother, you should rest. Hank will be there still when you wake."

"Can't." The word was harsh in his throat even though it came out as a whisper.

"Hmm. I am familiar with this malady. Ah, well. Sleep will come upon you if you ignore it. Annoying habit that sleep has." Kai shifted on his rock. "I would like to tell you some things. Everyone has been so concerned with injuries, I think they may have forgotten to tell you things." He leaned against the wall with a gusty sigh. "The first is that this was self-defense. You and Hank were viciously attacked by someone with vindictive purpose. Both of those fools will live, by the way. Their injuries are of their own making."

He waited, maybe to see if Ryld would say something, then went on when Ryld just stared. "Second is that Hank was not harmed by your shadows. Though I think some part of you knows that. Your shadows, listen to me carefully, little brother, your shadows *protected* Hank. Stood guard over him. They did not get away from you. Something new, I think."

It seemed to take a monumental effort to speak. "They trapped me. Hank was being hurt. The shadows came...and I remember. Not all, but I remember they broke the circle. They went after Cress. Then nothing. Until you came."

Kai considered him for a long moment. "You remembering something of it tells me that you... Ah, it's not that you go away or outside yourself when the shadows come. But I think your mind tries to protect itself for some reason. I don't understand this reason, but I've seen similar. And this time, because Hank needed you, you did not sink so far into the safer place your mind makes for you. Part of you was more present."

Ryld sat with the idea for a moment. It felt right. He looked at Hank. Sleeping, breathing evenly. Alive, if not well. Would he be, if the shadows hadn't come to break the circle? If they hadn't gone after Cress and left Hank untouched?

He must learn how to control his weapons. He must learn how to control himself.

"Kai Hiltas, you are drow. You know how I was made."

Kai didn't look away but he shifted as if uncomfortable. "The specifics? No. I was not a member of your court. I do know of the superstitions about drow born with your coloring. I know some particularly ruthless courts will...pair certain men with certain women, in the hope their offspring will be born with your power."

"White, black, gray, blue. The most common colors for drow hair. Their eyes all shades of red from light to dark, very few other colors. I was told I was bred from stock. Like an animal. *Sulitek.*"

Kai didn't flinch at the word, but there was a tightening around his mouth and eyes.

Ryld nodded. "The woman who birthed me was a slave, punished for a crime. She was chosen for her dark hair and white eyes, and not given a choice. The man who sired me had silver hair but no power. He went mad and was killed before I was born. I was the only one of their offspring who survived. The only one with power."

"The court mages..." Now Kai stared off into the distance. Maybe he was remembering things, too. "They don't understand genetics as the humans do, but those notions they have about coloring show a rudimentary grasp of it, even if they don't have the words. Your sire most likely carried the seeds of power within him, even though he could wield none of his own. Breeding programs among the drow are not as rare as I would like, though they are not always so brutal."

"Brutal. Yes, they were that. I was always smaller than others, and many believed I was simple minded, because I didn't speak until well past the age most drow children begin to speak. Because I couldn't control my emotions." He paused. He didn't like to speak of that time. Remembering sometimes made the past feel so close it was hard to tell what was now and what was then. Still, it felt important to tell Kai. If he could tell him how he had been treated, how he had lived, then perhaps he could begin to understand himself.

After a few moments he continued. "The one who owned my mother believed the experiment that brought about my birth had failed. She believed I had no value. Not until I showed the signs that I had power. Then a new experiment began. To find the ways to best use the weapon they had created. They observed and learned that when I became upset, the shadows would grow. The more agitated I became, the more power the beasts had. I don't know if there was a time that I had control of the shadows. Maybe the punishments took the control from me."

Kai opened his mouth to speak, closed it again, his foot tapping in an agitated fashion the entire time. His expression might have been angry or distraught. Ryld couldn't be certain. When he finally spoke, his voice was tight and strangled. "You should have been *taught*. Guided. Instead they punished you like a dog being trained for fighting." He stopped and held up a hand. "Forgive me. I'm not angry with you, little brother."

Ryld nodded his understanding. "You believe there is one who could teach me. I'm not sure I can learn. Certain things that were done…things to make me fearful, react strongly, immediately…I don't know if it can be undone."

"It may be that they cannot." Kai shook his head, chewing on his lower lip. "The damage done to you was egregious. However, consider this. When you first came to the city, you were so frightened you loosed a shadow beast in my department that had little form. Serpent and spider both. Amorphous and strange. Destructive. Mindless. In the short time you've made a life here, away from your former keepers, your beasts have already changed. Their forms are more defined. They begin to have purpose."

Kai held up his injured arm. "Ryld, they were wolves in the park. And they defended and attacked as a pack. As wolves would. They *had* shape and purpose. You have already progressed. Can these people teach you? Perhaps not. But if they can, even a little, you may be able to teach yourself the rest."

Ryld nodded. He reached out a hand and placed it gently on Hank's arm. He hadn't stirred while he and

Kai talked. Still deeply asleep from the powerful medicines they gave him.

"I will go to this teacher." The capitulation filled him with an odd dread but doing nothing would certainly be worse. For all that Kai tried to reassure him that he had done nothing wrong, and that the two the shadow beasts had attacked would live, Ryld knew it was only a matter of time before they did kill someone. Innocent or not, the humans, and many of the crossovers as well, might not be as understanding as Kai was the next time Ryld lost control.

"Good." Kai leaned forward and spoke more gently. "We will wait until Hank is well enough to travel. I have every reason to believe he would wish to go with you. *I* will go with you. While trust comes more easily to me than it once did, I can only trust so far and will *not* hand you off to people I don't know well." He gave Ryld a wry smile. "I, too, have only progressed so far."

* * * *

Hank zipped the suitcase shut, swearing under his breath when his shoulder twinged. They'd had to pick luggage up for him from *Needful Things* when he realized he didn't own a suitcase. He'd never had the need to travel out of the city. All this wide new world, and he had stayed rooted in place — just like at home.

A little anxiety niggled at him. Traveling was new, traveling by train something quite new — but he refused to give into it. He would be with Ryld. They would have Kai with them, who was by all accounts, an experienced and jaded traveler.

He'd helped Ryld with his packing first, which had gotten Ryld all turned around since he didn't know what he might want or need and was in danger of packing enough for a year. But once Hank had gone through some options and checked the weather out in Oregon with him, he'd settled into more practical selection. Ryld didn't show it in ways that most people did, but he was also anxious and maybe a little excited.

Going west to meet a teacher among the aelfe... Hank hoped it would be a good thing for Ryld. Drifting in and out of his medicated haze in the artificial cave, he'd heard some of his conversations with Kai. What he'd heard... *Ryld... My poor Ryld...*

He'd never known real parents. Never had a family. Never had someone who would hold him when he was upset when he was a kid. Goddesses, what a terrible way to grow up. Somehow, Ryld retained the need to be fair. To be kind. Even though his childhood had been filled with cold, uncaring adults and from his adolescence on had been filled with nothing but fear and pain.

So much pain.

It's stupid to hate all drow for what was done to him. I know that. But I don't think I'd be able to keep from punching some drow faces if I ever met those particular *drow.* Which also was never going to happen, so raging at them wasn't going to do anyone any good, either. Still, how could anyone be so cruel? It just wasn't something he could wrap his head around.

As he'd recovered, he made sure to take Ryld's hand whenever he was near and to coax Ryld up onto the bed for what the little guy called *"snuggling practice"* whenever he could.

The phone on the hall table rang as soon as Hank rolled his suitcase next to Ryld's.

"Mr. Onyx-Wainwright?" The kawauso driver's voice was one Hank recognized right away. Otter folk had distinct squeaks at the ends of their words and this driver had ferried them around several times before. "I'm out front for you when you're ready."

"We'll be right down, Yuki. Thank you." Hank turned to call into the apartment. "Ryld? Are you ready? It's time to go."

"Yes. I am ready." Ryld came from the direction of his bedroom.

Hank gaped at him. He couldn't help it. Ryld had pulled his hair back in a long braid, the silver strands glinting against darker and lighter strands. He wore a dark blood-red long-sleeved tunic embroidered with gold and black stylized dragons. A row of toggles down the front kept the tunic closed and it was fitted as if made for him. The Asian style suited him very well, as did the immaculately fitted black trousers.

"Hank? Are you unwell?"

"I'm just a little bowled over. That looks really good on you." Hank indulged himself, letting his gaze wander up and down. "Really good." He held his arms out with a laugh, looking down at his own plain black T-shirt and jeans. "And I feel underdressed."

Ryld tilted his head slightly. "No, you are covered." Before Hank had a chance to explain that wasn't what he meant, Ryld looked startled. "I forgot something." He turned around and dashed back into his bedroom, returning a moment later with a white box. "This is for you."

"Really?" Hank took the box and found himself at a loss. "Should I open it now?"

All he got back was a nod, Ryld's hands beginning to curl in on themselves. *Crud.* He was making Ryld nervous, so he opened the box and carefully folded aside the tissue paper to reveal a shirt — button-down, long sleeved, in a butter-soft black cotton with a faint gray pattern. Wolves. They were wolves. Shadow wolves.

"It's gorgeous. Your pattern?"

Another nod.

"Well, I'll just have to wear this now." Hank stripped off his T-shirt and stuffed it in the front pocket of the suitcase before he pulled on the shirt. It fit beautifully and felt... He couldn't put his finger on it, but it felt *good*. "It's too nice to leave in the box."

Ryld shifted from foot to foot. He stared without speaking so long Hank was about to ask if he'd done something wrong. Then Ryld brought a hand up and traced his fingers light as a breeze over Hank's chest.

"Seeing you in it makes me want to kiss you again," he said softly.

A pleased shiver ran down Hank's spine. He put a finger under Ryld's chin and tipped his head up. "A quick thank-you kiss. 'Cause we have to go."

He leaned down, his free hand covering Ryld's which he pressed flat to his heart, and claimed Ryld's lips in a gentle kiss, almost able to keep a pleased moan inside. Almost.

A quick kiss. That's all they had time for. Indeed. What he hadn't planned on was that Ryld would sway closer, press along the whole front of his body. It took an act of sheer will not to wrap him in his arms and pull him up tighter. Instead he made himself pull back.

Ryld stood completely still and looked as shellshocked as Hank felt.

"Can we leave later?" Ryld asked.

"No, hon." Hank gave him a quick kiss on the nose to temper his words. "Kai's waiting for us at the station, and the trains leave at specific times. So later won't work. But we do have a room on the train. And we could, um, pick this up tonight."

"Tonight." Ryld managed to pack a wealth of feeling into the single word, very much testing Hank's resolve. Somehow they got down to the waiting car and off to the station with Hank every bit as distracted as Ryld usually was.

Parts of him were definitely acting like horny teenage half-goblin parts, and that wasn't at all how he wanted to walk through Penn Station for the first time. Luckily, he'd managed to think about cold ponds and that revolting strawberry soda one of his work colleagues had loved so much and he'd calmed down enough not to embarrass himself when they got there.

He'd seen pictures, of course, but the reality of the station was so much more astounding. Huge, vaulted ceilings of glass and steel, enormous spaces so large, Hank was afraid they might be swallowed up. Standing in the middle of the entrance hall, somehow taking up far more space than his slender body could account for, was Kai, checking his watch and searching the crowd.

In a day of surprises, Kai managed to shock Hank, too. He wasn't wearing a suit. Didn't mean he wasn't sharp and stylish in a tailored red shirt and black pants, but still. Hank hadn't been able to think of Kai without his designer suits before now.

Maybe it was a genetic thing. Drow and stylish clothes.

Ryld also spotted Kai and smiled. "Kai Hiltas. We are not late, despite the kissing. Are you ready to travel?"

Both of Kai's snow-white eyebrows shot toward the ceiling. "I suppose Tenzin would say that's not my business." He still shot a narrow-eyed glare at Hank. "Though do be cautious, you two. No, you're not late. I simply like to have plenty of time to find the right platform." Kai gripped the handle of his bag and turned sharply toward the escalators. "Come along then."

Ryld followed, still smiling faintly, seemingly unconcerned. Hank suddenly had concerns though. His business or not, that look hadn't been altogether friendly, and having a drow as powerful as Kai angry at him was high on his list of things to be avoided.

He kept one eye on Ryld, who walked in Kai's wake with his head tilted back, engrossed in the structure of the building and oblivious to the people streaming around them.

A few times Hank was sure there was about to be a collision, but people seemed to veer away as soon as they strayed too close. Hank squinted but the few shadows around Ryld were tiny and could just as well have been created by the light.

Nope. Wasn't Ryld. Kai was actually creating a wake as he strode through the station, a tiny bit of power shoved in front of him as a wedge, clearing a path. Hank couldn't help a smile. He'd come to know Kai as the person who sat with Ryld and spoke with him in soft, gentle tones and he'd had trouble squaring that drow with the one people always talked about— arrogant, high-handed, impatient. Made him wonder how much of that was just social armor.

The trip would take three days but they had a private bedroom suite so they could avoid other travelers for the most part if they wanted to. That suited

Hank and he could guess that Kai would be happy to shut himself away for the duration as well. Ryld was another story. The train, the noise, the crowds, the nervousness of going to a new place had him on edge. A stranger might not be able to tell—he was still and quiet for the most part—but Hank could see the tension in the way he held his shoulders, the wideness of his eyes, the way he kept his hands clasped and arms down, controlling the urge to twitch. The only thing that didn't betray his nerves was the shadows, which were still small and unmoving.

As they stood in the small compartment that was currently set up to be a living space, he pointed it out.

Ryld nodded. "I am trying very hard to make sure there isn't *a scene.*"

"You're doing so well." Hank took his hand and gave it a little squeeze. "So incredibly well."

The look Ryld gave him was hard to read, but Hank thought there might be some relief there. His own relief only lasted until Kai pointed to the hallway.

"Mr. Onyx-Wainwright, a word, if you please. Ryld, we'll only be a moment."

Oh great. Here it comes. Hank sent Ryld what he hoped was a reassuring smile and slid the door shut behind him when he stepped out into the hall. "Sir?"

"I didn't think you the sort, Hank. I truly did *not,* young sir," Kai hissed at him, his words short and clipped. "Taking advantage of someone so... inexperienced. Someone who trusts you."

"Um. Well." Hank ran a hand over the back of his neck, hoping his ears weren't turning red. "I didn't. I really didn't. Ryld is very... Well, you know how he is. Direct. Right to the point."

Kai's gaze narrowed. "You're saying he initiated *this*?" One slender, mahogany hand waved at the door, at Hank, at the world in general. "Whatever this is?"

"He asked if we could have sex. I said we should start with something smaller. Kisses, as he said." Hank heaved a long sigh. "He's not a child, you know. Different, yes, but he knows what he wants."

A huff and an offended sniff later, Kai's combative stance relaxed. "No, I suppose he's not. I see him as a child. In drow terms, he *is* still young, all other things aside. My apologies. He is vulnerable in so many ways, and I find myself more…protective than I normally would be."

"It's okay. I get that." Hank gave him the start of a smile. "I feel the same way."

"And more? Or do you simply indulge him in his requests?"

Hank considered saying it was none of his damn business. But that would be stupid. In close quarters, Ryld's wellbeing was the business of everyone involved and he knew Kai had grown attached in an oddly paternal way. "I like him. A lot. I…don't know if it'll be more than that. Or is more than that. But he's wonderful and talented and so smart. And sometimes he takes my breath away."

"Very well, then. I shall, as Quinn says, take my drow nose out of things." Kai patted his arm awkwardly and reopened the suite's door.

Ryld stood in the center of the small room facing the door. He was completely still. His finely arched brows were drawn together. Hank had seen him display emotions in somewhat unpredictable ways, but this one was easy. He was mad.

"Kai Hiltas." His voice wasn't loud, but there was a sharp note to it Hank had never heard him use. "Eavesdropping is not polite, but sometimes can't be helped. I do not wish you to be angry with Hank."

"I am no longer angry with Hank." Kai gave him a tiny hint of a bow with his hand pressed to his chest. "I misunderstood and have been corrected."

"I know. Thank you. Yet this" — he made a gesture that seemed to encompass his body — "won't go away. It's irrational, and I don't know why it won't go away."

Kai tilted his head to one side like a curious raptor. "It won't...? Ah. Often, our body's responses aren't rational, little brother. Physiological response has to do with hormones and signals from the more instinctive parts of our brains. This happens when we have been frightened, too. The danger is past or has proved to be nothing, and yet our hearts still beat like trapped birds for several moments after."

The little furrow between Ryld's brows smoothed. The set of his body shifted so subtly it was hard to identify what changed, but Hank could just tell the threat level had been downgraded from about a three to perhaps a four. Keeping him at a steady, calm five for this trip might take some doing. The stress was enough to make him weary, for Ryld it had to be that much worse.

"I will wait for it to pass. I don't like the way it feels at all."

"Not a good feeling." Hank didn't hesitate to agree. He hated feeling mad more than anything else and usually he could let it go pretty fast. Unless he thought about someone like Cress again. *Not going there.* "Why don't we get settled? The train'll be leaving soon. Then you can watch out the window as the city goes by."

Thankfully, Ryld was willing to allow himself to be mollified by this suggestion, and they finished stowing their bags and got comfortable. By the time the train was pulling out of the station, Ryld seemed to have gotten over his anger and, just as Hank had suggested, was watching out the window.

Hank sat with him at the window in their shared living space. Not a bad way to travel. Not at all. He knew if he'd been traveling on his own, he would've only had a seat in coach, crammed together with all the other travelers, sharing a bathroom. He knew it was Kai's money paying for a private space and for that, he'd forgive Kai Hiltas a *lot*. The drow mage had retired to his side of the suite, probably not for the night, to make a phone call. From the tone of his voice—just a little wheedling, soft and even sweet at times, Hank knew exactly who Kai was talking to.

It was adorable how devoted he was to Tenzin. Not that he would say that to Kai's face. Ever.

Soon the city was behind them, and Kai emerged to take a seat on the bench across from them. If his eyes were red-rimmed, Hank didn't think it would be kind to mention it.

"He worries. I suppose I've given Tenzi enough reason to over the years." Kai blotted at his eyes with a handkerchief, something Hank thought had been consigned to historical TV dramas. "A phone call and a portal away, I've reminded him, if the separation becomes unbearable for him."

Or for you. Again, Hank didn't say it. He wasn't sure how he would've reacted if Ryld had gone without him. Not something he'd had to think about before, really. Not something he'd expected to be thinking about. Ryld had managed to nestle up against Hank's heart good and tight, and there wasn't anything he could do about that now. Nor did he want to.

"Today has been difficult for you, too," Ryld said. "Look at all of the green and blue outside…and we are here with you. Beautiful things are even more beautiful with someone to share them."

Kai sat back, took a slow breath and turned his gaze out the window. After a few moments, he murmured, "Thank you."

For a long time, the only sounds were the ones the train made as it rushed along the tracks.

* * * *

The swift and sharp bite of anger he had felt when Kai spoke to Hank in the hallway had disturbed Ryld a great deal. Kai was one of only two people he trusted, certainly the only drow he trusted. To find himself at odds with him was upsetting, and thankfully brief. This was what Hank had meant about people knowing about the kissing and cuddling and believing Hank was *taking advantage*.

The feeling that had swept over him was more complex than simple anger though. Kai, of all people, should have known better. Should have known Ryld was capable of making his own decisions and knowing his own mind. That anger had been colored with disappointment. Once Kai had stopped being angry at Hank, and touched his arm, a different sort of anger nearly overwhelmed Ryld, much hotter than the first. The unsettling image of physically biting Kai's hand for daring to touch Hank, just as his shadow wolves had already bitten him, came unwanted and unbidden to his mind.

Strange. Kai had done nothing wrong. He hadn't hurt Hank. He hadn't driven him off with words. Hank was not in danger from Kai. He didn't need protecting. Yet Ryld struggled with an urge to grab Hank's arm and pull him away, hide him and guard him. He knew it made no sense and might even test Hank's seemingly endless patience. Once the anger cooled, he decided to tuck the feeling away for later. Perhaps he would discuss it with Hank, or maybe with Kai.

The rest of the day had been pleasant. There were so many interesting things to look at outside the window. Some of them he wished they could stop and look at closer. That was not possible as others on the train wouldn't like to wait, but Hank had said maybe another time they could go to those places.

At some point food arrived. Ryld ate absently, although it tasted good. His thoughts seemed so full, and it was hard to think of one thing at a time as they kept tumbling around in confusion. He decided this was the result of being up earlier than he liked and spending a full day with all new things around him. He would have liked it very much if the cabin could become the little cave in the AURA building.

The sky outside had taken on the blue gradient of early nightfall, and Kai stood from his seat, folding his napkin carefully before returning it to the tray the food had come on. "I think I'll take a walk through the train. Perhaps to the observation car eventually where one might see stars. I do miss stars."

He put his phone in his pocket before sliding open the door to the corridor. "Call if you need me."

Ryld fidgeted. Looking at the closed door, the table, the window.

After a moment Hank asked, "Ryld, would you like — ?"

Ryld cut him off. "Could we practice cuddling now? Please?"

Hank chuckled and kissed Ryld's cheek. "Of course. Do you want to help me get the beds down?"

"The beds down?"

"Yes. There are beds. Personally, I don't want to sleep on a bench." Hank gathered up the food tray and set it in the corridor, then showed Ryld the latches for the beds on either side of the suite. "These will be the beds."

It was just the sort of cleverness that ordinarily would have had him fascinated and examining all the details of how it actually worked, but his mind was already overstimulated, and as soon as Hank was done lowering the bed, Ryld circled his arms around Hank and pressed his face into his chest.

"That feels wonderful," Hank murmured against his hair as he wrapped Ryld close. "You're so warm."

Without letting go, Hank walked them the three steps over and pulled a partition down the center of the room, leaving the door to the corridor on the other side. "There. Now if Kai comes back late, he doesn't have to wake us. And if it's early, he can have his privacy. And so can we."

Hank's strong hands stroked along Ryld's back, easing muscles he hadn't realized were so tight, his lips tracing a soft line along Ryld's brow.

The tumbling thoughts in his head evaporated, nothing left but the hyperfocus on the feel of Hank's lips and hands where they touched him. Ryld settled his hands on Hank's hips and closed his eyes, letting

Hank anchor him. His soft kisses trailed from his brow to his temple and brushed close to the edge of his ear.

Ryld shivered, and when Hank turned his head he kissed him, not quite as carefully as he had done before. He thought he understood now what Hank meant about devouring kisses.

With a strangled gasp, Hank pulled back. "Hey. Hi." He was panting, but his smile was warm and maybe a little amused. "Wow. Ryld, I want to touch more of you. All of you. With fewer clothes involved. But I won't rush you. What would you like?"

Words were sometimes a less convenient method of communication. Ryld deftly undid the toggles fastening his shirt closed and shrugged it off his shoulders. He let it fall and unbuttoned Hank's shirt just as efficiently.

"I want fewer clothes, too," he murmured.

"Oh, thank goddesses." Hank winced a bit as he tried to slide out of the shirt and didn't complain when Ryld helped. His shoulder was much better, the scar a puckered line against his gray-green skin, but it was obviously still sore sometimes.

Hank let the shirt fall and sank to his knees to undo Ryld's shoes and remove them, one and then the other, with such great care that Ryld wondered if he liked feet best. But he didn't linger, rising back up on his knees to undo the front of Ryld's trousers, sliding the zipper down carefully and tugging the material down to his ankles.

Ryld didn't think much about his body. It was…functional. He had never minded being small compared to most other drow, except for the occasional wish for greater strength. He liked Hank's body though, the smoothness of his skin, the shape of his muscles under it. Looking at Hank definitely stirred his arousal but having Hank touch and kiss and nuzzle him was infinitely more so. When Hank looked up at him, Ryld took his face between his hands and leaned down to kiss him. "You are perfect. Everything is perfect, Hank. I want this, want you, want... everything."

"I do too." The gold in Hank's eyes was darker, something fierce and bright shining there. "You're so beautiful. Sometimes, just thinking about you makes me want." Hank rose, undoing his jeans as he did and letting them fall to the floor under the weight of wallet and keys. He kicked them aside and took Ryld back in his arms. "Bed?"

Ryld drew him over to the fold down bed and slid over, making room. As soon as Hank joined him he ran his hand down his chest, over his taut abdomen. "I like your shape."

"Mmm." Hank's head fell back, his breathing careful and slow. "I like your hands on my shape. A lot."

Hank slid his hand down Ryld's side to rest on his hip, then leaned in to kiss him. Where Hank's fingers touched, it felt as if tiny bits of lightning were running over his skin. He wanted more of that and pressed closer. He knew where Hank would be most sensitive and slid his hand lower. He kept his touch feather light. If Hank thought he was warm before, nothing compared to the heat that flushed through Ryld now.

A sharp hitch in Hank's breaths made him still, but the gasp turned into a soft moan as Hank rocked his hips into Ryld's touch. Hank slid his hand lower to grip Ryld's backside, nothing hard or painful, but enough to pull Ryld closer still.

Ryld rolled his own hips, craving the sensation of their bodies sliding and pressing together. Touch was a tricky thing. For most of his life touch had been startling, painful, unwanted, yet at the same time, he was starved for touch. To have so much of Hank touching so much of him felt like drowning, like he was a parched patch of ground trying to absorb a sudden summer rain. All his senses were engaged, turned up so high his head hummed. He wanted to stop and examine every new thing but couldn't wait for the next. Hank's scent made him dizzy. He knew Hank's scent, and yet he smelled different now... Like spices, as if Ryld might burn his tongue if he licked him. He had to try it and see. He licked a wet line over the smooth skin of his chest and the hard little pebble of his nipple. Hank gasped again, and Ryld decided he liked that sound almost as much as he liked his taste. He curled his fingers around the stiffening flesh of his penis, stroking the silky skin back and forth.

"I should've unbraided your hair before we started," Hank whispered. "Have it draped all over me – maybe next time."

He leaned in to claim Ryld's lips again, sliding his hand between Ryld's thighs to cup his sac. Part of Ryld was grateful that Hank went slowly. The other part wanted everything, now, faster.

"Hank..." Ryld's own voice sounded strange in his ears. Thicker, husky. There were things he wanted to say, to ask, and only a smattering of nonsense in drow came out. He gave up on talking. They were so close it was easy to maneuver Hank so that on the next roll of his hips, his penis slid between Ryld's thighs. He pressed his legs together, and moved, stroking him with the muscles of his inner thighs.

Against his ear, Hank murmured words Ryld didn't understand, probably in an unfamiliar goblin dialect, before he nipped gently at the point of Ryld's ear with one of his tusks. Hank's tongue followed the spark of almost-pain with his tongue, tracing the outer edge of Ryld's ear while his strong hand closed about Ryld's erection, matching the rhythm of his hips.

That felt so amazingly good every other thing left Ryld's head. A thrill of pleasure that felt scorching hot and left his skin tingling raced through him. He gripped Hank's biceps with one hand and the back of his neck with the other as they moved together in a building rhythm.

"Ryld." Hank's whisper had taken on a note of desperation. "Goddesses..."

The rhythm of Hank's hips changed, jerking and bucking instead of moving in a slow roll and Hank's lips fastened around the tip of Ryld's ear, sucking hard.

"Oohh..." Ryld exhaled a soft moan. The rain of sensation became a downpour, a flood, and he was sinking, until bright sparks burst inside him and slicked Hank's stroking hand with a different sort of flood. Ryld gasped, his breathing ragged, the pleasure shuddering through him for a few moments before ebbing and leaving him feeling like he could float right down to sleep. He fought the urge, wanting to savor the pleasant lassitude.

Hank let out a sharp cry, his hips jerking once more before he melted against Ryld, panting. He slid an arm around Ryld's waist and just held him, his heavy breaths evening out a bit more with each inhale.

"Thank you. That was wonderful." Hank lifted one of Ryld's hands to kiss the tips of his fingers.

"Mm…" Ryld felt too sleepy to do anything, but after a little while he said, "Hank?"

"Hm?"

"I think we are very good at snuggling now. But I still want to practice. A lot."

"Can never get enough practice." Hank pulled the covers over both of them and fidgeted around until he had Ryld fitted against his side, head on his shoulder. Not too many breaths later, Hank's breathing had evened out into sleep.

Ryld yawned, listening to all the little unfamiliar sounds. Hank felt solid next to him, and the small compartment, dark with night, was almost like their own little cave. He too was soon asleep.

Chapter Nine

The trip had been surprisingly uneventful, something for which Hank was more than grateful. He'd lived such a mundane, quiet life up until the day he'd been fired. Not that he'd go back and change anything. Fine. A couple of things. Like getting jumped by a gang of not-quite-grown goblins. Though then he probably wouldn't have come to Kai's attention and wouldn't have met Ryld.

It was like one of those time-travel books. Go back and change a bad thing and everything changed. Often not for the better.

They were all watching out the window when they pulled into Oregon Station. It was...small.

"Great Mother." Kai pulled in something between a hard breath and a sniff. "That's hardly more than a shed."

"There are a lot of trees," Ryld pointed out. "Where is the city?"

"It's a smallish city." Kai waved in a disgruntled fashion toward the northwest. "Over there somewhere,

I'd expect." He stood as the train lurched to a stop. "But we won't be going into the city. We have a car coming to take us to Pacific Elvenhome." As he gathered his luggage up, he muttered something that sounded like, "I hope."

Hank had a hold of both his luggage and Ryld's, since Ryld seemed to have forgotten it existed in the excitement of getting off the train after being cooped up so long.

"Do only elves live at Elvenhome?" Ryld asked.

Kai nodded as he slid their room door open. "Well, the majority of the population, at any rate. All different sorts of elves, though. There are some goblins who, as I understand it, serve mainly in security roles. Perhaps some other employees. But most of the residents are elves."

Ryld's mood shifted from excitement to caution. Hank could see it in his expression. Apparently Kai noticed too because he stopped and focused on Ryld. "They work there of their own volition, Ryld. Paid employees rather than captured slaves. I wouldn't bring you or Hank into danger."

Ryld nodded, but still looked guarded. "They will not try to make Hank work security." It was a flat statement, not a question.

Kai's smile was a spare one, wry and amused. "No one will take your Hank from you. Any staff on site will be contracted with the courts and, with perhaps a few personal exceptions such as a paid secretary, court bankrolled. Hank's only arrangements are with you."

Ryld's Hank, was he? While a little part of him warmed at that notion, the phrasing made him uneasy. "If I ever wanted to take another job, bud, would you be upset?"

Ryld went completely still. "Do you not want to be my companion any longer?"

"Hon..." Hank rubbed the bridge of his nose between thumb and forefinger. "Of course I still want to be your companion. I didn't say I didn't want to. But I'm not a...a thing you own, either."

Ryld's brows drew together. In confusion, not anger. "I know you are not a thing. You are Hank. Owning people is illegal here. But...I don't want you to go away and work for someone else."

"Then that's what you say to me instead of telling other people what I will or won't do—" Hank cut himself off at the unexpected sharp tone in his voice.

They'd reached the platform and had walked around the tiny station where Kai's gaze searched the appropriately small parking lot. "Peace. The two of you. Ryld, you are experiencing something all drow struggle with. Some more successfully than others. We are naturally possessive. Jealous. We have difficulty sharing certain things, especially those close to our hearts. This is why drow do *not* have *senrists*."

Ryld rocked from foot to foot. He was silent, but Hank could tell he was nowhere near at peace. Even if he couldn't see it already in Ryld's face, he could tell by the way the small shadows around his feet shifted restlessly. Kai must have finally noticed as well because he stopped looking for their ride and looked at Ryld instead.

"Ryld."

Ryld squeezed his eyes shut and put his hands over his ears, then pulled his arms down again. "I don't know what I did wrong." The words came out almost a shout and before either he or Kai could respond, Ryld gave them a horrified look, turned and took off running for the tree line.

"Well. That could have gone better." Kai made a weary gesture. "Go after him. He won't want to see me, most likely."

And your wingtips might get muddy. But Hank kept that uncharitable thought to himself since he knew Kai was right. He sprinted off after Ryld, his longer legs gaining ground quickly. As soon as the impatient words had left his mouth, he'd regretted them. Getting angry with someone else always felt awful, like there were hot coals in his stomach, but getting angry with Ryld felt so much worse.

"Ryld!" Hank called after him. "Please, I didn't mean to upset you! Please stop and talk to me!"

Ryld stopped but only once he'd reached the trees, and Hank didn't think it had much to do with Ryld hearing him. Ryld dropped to his knees in front of a huge spreading oak and bunched his fists into his hair, which had to hurt even more since he had worn it braided today.

"Ryld, don't…" Hank tried to disengage Ryld's fist, and Ryld snarled at him. "Okay, okay, I won't make you, but please, just talk to me."

This got him another frustrated snarl, this one accompanied by tears. At least his eyes were still blue.

"Okay, I'll start. Can you tell me why you're so upset at the idea of me getting another job?" He wasn't sure this would work at all, but he had to try. If he could keep Ryld here with him by talking, maybe he wouldn't escalate to the point that he totally lost control of the shadows now dancing around him.

"I don't want you to go. I don't want you to leave me."

"Sweetheart, even if I had another job, I wouldn't leave you. Those are two different things. Kai and Tenzin don't work together, but they see each other when work is done."

"I scare everyone away."

"Ryld, you're not listening to me. I'm your friend, remember? More than a friend. If I was no longer working as your companion, that doesn't mean I stop being your friend."

Ryld didn't say anything to that, but he did loosen his grip on his hair. Tears still rolled down his cheeks, but he no longer looked quite so anguished.

"Is that what you thought I meant? That if I got another job, it would mean you wouldn't see me again?"

Ryld nodded.

"That's not what I meant. Okay?"

"You're not going to leave?"

Hank reached over and gently brushed away a tear with his thumb. "I'm not going to leave. I'm right here. No matter what jobs you or I might have in the future, I'm not going to leave."

Ryld swallowed and reached for Hank's hand with both of his. He let Hank pull him up to his feet, then wrapped his arms around his neck and buried his face in his chest. Hank put his arms around him, holding him gently, running a soothing hand over his back. His hair had come half-loose from its braid and there was a dry leaf caught in it, and his pants were wet and slightly muddy from the knees down. Probably not the best look for a first impression, but Hank wasn't at all sure trying to get him into a bathroom and cleaned up wouldn't stress him to the point of meltdown again. Better just to get him back to the Kai and into the car.

"Hold on to me," Hank offered as he tucked Ryld's hand into the crook of his arm. "We're going to be just fine. Let's not worry Kai too much today."

Ryld held on, and Hank led him back toward the parking lot, which took longer without the surge of adrenaline that had sent him after Ryld.

"Why would Kai be worried?"

"I think he worries a lot. About everything. Even though he doesn't say so." Hank patted the hand on his arm. "Right now, he'd be worried about you, that you were upset and ran off. And if you were all right. And probably if he'd done part of the upsetting you."

"I'm not upset with Kai. He is right. I *don't* want to share you with anyone. I want to chase away anyone who gets too close to you. But I know that would make you unhappy, and I don't want to make you unhappy."

Hank leaned over to kiss the top of his tousled head. "Kai was explaining that it's part of being drow to feel like that sometimes. I think it's okay to *feel* like it, and I'll try my best not to do things that would make you feel jealous, as long as you don't act on it. Humans have that tendency, too. They have so many stories where jealousy gets out of control, and someone gets hurt."

"I will also try. I never ever want to hurt you, Hank. Even the shadows know I don't want to hurt you." He paused, then admitted, "I can't promise not to hurt someone that tries to hurt you, though."

"I can't promise not to hurt someone who tries to hurt you, either. Honestly, if someone stabs me, I'm not going to be annoyed about you hurting them. That's not the same thing as jealousy, if you try to protect someone you lo—really like."

"Jealousy is when you are afraid someone will take something from you."

"Well, that's about the size of it, yes."

Ryld seemed to mull that for a moment before he said, "If someone tries to take you from me, can I just send a *little* shadow after them?"

"A very small one. Maybe gnat-sized." Hank chuckled and moved his arm around Ryld's shoulders to give him a little squeeze. "I won't let anyone take me from you. And if it's more physical, like smacking me over the head with a bat and trying to stuff me in a panel van, well, that's a different kind of taking."

"Let's hope no one is in danger of being kidnapped," Kai said drily as they reached where he was waiting for them.

"First hypothetical I could think of." Hank shot him a grin. "Not like I owe money to loan sharks or anything."

"Of course not." Kai sniffed. "It would have come up in the vetting process." He raised a hand toward the parking lot and a vehicle just turning in. "Ah, finally. Here's our car."

A sleek, black car pulled up to the station's shed — one of those things they called a limousine car without the extra length. *Fancy.* The driver hopped out — full adult goblin, warrior caste, so he was big — and gave Kai a salute.

"Mr. Hiltas? This all of you?"

"Yes, thank you. Was there a delay?"

"No, sir. Train's just not usually early."

The goblin, who wore a sharp green livery with gold buttons, loaded their luggage in record time and hustled them into the car.

It had been quite a while since Hank had been near an adult goblin. He was immediately struck by a stab of homesickness.

Ryld held on to his arm even after they got into the car, and Hank had to wonder if it was for comfort or possessiveness. If it was the latter, he didn't exhibit any further hostility, engrossed with looking out the window at the scenery. They hadn't gotten far when Ryld said, "It's very, *very* green here."

"It is." Kai took his sunglasses from his shirt pocket and put them on as they drove under the leaf cover, the sun spearing through in fits and starts. "Elvenhomes were set up mostly as homes for the aelfe, since there are far more of them here. This is their sort of domain. Little brother, would you allow me to redo your braid?"

Ryld touched his hair, probably noticing for the first time it was in disarray. "Yes."

"Turn for me, please." Kai undid the tie, and his elegant, dexterous fingers soon had the braid out. From his messenger bag, he produced a fancy-looking, two-sided brush and began smoothing Ryld's hair with practiced ease. "The kolle have a village up in the hills nearby and the vasse a small settlement beside the river within shouting distance of the aelfe tree homes. The drow, I'm given to understand, have claimed a farther corner of the preserve where they could expand an existing cave system." His fingers flew as he redid the braid, something he'd obviously done thousands of times with his own hair. "It appears to function in a more amicable way than the first Elvenhome, where everyone was simply crammed together in the same village."

"What if a drow wanted to live with the kolle, or the aelfe? Would they be allowed?"

"I'm not at all certain it's come up." Kai tied the end of the braid off in a neat bow. "Crossovers tend to want familiar things. Their own people, even if other crossovers aren't truly their own. It would be up to the matriarchs to decide whether it would be allowed." Kai put his brush away and turned forward again. "I think in your case, since the Lady of the aelfe understands your circumstances, that she would allow you to live with the aelfe if you ever wished to. The kolle tend to be more wary and probably would not accept someone unlike themselves, though the kolle in my world lived closely with the drow. And the vasse are strange. I don't know them well enough to guess."

"The goblinkind can live where they want?"

"They seem to live mainly with the drow and the aelfe, but I'm sure they are permitted to make their homes as they wish."

Hank filed Ryld's questions away for later. Maybe they were just curiosity or maybe Ryld was thinking about...options. Maybe it would be less stressful out here for him, in all the green, but it seemed to Hank that Ryld had adapted amazingly well to city life. It would be sort of a shame to take him away from what he'd built.

The crunch of gravel replaced the sound of asphalt beneath their tires as the road ended in a curved drive of hard-packed white stone. The drive turned in a semi-circle around a clearing with a garage on one side. Hank counted seven doors, so there were several of these fancy cars or perhaps other vehicles.

"This is as far as I can take you, Mr. Hiltas." The driver turned in his seat as he parked beside a path that led into the trees. "No motorized vehicles are actually allowed inside Elvenhome."

"Ah." By the lift of his eyebrows, this was news to Kai. "How...selective. Computers, but no cars."

"Her ladyship is picky, yeah. Cars are loud, and they smell bad. I've tried to suggest electric cars, but she says they still stink." He opened their doors, talking as he got the luggage out. "You take that path there, Mr. Hiltas. About three hundred yards on, you'll come to another clearing. There'll be a light carriage waiting for you to take you the rest of the way. Her ladyship didn't think you'd be dressed for riding. Her residence is about four miles in."

Kai thanked him, and as the driver hurried off to put his car in the garage, Hank realized he'd never given his name. *Odd thing for a goblin to do.* The walk through the trees put it out of his mind, though. Birds called and rustled above them. A little snake wove through the grass at one side. A curious squirrel came down the trunk of one of the huge evergreens to scold them for interrupting her day.

Truly idyllic. Peaceful. Not quite like home, where the trees would've been smaller and the undergrowth mostly blackberries and rambling wild roses, but enough to let him draw a deep breath, something loosening inside that he hadn't realized was tense.

True to the driver's word, a pretty carriage waited for them, all carved wood, even the leaf springs underneath, decorated in leaves and bursts of flowery fancy. The aelfe in the driver's seat gave them a nod but didn't speak as Hank heaved the luggage up for his smaller companions and made sure they were able to clamber up before he took a seat as well.

The horses were snow white, a matched pair, stamping and impatient to be off. They surged forward at a trot down a wide path of mixed mulch and wood chips, sending up the scent of pine with each step.

Kai didn't react to the aelfe's silence, so Hank guessed that this was either normal or it would be rude to question. He sat back with an arm around Ryld and enjoyed the scenery. The woods became dense, nearly evening dark, before the trees thinned again a few miles farther on. The horses whickered and quickened their pace, probably anticipating being home soon with harnesses off.

Sure enough, the forest opened up into a clearing far larger than the one where the cars were kept. An entire village could've gathered here for a bonfire and not endangered the forest. At the far end, platforms were just visible in the trees, some covered, some open to the sky, and beneath these, a house sat on an elevated wood foundation. Maybe house wasn't the right word. Though it appeared to be wood as well, the building looked more like a fairytale palace with towers and rounded domes and elevated walkways.

Residence? Someone thinks she's a princess. More like a mansion.

Ryld was the first of them to speak. "This took a lot of resources to build."

"I bet it did." Hank leaned around him to address Kai. "Any idea how long it took?"

"I could only venture a guess." Kai gestured toward the residence. "Something like this would most likely have required artisan mages. Lady Jessamine is lucky to have them."

The carriage came to a stop some distance from the main structure, just far enough to have them walk through a short natural corridor made by the overhead canopy of trees. Ryld took hold of his bag when Hank got it down for him, and Kai took his. Out of habit, Hank took in his surroundings, both above and around them. Although they were well hidden by aelfe standards, Hank picked out at least two archers up in the trees. They weren't pointing arrows at them, thankfully, but they were watching closely. For all the beauty around them, it struck Hank as awfully quiet.

There were no curious kids gawking, or even any adults sitting outside enjoying the day as they started the walk up to the *palace*. Yeah, mansion wasn't fancy enough.

They got no more than a few steps when Ryld said, "The trees have many eyes."

"They do," Kai murmured. "Aelfe do like their sentries. Try not to mention that you've seen them, though. They believe themselves hidden."

Ryld nodded. "If goblins live among them, I wonder why they haven't taught them how to hide better? None are better at staying unseen if they don't want your eyes on them."

"Hush now. Aelfe are proud and would not take well to others teaching them. It's amazing we get any through the police academy at all."

About halfway up the short walk, two goblins emerged from the building. "Welcome to Elvenhome," the taller of the two greeted them. Though the greeting was friendly enough, it was obvious the pair worked in security by the way they were dressed — liveried uniforms subtly different from the driver's, and the visible weapons they carried. "Lady Jessamine will meet with you in the garden, but I'll take you to your rooms first."

Hank expected bedrooms, probably nice ones, but *rooms* really meant plural. Ryld was given a suite with a bedroom big enough for a tennis match and a balcony, along with a front parlor, a lavish bath, and a little room off the parlor their guide described as *for your servant.* Hank was pretty sure that meant him. He was fine taking on that role for now. Made him invisible, in a way. Also, more fool them. He was going to end up in that massive bed with Ryld regardless.

Kai's suite was across the hall, equally lavish, with the addition of a little office, all set up for computer access. To say Kai was pleased was downplaying that sharp gleam of unholy joy in his computer mage eyes.

The goblins who were doing their best to pretend they weren't guards left them to freshen up and unpack.

Ryld sifted through his clothes. "Do you like it here?"

"It's really pretty," Hank called from the bathroom where he was washing his hands and face. "But we just got here. I can't really say yet."

"They are well protected, but there are many shadows. Everywhere. What are they protecting against?"

"It's hard to say, again. I don't know these people." Hank came out, drying his hands on the fluffiest towel he'd ever buried his face in. "But remember we talked about trauma from our original worlds and how we all carry it? I've known elves who come through from worlds that have been at war for centuries. They tend to be wary, just in general. Maybe a lot of these elves haven't had time to relax from that always-at-war vigilance."

Ryld seemed to accept this, or perhaps was just distracted by finding the shirt he wanted. It was a dark, ultramarine-blue long-sleeved shirt with tiny silver butterflies at the cuffs and collar. The dark color brought out all the metallic silver strands in his neatly braided hair. Usually Ryld wore a lot of brighter colors that distracted from the true silver of his hair.

He changed his pants too, into a black pair that fit him like they were tailored for him. *Maybe they were.*

Hank thought about changing but decided being drab in his khakis and black chamois shirt suited his blend-into-the-background strategy. He wanted to be able to stay and observe through whatever happened and calling attention to himself was a sure way to get mages all squirrely and him sent out of the room when they started to teach Ryld. He smiled. Not that his little self-appointed protector would likely let them.

A half hour or so later there was a knock on the door. Hank opened it, expecting one of the goblins who had shown them in, but this time an aelfe greeted them. He gave Hank a little nod and Ryld a deeper bow. "I hope you find your rooms satisfactory. Lady Jessamine would like to formally welcome you, if you'd like to follow me?"

Ryld wished he'd remembered to bring sunglasses. The garden where they'd been led was a sunny inner courtyard. Flowers bloomed in profusion everywhere he looked. Pink, yellow, white, red, purple and all shades of those colors and more. They perfumed the air with a riot of sweet scents and big lazy bumblebees flew drunkenly from bloom to bloom.

Under a short flowering tree was a table set with a tray of tea things and a plate of small cakes and other treats. It was all quite beautiful, if a little overwhelming to Ryld's senses.

"Oh goddesses!" An aelfe rose from a seat under the tree. Somehow Ryld had missed her in the overload of flowers and the blinding sun. She was taller than Hank, willowy, and beautiful with her sun-gold hair and eyes the color of lilacs. "I forget how sensitive drow eyes are. Clematis!"

"My lady?"

The tall aelfe flapped a hand at her. "Go and fetch the awning. Hurry."

"Lady Jessamine, so lovely to meet you in person," Kai said as Clematis rushed off. "May I introduce Ryld Varjo?" He gestured toward Ryld and Hank, who was standing just slightly behind him. "And his companion, Hank Onyx-Wainwright."

Ryld took a small step forward. Although the aelfe and drow were different in many ways, they also shared enough similarities that shared social structures were common. In this world, so disconnected from their homes, many of the elvenkind didn't observe any of those structures, but being brought to a court with an elven queen, even if she was aelfe, Ryld couldn't help following old patterns.

He gave her a respectful bow, hand held lightly over his breastbone. "Lady Jessamine, I'm glad to meet you."

"Ryld." She smiled brightly at him. "I've heard so much about you. Welcome. And my dear Kai. So lovely to see you. All of you, not merely a face on a screen. Come. Come sit with me. Your companion is welcome as well. So charming. Companion. Such an old-fashioned title."

They all sat, and Ryld remembered to be polite. "Thank you for inviting us."

"You are most welcome, Ryld. I'm hoping our mages can help you. You must let me know if there is anything you need while you're here."

Ryld nodded. She reminded him of Miranda, although she looked nothing like the woman who managed Needful Things. It was the kindness in her voice.

"Have you lived among the humans long?" she asked as she motioned to another servant to pour tea.

"I have lived in this world several years, my lady. First in the mountains, then I was brought to the city of New York."

"Yes, and how do you like it there? I can't imagine it's pleasant with so much noise and all the poisons in the air. Especially for someone like you."

Ryld looked at her. He didn't like having his differences pointed out, but he saw nothing malicious in her expression, only concern. Lysander had explained that many people did not know how to treat someone who was different and so he must be patient. Patience was hard.

"It was hard, at first. But there are many wonderful things to see."

She nodded graciously. "There are many wonders in the human world, to be sure. I do find I like the quiet of the forest better, though." Lady Jessamine turned her sunlight smile on Kai. "And how is your husband? Such a dear. I missed chatting with him this past week."

"He's quite well, my lady." Kai's own smile was fond, a more gentle one than he often showed. "Busy, of course. His department is forever short-staffed and forever overrun, but he loves the work."

Clematis returned with a large canopy and poles and began to set them up to provide some protection from the afternoon sun. There was a hand crank involved and little buttons than clicked into place and the canopy itself was designed to flow down more poles set overhead. This meant they didn't even have to move while she set the shade up, and Ryld was far more interested in how it was put together than in the conversation.

Lady Jessamine and Kai were discussing travel by train, and Ryld slid out of his seat to go examine how the long poles set in the ground and connected in the center.

One of the dainty carved wooden teacups nearly disappearing in his hand, Hank watched him with a little smile. He still had said nothing, and Ryld wondered about that. Maybe the aelfe queen made him shy.

Looking at Hank's smile made a little wash of warmth spread through his middle. Lady Jessamine seemed nice enough, she certainly liked nice things around her, but she was also…boring. He'd rather be talking to Hank. Hank was never boring. Hank never talked to him like he was a child either.

He turned back to Kai and Lady Jessamine as she was telling him about how special some of the roses in the garden were. "Is the one who thinks he can teach me going to join us?"

"Not this evening, my dear." Lady Jessamine turned to him, her wide sleeves swaying. "You'll meet them in the morning. Twins. Very unusual and even more so that they crossed over together."

"They are aelfe?"

"They are, yes." Lady Jessamine turned to Kai with a silvery laugh. "Kai, did you not say so?"

"I believe I mentioned it. Ryld does well to confirm."

"How do the aelfe know how to control drow magic?"

She hesitated, though she did look like she would answer, but a servant hurried in, interrupting them. He knelt by Lady Jessamine's chair and offered a scroll, which she unrolled. Her smile vanished. With a look of distaste, she turned back to Kai. "She wants to see you."

Ryld had no idea what that meant, but Kai nodded and put down his teacup. "Ah. That was perhaps sooner than I anticipated."

"Will you go to her?" Lady Jessamine asked with a breathless hiss.

Kai nodded. "It would be more than rude not to. I'm not here to cause a diplomatic incident. I'll go see her this evening."

"Who?" Ryld finally blurted out.

"The drow queen. Ksatha." Kai rose, brushing cake crumbs from his trousers. "She has heard of my arrival, and while I owe no allegiance, it would be improper to ignore her."

On a logical level, Ryld knew that there were other drow living in Elvenhome. Until that moment, he hadn't put together that he might actually have to see them, interact with them. Most importantly he hadn't thought he might be required to meet the drow queen and be expected to act polite and sane in her presence. He couldn't do it. The thought that he might be expected to had him frozen and all the shadows under the canopy, in the bushes and leaves were suddenly dancing erratically around him.

Hank put his cup down as well. "Ryld, breathe. Kai didn't say you had to go."

Ryld closed his eyes and drew a breath. In through his nose, exhale through his mouth. He was still shaking, but was less afraid with Hank's words reassuring him, and after a moment he opened his eyes again.

Lady Jessamine was watching him carefully, though he couldn't read her expression. A fleeting moment and her attention flicked to Kai again. "I'll lend you a horse and a guide. You do ride, Kai? I shouldn't assume, I suppose."

"I haven't in years. But one doesn't forget such things. Thank you, my lady." Kai stopped by Ryld to murmur, "The Elvenhome drow will not come here to this bright court. You're safe. Stay with Hank. I won't be long."

"But are you safe, Kai Hiltas?" Ryld asked, his voice trembling.

"I have no reason to doubt my safety. They would avoid diplomatic incidents as well." Kai offered a hint of sharp teeth in his smile. "But I am slippery. They will not hold me if it comes to that."

Ryld nodded, shivering, some of the brightness leached from the day.

Chapter Ten

The aelfe loved their white horses, so Kai was pleasantly surprised when the one the stable hand brought out to him was coal black, some sleek human breed instead of an aelfe battle steed, of course. Elven horses generally did not survive the crossing, and the few that did seemed unable to breed.

He'd changed into leathers and boots, which were perhaps not the most appropriate clothes for a court visit, but he wasn't ruining good wool slacks riding. The horse shied from him until he spoke to her, assuring her that he was no threat even though he smelled of strange places. His guide, a young aelfe, equal parts nerves and contempt, was not so easily won over.

"She's very fast. Are you certain you can stay in the saddle?" the youngster sneered as Kai vaulted onto his mount's back.

Kai was far too tired already to waste polite conversation on him. "Child, I was riding for centuries before you were born. Horses. Tzok lizards. A giant spider who liked my company. Lead on."

The guide blinked in shock, but with the bravado of the young, kicked his horse into a gallop as if daring Kai to keep up. Leaning over his horse's neck, he whispered in her ear, and she leaped to follow, through the trees and the gathering dusk. The dense forest gave the impression of being impassable, but there were paths hidden in the undergrowth and the aelfe youngster obviously knew them well. They rode for perhaps an hour before they reached another huge clearing, though no beautiful palace rose up to greet them here.

The ground had been rising steadily as they rode and at the far side of the clearing it rose sharply to steep-sided hills. Several arched entrances had been carved into these hills, precisely and with meaning to their shape and angles. The entrance to a drow court, written in the stone for any who could read it.

"I don't go in there." The guide nodded to the cave mouths. "An hour. I'll wait that long. No more."

"If you make me walk back, Lady Jessamine will not be best pleased." Kai tossed his reins to the aelfe and slid from the saddle. "But I don't think this will take terribly long."

He was watched. He knew that. Though the sentries were far better concealed than the aelfe in the trees had been. *A bit of swagger, then. It never hurts.*

He took the central tunnel down, the one clearly marked as the way to the court proper, steeling his resolve, pulling all his arrogance around him. Quite frankly, he was scared out of his mind.

The tunnel opened up here and there to other passageways, other rooms, but none of those distracted him. Down and down, into the heart of the earth, until he came to a guarded door of black metal and silver.

"Kai Hiltas," he told the guard. "She's summoned me."

The drow guards nodded, polite enough, and opened the heavy door for him. The cavern beyond glittered with quartz and mica trapped in the stone, a soaring chamber big enough that the edges were lost in darkness. Not her, of course. She sat in the center under the lamplight, on a high seat as white as bone. It might have *been* bone—such was tradition.

Kai had never spoken with this queen in person before either, not even on a video call, although he had had correspondence with her. And of course he knew what she looked like because research was after all what he did. The photos didn't do her justice. She was a young queen, younger than Kai at least, but not as young as Ryld. She could have been a direct relative. She looked so similar to Kai, midnight skin and crowned with snowy white hair. Her eyes were a more common red, although so deep a crimson it was like looking into heart's blood.

She did not stand on ceremony and welcomed him herself, rather than the traditional announcements and scrapings of court. "Well met, Kai Hiltas," she said in drow.

Not to be rude, he answered in kind, with a hint of a bow, "Lady Ksatha, an honor. I came as soon as I was apprised of your summons."

One of her slim brows rose. "Summons? More of an invitation." She paused. "Ah, I see. Read the note I sent for you, did she? Jessamine *does* love her dramatics. No matter, thank you for coming so soon. I hear you have a young drow in your company?"

"Yes." No reason to deny it. She knew already. "We will be visiting with the aelfe for a short while."

"I'm aware of your goals, even if you didn't seek my advice." Her lips twitched into a sardonic half-smile. "She's promised her sorcerers can bring your silver drow to heel, is that not so?"

"Lady Jessamine has promised nothing," Kai said, as neutrally as he could manage.

Ksatha shifted her indolent slouch in the throne, leaning in more toward him. "Come now, there is no need to be so stiff and guarded here, among your own." Her words poured into Kai's ears like warm honey. "You are a mage of some renown. If you're seeking the help of the aelfe with a weapon the drow created, the situation must be quite desperate. How mad is he?"

His blood screamed at him to fall to his knees and spill out all the thoughts in his head. This was no pretender, but an actual drow queen, young though she was. But his blood could go sing to someone else. "He is not mad, my lady. That much is certain. Though they tried their best to make him so."

"Control through fear has its uses in the short term, but I've found it exceedingly limiting. Long-term loyalty is best earned through other means." She smiled. "I can see you don't believe me, but don't worry. I don't blame you for your mistrust, no matter how nobly you try to hide it. I take it the silver born was too terrified to come with you?"

"I would not have brought him in any case." Kai tipped an eyebrow up at her. Eyebrow for an eyebrow. "Your interest in him is far too transparent, my lady."

She laughed, not true mirth, but a shivering power in the sound that made Kai lock his knees. "Yes, well. You would mistrust my intentions either way so why go to the effort to hide them? I don't wish him any harm, though I dare say that won't set your mind at ease. I will say I'm not the only one that seeks to tempt him to stay here in Elvenhome."

Point to her ladyship. Kai inclined his head in acknowledgment. "I'm well aware of such possibilities. The courts will always be the courts, wherever they happen to be transplanted. He is not here to stay. I intend to continue to make that clear until we depart."

"I'll make no move to force the matter. However, I have an offer. I would like you to spend some time here, in my court, while the aelfe pretend they know how to teach a drow his magic. When they fail, and if you find my home safe enough, I'll help him."

There was a subtle insult hidden in her gracious words. As if Kai hadn't tried to work with Ryld himself. As if Kai weren't enough of a mage to teach him, but Ksatha thought *she* could. Offense was not something one showed in a drow court, though, unless one was in a position of unassailable strength.

"My lady, it is not a matter of my endorsement. Or my approval. Ryld *will* not. The circumstances of his upbringing make such a thing impossible."

She leaned back on her throne, drumming her fingers slowly on the armrest. "I see. He doesn't fear all his kind though, or you wouldn't be allowed near him, either. So, either a queen or some other woman abused him. What do you fear will happen if he did come before me?"

The urge to tell her everything was nearly overwhelming. Nearly. "Disaster, my lady. Destruction."

They both fell silent, sharing a moment of things said without being spoken. Kai knew of the particulars of Ryld's birth now, most of them anyway. She might not have the same information, but most drow had heard something or other of the silver born. She would know Ryld was rare, that of those who were born with his genetic traits, most didn't survive to adulthood, and of those that did, they had a high chance of both enormous power and madness. Ryld might not be neurotypical, but he wasn't mentally ill. If there was another drow like Ryld in either this world or the one Kai had come from, he didn't know of them.

"He must indeed be very powerful then," she said at last. "My offer still stands though, as does my promise not to force him to come to me. I still extend my hospitality to you, Kai. Drow are not as common in this world as the aelfe. We should be able to gather civilly together."

You have neither the power nor the right in this world to force anything, my lady. But that, Kai prudently kept to himself. He swept her a formal bow. "I do thank you, my lady, and will attend you upon invitation. Perhaps to regale you with tales of this world and the drow I have met."

This time the smile she bestowed upon him was genuine, and even held some warmth. It hit him like a shock to the system and he had to force his own smile.

"That would be lovely. Thank you for your company, Kai. I do believe the young aelfe outside has worked himself into a nervous lather while we talked and might be about to bolt like a scared rabbit. Until we meet again…"

He allowed a small chuckle, since his guide would definitely find offense in being called a rabbit. "Until then, my lady."

Kai backed three steps from the throne as was proper, before he turned and strode out. Relief and wars of allegiance raged in his blood and his knees were weak when he reached the surface, though he hoped to all gods it didn't show. He couldn't put his finger on it yet, but something was…odd. Best to keep lines of communication open until he knew more.

* * * *

"A short visit and not a dreadful one." Kai waved his fork vaguely before spearing another asparagus. "And I am safe, as you see."

He'd joined them in their suite for breakfast, much to Hank's relief. It just felt better to have them all in the same place. The whole place made him uneasy, lovely though it was. Probably the woods or the presence of royalty or sleeping in unfamiliar beds. Or all of the above and just being worried about…everything.

The bed had been wonderful—soft and big enough for several of him with several Rylds snuggled up close—but he'd hardly slept, listening to night birds calling, ones he couldn't name.

"Good. Didn't make me happy, you going off on your own." Hank sipped his coffee, another surprise since he'd assumed the elves would only have tea, and tried to convince himself he had an appetite. The bread was excellent, and there was honey. He'd stick to that. "I know. You're used to getting yourself out of bad spots. Still."

"My apologies." Kai inclined his head. "Though I may need to meet with her again. It's all maneuvering. Nothing to fear in a physical sense." His eyes flicked up toward the window where the sun was starting to creep in. "Ryld, are you ready to meet your prospective teachers?"

Ryld had eaten more of the food on his plate than Hank had, though he noticed he was also just picking now. He was probably more nervous than he looked.

"I am ready."

He said it so solemnly, as if he were saying he was ready to go to his doom, that Hank had to smile. "It won't be that bad," he reassured Ryld. "They only want to help you."

"Mm." Ryld made a noncommittal sound, and Hank knew he was reserving judgment on that score.

Kai leaned back, toying with the handle of his coffee cup. "Do you wish us both to be there? Or just Hank?"

"Both, to meet them, please. Hank will see them one way. You will see them another way." Ryld paused, then added as if for clarification, "I see more than most people think, but not everything."

"Wise thought. Good." Kai folded his napkin in that precise, fussy way of his, and stood. "Very well. Lady Jessamine has taken pity on our collection of night-adapted eyes, and we are to meet her mages in the room they use for weapons practice. It will be far less sunny since there are no windows. Half an hour, gentlemen, and someone should be up to collect us."

Kai left for his own suite, probably to rethink what he was wearing. Hank sighed inwardly. Drow and clothes. Right.

"You all set with how you look?" he asked Ryld, though it didn't need asking. If Ryld was going to pick something else, he'd start sorting through his clothes without prompting.

"Yes. If there is a test, these clothes are comfortable. Although they are not beautiful."

"You look beautiful no matter what you're wearing."

Ryld smiled. "Thank you." He was quiet then said, "If you were my clothes, I would only wear you every day."

If Hank thought he was too grown up to blush, Ryld proved him wrong as the heat climbed his face. He knew what Ryld was saying, but it was a very drow thing to say. "Uh, thanks. That would be, um, interesting."

It was exactly half an hour, somehow Kai had known, that a servant knocked on the door and bowed them out into the hall where Kai already waited. The servants all gave Kai extra space, and Hank couldn't decide if that was respect or insult.

Down the stairs, through lavishly carved hallways, and down the stairs again to more utilitarian hallways, probably for storage and such. Finally, they stopped at a heavier, brass-bound door. The servant bowed them inside where they found a room with stone walls and floor, weapons racks along the far wall and lumps stacked in a corner that were probably practice targets.

In the center of the room, Ryld's teachers waited. They'd been warned, but Hank still had a little jolt seeing them. Sometimes he had trouble telling aelfe apart, but these two were identical. Mirror copies of each other. Both tall and slender, with the elegant, dexterous hands he associated with mages, their long, ice-blue hair hanging loose at the exact same length, their new-grass-green eyes regarding them with the identical expression of appraisal and mild contempt. They even stood in the same hipshot stance. He had to wonder if it was normal or something they put on to confound strangers.

The one on the left made a gesture that wasn't quite a bow. "I am Yarrow, and this is Yew. The little one is Ryld, we assume?"

"I am Ryld Varjo," Ryld said. He didn't snap, but his volume was a little louder than normal, and the one called Yarrow snapped his attention to Ryld, his hand vaguely fluttering over his chest as if he thought Ryld might bite him. Hank suppressed the chuckle, and also the warning that if they weren't careful Ryld might indeed bite them.

"I see…" The aelfe seemed at a loss now that he had to speak to Ryld directly. "Well…shall we sit? Lady Jessamine has told us a bit about you, but I'd like to hear from you what you hope to accomplish with proper lessons."

There were cushions a bit farther in, and they all settled, though Hank noted with some interest that Kai took his cushion a little farther off. He was making it clear that he wouldn't interfere. This was all Ryld.

Direct as always, Ryld said simply, "I need to control my shadows."

Yarrow peered at him more closely. "Your shadows. The ones…"

"They flutter around you," Yew finished, his hands making fluttering motions in response.

Now Hank spotted the difference and couldn't unsee it. Yarrow looked at them directly. Yew would not.

"Always," Ryld responded. "Sometimes more, sometimes less. They move and grow, and sometimes they escape."

"Escape. As in escape your control?"

"They are not in my control. I-I hold on to them…" Ryld was clearly struggling to explain something that was as natural to him as breathing to someone who didn't understand the concept.

"And what happens when they escape?"

"I wonder why you ask what you already know?"

"I wish to hear it from you, what you think."

Hank glanced at Ryld. His face was smooth, expressionless. Not upset exactly but perhaps annoyed. He wondered if he should warn the aelfe that they really shouldn't annoy him. He decided to keep quiet for now. Kai was probably right in taking a hands-off approach.

"The shadows grow teeth and claws. They bite and rend and kill until they are stopped."

Yarrow glanced at Yew who made an unfathomable gesture with both hands. When Yarrow turned back, he asked, "Ryld, you say you hold the shadows. Where do they come from?"

Ryld cut his eyes away. "The darkness."

"Hmm. Yes. Shadows are the dark." Yarrow cocked his head, gaze intent on the air around Ryld. "We all have shadows. Carry the dark."

Yew's leg twitched, his tone flat and without the polish of his brother's. "They're yours."

"They come to me…"

"No, the shadows in this room are only the absence of light. Your shadows are different. They come from you."

"I am small. The shadows can be much bigger. They don't live inside me."

This was actually interesting. Hank wasn't sure what he'd expected. Blah, blah, blah, magic theory, boring stuff about firmaments — but the twins were surprisingly astute and direct in addition to being unsettling.

"Hmm, no." Yarrow raised a hand, palm up. A tiny spark burned above his fingers, flickering blue-white before it grew into a red, swirling fireball the size of his head. "The fire does not live inside me. I use the magic in the air around me to manifest it. But it is mine. I have made this fire. It did not come to me on its own." He banished it and called a miniature rainstorm over his hand. "Nor the cloud. It cannot simply come to me. I must make it from air and water and from what is in me."

"I do not make the shadows. They come to me," Ryld insisted.

The twins went quiet, both looking at Ryld curiously.

"You fear them," Yew said.

"*You* should fear them, too," Ryld told him, maybe a little more forceful than his usual tone.

"But they do not hurt you? Is that not so?" Yarrow said.

"They don't hurt me. They hurt others. Anyone in their path."

"Why do you think it is they don't hurt you, if you are not in control of them?"

Ryld stopped his agitated twitching and stared — more accurately *glared* at him.

"A seed planted must grow," Yew said.

"Yes, I think that's enough for now. This was not meant to be a lesson, more of a meeting, but it has turned into a teaching nonetheless. I would like you to meditate on this, Ryld, and meet us here again tomorrow."

Hank rose first, offering a hand to help Ryld up, though he either didn't see it or was too agitated to respond to it, rising on his own and stalking toward the door. Hank knew what the twins were saying. He even agreed. But it wasn't going to help unless Ryld's worldview shifted so he could see it, too. The shadows were very much Ryld, part of him that Hank had almost become accustomed to.

No. That wasn't right. He had become accustomed to them and to watching them for signs of Ryld's distress. They were a Ryld barometer, and most of the time Hank didn't find them scary. Not anymore.

Now it seemed as if Ryld were bent on outrunning the flickers of dark that skittered along like small mice behind him. He was definitely upset with the meeting, which didn't bode well considering it took all of fifteen minutes.

"Ryld?"

"I want to go outside. Out of this place," Ryld said, tone completely flat.

Hank jogged to get ahead of him. "All right. We'll go out. I saw a door near the stairs on the way down. Kai, you still there?"

The snort from farther back was confirmation enough. "Behind you. Yes. Though if you insist on running, I may just catch up to you later."

Ryld slowed his steps. Hank led them out of the door and into the sunlight, and all three winced. This time Hank had remembered both his own sunglasses and Ryld's, and of course Kai was already reaching into his pocket.

"Thank you." Ryld put the glasses on. They were the pink ones with the rhinestones around the frames. They were only three paces away from the building when Ryld said, "I don't think they are telling the truth."

"About what, specifically?" Kai asked in a tone implying that probably no one in this place told all the truth.

"The shadows are not a part of me." Ryld made a cutting motion with one hand to emphasize the point.

"Why do you believe they are not?" Kai asked softly.

Ryld spun around, the look of betrayal he shot Kai evident in every line of his body. "Kai Hiltas, they are not me. They are *not*. I don't want to hurt people. The shadows…that's all they want."

Kai lifted a hand, gesturing for peace. "Very well. But I have commanded dark magics in my time. So very dark. If the shadows are called from elsewhere, I should be able to call them, yes?"

Although Hank agreed with Kai, he very much wished he hadn't pushed Ryld on this. Without thinking he put a hand on Kai's arm, instinct to pull him out of the way of danger.

Both drow snarled, Kai most likely out of old instinct, and Ryld because Hank had touched Kai. *Oh crap.* The edges of Ryld's eyes darkened, and Hank lifted his hand and backed away.

"Ryld. Shadows. I can see them. Take a breath."

Ryld took a breath all right. Like he'd just sprinted a half mile. His eyes went completely black, but at the same time Ryld grabbed his head and crumpled, drawing his knees up and making himself into a small tight ball. The shadow that leapt from him toward Kai was about the size of a small rat but shaped like some sort of sea monster with many whipping legs.

Kai hadn't been without warning, at least. He dove and rolled to the side, managing to get a hand up even as the shadow thing shifted direction in midair. The mage ball Kai threw at it wasn't elegant or even nicely formed, but it did the trick, smashing into the ferocious little shadow and reducing it to fading wisps.

"Lovely," Kai spat out as he sat down hard in the grass. "Tell me again, child, that that wasn't *you*."

"Easy, Kai." Hank patted at the air. "You're all right. Don't make it worse."

Ryld was still tucked into a little ball, but his head came up and he bared his teeth in a snarl at Kai. However, the shadows stayed put, clinging to him like stringy lines of tar. The standoff went on for several seconds and finally Hank asked, "You ever seen this happen with him before?"

"No." Kai shook his head, his voice soft again. "But Ryld has never been so...conflicted at any time since I've known him." Kai flicked a look at Hank. "Nor has he had cause to be jealous before."

Ryld growled but the growl turned into a moan, and he dropped his head down, rocking on the balls of his feet. Hank debated if touching him would help or hurt, but before he could decide the little sounds of distress quieted, and Ryld was back with them, looking confused as to why he was practically sitting on the ground.

"Hi." Hank offered a little smile as he hunkered down in front of Ryld. "You all right there?"

A bewildered nod was his only answer.

"Now. I'm not saying I agree or disagree with what anyone said today. But Kai ticked you off a bit. I was dumb enough to take his arm. And this scary little kraken shadow attacked him." Hank sat all the way on the grass. Might as well join them. "Sweetheart, tell me that's coincidence."

Ryld looked from Hank to where Kai sat, a worried frown on his face. He must have thought Kai looked all right because he dropped his eyes, shamefaced.

"I—I'm sorry."

"I'm well, little brother." Kai heaved a long sigh and, shockingly, lay back in the grass. "My apologies for not knowing when to end an argument. Tenzin says I always have to have the last word."

"Tenzin is wise," Ryld said.

Kai laughed.

"If the shadows are not me, why am I sorry?" Ryld said in a tone so soft it was almost a whisper. "If they are me, I am as much a monster as they are."

"No, hon." Hank reached out and took his hand in a gentle grip. "No. Someone put a machine gun in your hands, blindfolded you, put you in a dark scary place and didn't teach you how to use the damn thing. Those people are monsters. Not you. You're still not all the way aware when it happens. That's how badly they crippled your power."

"I don't want them. I don't want to be me anymore. I know why the others like me go mad. Every day, every minute, I have to hold on, and my hands are tired."

Cracks rippled across Hank's heart at the anguish in those words. He drew Ryld close, wrapped him tight, rocking him gently. "I'd be very sad if you weren't you anymore. And I'm sorry it's been so hard. All your life. So hard. But that's why we're here. To see if maybe we can...can help you unclench your fists safely again."

Ryld laid his cheek on Hank's chest and let himself be soothed. The three of them stayed like that. Listening to the wind sigh in the trees and the birds twitter and play. Eventually the tension level eased. When Ryld lifted his head again, Hank asked, "Would you like to go for a walk? Sometimes walking helps me to relax."

"I would like to go for a walk, yes," Ryld said. "Kai, would you like to walk with us?"

"Thank you, yes. I do believe I would."

They walked straight out into the trees, following a little footpath obviously used by frequent pedestrians, Hank with Ryld tucked under his arm, and Kai strolling a few steps back, hands clasped behind his back, taking in the forest life.

It was a pensive ramble, no one in the mood for talk, and all wrapped in their own thoughts. Hank was working on some theories of his own about what had just happened and why. Ryld didn't want to hurt anyone. He'd said so often enough. Yet a part of him did want to hurt people, of course. The people that had originally made his life such hell to begin with, probably. Maybe accepting that was just too much for his mind to handle, and so to protect him, his mind tucked that part away. Hank wasn't sure that making him face it was right though. After all, if his theory was correct, his mind had protected him from that part of himself for a reason.

Such dark thoughts seemed out of place on such a perfect day. They saw more birds and squirrels and even a small herd of deer across a clearing. Wildflowers bloomed in profusion and butterflies floated above them. Wait. Not butterflies.

"Ah. Hello, little one," Kai was saying to a bright yellow something flitting around his head. "So you live here as well? Oh? Well, yes, I have a troop who lives with me. I suppose I might smell of flower fairy a bit."

The air was suddenly filled with bright wings and high-pitched calls. Ryld stopped, frozen to the spot as pink, blue and yellow fairies swooped around his head. He had the same delighted look he'd had on his face when he'd found the perfect color or created a pattern that especially pleased him. He held up one hand and a tiny blue fairy landed on his palm. She looked as quizzically at Ryld as Ryld did at her.

"Hank..." Ryld whispered excitedly. "Hank... Hank, look..."

"They're beautiful." Hank leaned his chin on Ryld's shoulder for a closer inspection. "Hello, tiny miss."

"There are so many of you here," Kai breathed out in wonder as he stepped off the path into the glade. The flower fairies immediately swarmed him, tugging at his hair, their tiny voices becoming a constant high-pitched buzz. Kai looked like he was walking inside a multi-colored, moving cocoon.

"You understand what they are saying?" Ryld asked.

Within the odd dome of fairies, Kai turned his head. "Yes. It, ah, took some practice, but you most likely can too if you listen quite closely. The trick is to listen to one at a time, which can be a bit difficult since they will insist on all talking at once."

Hank swept a glance around the glade. "Look in the trees...there must be...I don't even know how many. They must live here, or nearby?"

The tiny fairy still perched on Ryld's hand said something and Ryld's eyes widened. "Oh, I do understand them..." He looked up. Hank looked up too. Above them was a large nest with various bits of wood, leaves, vines and less natural items like bits of colored glass and mirror. Once Hank saw it, like the fairies themselves, he saw them everywhere.

"I didn't know there were so many fairies in this world, much less living all in one place." Kai had wandered over to a bramble, examining the nests there.

"Since they're so small, they tend to be pulled over during Events in multiples rather than singly as most of us larger beings are. Add to that a good nesting environment as you see around you, and they do tend to be rather fecund."

"Rather...what?" Hank would've looked the word up under other circumstances, but he didn't want to let go of Ryld.

"They breed faster than rabbits."

Ryld lifted his hand up a little higher, so he was eye level with the fairy. "You are so beautiful. I love your color."

Kai had wandered closer again and had stopped at a nest that a particularly insistent fairy wanted to show him. Craning his neck, Hank could make it out, a larger one, but instead of a down-lined hollow at its center, the nest had been filled with flower petals.

"What's happened here?" Kai asked the insistent green fairy. He listened—his forehead creased in concentration. "Oh dear. I am sorry. No, no, I'm not a healer. That's very sad."

"What's sad, Kai?" Hank called over, though he was afraid he knew what the answer would be.

"This little queen has lost half her troop. The petals cover their bodies until they can have a proper burial."

"So many...?" Ryld murmured. "What happened to them? Were they attacked?"

Kai bent his head to listen again. "No, they simply died in their sleep. It's...unusual to happen in such large numbers, but she says it simply happens sometimes." He returned to them slowly, some of his entourage peeling away to join the flocks in the glade. "I do wonder, though. I hope there's not an epidemic brewing. We'll ask Lady Jessamine to send a healer out to be sure."

By the time they got back, it was still early but felt much later. A long day filled with highs and lows. Ryld looked positively ashen, and Hank told Kai they would meet him later for dinner, if he was free, and took Ryld back to their rooms.

"What would you like, sweetheart?" Hank asked once he'd closed the doors. "Hot bath, some food, or a nap? Or all of those."

"A bath. One of my favorite things used to be to go down to the hot springs. Have you ever been to hot springs?"

"I can't recall ever going. Maybe Mom and Dad took me when I was little, but we didn't have any nearby." Hank scratched his head. "I don't know if they have them here, either."

Of course *that* was solved simply by asking one of the servants passing in the hall, and it turned out that yes, they did, and yes, it would be down the same staircase they'd taken to meet the twins that morning, first door on the left.

The trip back down all those stairs was worth it. They had the chamber to themselves, and Ryld was obviously pleased. There were niches carved into the stone walls that held oil lamps and low wood benches near the pool of steaming water. Pegs were conveniently anchored in the walls to hang clothing.

Ryld shed his clothes quickly, then dipped his toes and oo-ed and hissed at the heat, but still seemed to be enjoying himself.

Hank shrugged out of his clothes at a more leisurely pace, taking in their surroundings. There were steps in places, little shelves beneath the water that could serve as benches. All rather well constructed. He sat on the edge of the pool and let his legs dangle, trying to work himself up to actually getting in.

Ryld stepped down onto one of the ledges, the water coming up to his knees. "Oo, ah…hot…" He took another step down, the water coming up to his waist this time. "I wish our apartment had a hot spring."

"That'd be an interesting thing to try to convince the building owners to do." Hank slid in and sat on the top step, letting the water lap around his body and telling himself he was not a crab in a pot. "I guess some people have hot tubs, which are like tiny hot springs."

"Yes. I would like a hot tub." Ryld's fingers glided across the surface of the water as he moved toward Hank. He sat down on the shelf next to him and leaned back with a contented sigh. "Does your shoulder still hurt?"

"Sometimes." Hank sank a little lower into the water, now that Ryld had him thinking about the remaining stiffness. "Mostly when I forget and pick up something heavy."

Ryld leaned over and kissed Hank's shoulder, just above the edge of the water. "Now the pain will go away."

Hank grinned. It had been a long time since anyone had kissed his boo-boos better. "Thank you."

"You're welcome."

He opened his arms and waited for Ryld to duck under and settle against him, the comfort of holding Ryld going a long way to improving what had been a really odd and anxious sort of day.

Ryld squirmed around to face him. Hank was more than happy to open his knees and let Ryld settle between his thighs, his heartbeat kicking up as their cocks settled together in the best way.

Ryld moved against him, flexing in such a way that ground pelvis to pelvis. "Hank…"

"Mm-hm?"

"My heart always wants to be near your heart."

For someone so literal to say such a poetic thing, about him, for him, Hank's eyes stung with the threat of tears. He tightened his arms around him and buried his face against Ryld's throat. "Mine too, hon. Mine too."

Ryld wrapped his arms around Hank's neck, the full length of their bodies from neck to hips pressed skin to skin in the heated water. For a while they stayed just like that, the steam rising around them. When Ryld did move again it was more of a wriggle, a sway of his hips that did delightful things where they touched under the water.

Hank lifted his head, and Ryld cupped his checks with both hands, looking at him closely before closing his eyes and kissing him. To an outsider, Ryld probably seemed aromantic, but once Hank learned his language it was easy to see that wasn't the case. He spoke in small ways, like showing him the patterns he made, then making one just for him. By paying attention to the things he liked and remembering them for later, even though he had difficulty paying attention. In his own way, Ryld tried to take care of Hank, and he had from the start.

It had been a long time since anyone had cared at all, and Ryld cared more than any lover Hank had been with in his old world or his new one.

He rocked his hips up to meet Ryld, letting the heat and the surging passion claim him, his cock and Ryld's trapped between their bodies creating delicious friction as they rubbed together.

The warm water helped to melt away all the stress of the day, and apparently Ryld felt the same because neither of them made a move to change up their position. It wasn't necessary anyway — the lazy glide of their bodies together was working to edge them toward a different type of stress relief.

"Ryld," Hank panted as he got close. "I want...I want your teeth. Right at where neck meets shoulder. Not...not so hard you break skin, but, you know... hard."

Ryld's blue eyes were dark, with passion, not shadows. He seemed about to ask a question but must have changed his mind. Instead, he lowered his head, at the same time picking up the pace and grinding harder against Hank. Ryld's breath was almost as warm as the steam against Hank's skin where his lips hovered at the crook of his throat.

Was the hesitation uncertainty or...?

Ryld dug fingers into Hank's shoulders as he nipped, then bit harder, right where Hank had told him to.

"Oh...goddesses." Hank gasped and moaned, letting his head fall back on the stone lip of the pool as his hips ground up hard, nearly whiting out as his orgasm climbed unexpectedly high before exploding from him in heavy waves.

Ryld sucked hard at the mark he'd made with his teeth, his hips jerked erratically through his own peak before slowing to a lazy glide again, then going still, panting where he was draped across Hank.

"Mmm." Hank kissed his face, lazy and thorough — forehead, cheeks, eyelids, mouth. "This was the best idea anyone's had in days."

Ryld made a happy sound of agreement. They lay submerged for some time, until they were both pruny and so loose and relaxed it was hard to drag themselves out. Later, when they met Kai for dinner, his eyes went right to the mark on Hank's neck, but he said nothing, of course. Only the hint of a knowing smile slipped across his lips. The big soft bed was welcome when they finally climbed in, and Hank slept better than he had the night before.

Chapter Eleven

"I see the companion is with you today." Lady Jessamine quirked a golden eyebrow at Kai. "Does this mean the lessons are going well?"

Only long practice allowed Kai to control his features. Her continued contempt for Hank irked him, an annoying flaw in an otherwise bright persona. Though he supposed it was normal for aelfe royalty and Elvenhome hadn't provided any incentive to break the habit. For his part, Hank stayed outwardly serene, pretending he didn't notice as he ate the dainty sandwiches on offer for lunch. He was a little too good at the calm mask. Far too much practice, Kai presumed.

"I believe there have been steps forward." Kai sipped at his orange blossom tea. Quite nice. He preferred something stronger, but it was pleasant. "Yarrow and Yew give Ryld much to consider, things he has not been able to face before. He has asked for us to leave him in peace so that he might meditate on these things."

"That *is* good news." She beamed at him—her regard nearly blinding. It was all Kai could do not to reach for his sunglasses. "I had hoped, since Yew is perhaps very like Ryld in some ways, that they would be able to communicate well."

"So far, I'm encouraged." Kai set his cup down. "I wonder, my lady, if I might impinge on your good will just a bit more."

"Kai!" She let out a silver-bright laugh. "You are my friend. If you require anything, please ask."

He gave her a nod, gratitude and acknowledgment. "Thank you. And perhaps you will wonder at my concern, but I have reason. We came across a...hmm, what amounted to a small city of flower fairies yesterday. So many living in one grove. I've never seen such a thing. The little queen told us that many of her people have died, and I fear an epidemic in their community. Would you have a healer willing to visit them? To see if they might root out a cause?"

Her frown was one of concentration, perhaps worry. "I'm happy to send a healer for you, my dear Kai. But I'm afraid the cause will be as it has been these past few years. I have warned the little ones about overcrowding. Flower fairies were never meant to live together in such numbers. And yet they insist on it."

"Have they told you why?"

"Safety, their queen claims. Something about this forest. She's never been terribly clear." Her smile took on a wry note. "I do try to assist those within my reach, you know. Aelfe or not. We assist the vasse when they need it. The kolle when they allow it."

Kai asked in his driest tone, "And the drow?"

"You know *she* would never accept help from me." Lady Jessamine made a sour face, though her smile returned swiftly. "I've even established an orphanage, near the edge of Elvenhome. No child is turned away, no matter what race."

"That must be quite an undertaking." Kai knew how logistically complicated caring for children could become. AURA struggled every year to place those younglings who crossed over alone.

"I have administrators, of course. Proper childcare professionals." Her laugh was too regal for a giggle, but it came perilously close. "I would never attempt such a thing on my own."

"Of course, my lady. Still, I commend you for your civic mindedness."

She brightened even further, an idea obviously occurring to her. "Would you like to visit the orphanage? It would please me to have you see the work we've been doing."

Visit a building full of children...perhaps not his favorite way to spend the day. But... "Hank, would you like to go?"

Hank put his plate down. He seemed startled to be addressed directly. "Um, sure, Mr. Hiltas. I'm kind of at loose ends today."

"Good. Thank you. We would find a visit of great interest, my lady." He was going to have a talk with Hank about the subservient role. It puzzled him that Hank would take it on willingly.

"Wonderful!" Lady Jessamine clapped her hands. "I'll have horses and a guide waiting for you in half an hour. Would that do?"

"Perfect, my lady." Kai rose and offered a bow, waiting until they were well down the corridor before he murmured to Hank, "Mr. Hiltas?"

Hank shrugged. "They don't see me as a person, in case you didn't notice. It seems, I dunno, safer somehow to play faithful servant."

"Hmm. So long as it's not unduly distressing, I appreciate your discretion. Perhaps, ah, keeping you under the radar is best."

"Kai?"

"I don't... Something is itching under my skin. Which generally means something is not right. But I can't imagine what yet. Eyes and ears open."

"Yes, sir." Hank gave a serious nod.

"If you persist with the servile playacting in private, I may smack you."

Hank only laughed.

True to her word, Lady Jessamine had horses waiting—the lovely beast Kai had ridden previously, and a draft horse for Hank. It was, of course, a beautiful draft horse since it lived in an elven stable, but the message that Hank's size and station didn't merit an actual riding horse was clear.

Kai turned to Hank with a belated thought. "You *can* ride? Apologies, I should've asked."

"I can. It was Dad's mule, mostly, but I'll manage." Hank eyed the draft horse with poorly hidden concern. "Though he's a big fella, isn't he?"

"As suits your warrior heritage. Remember that all draft horses were battle steeds once."

"Not making me feel better, Kai."

The guide was another surly youngster—where did she keep finding them?—and the ride pleasant, through one dappled grove after another. For most of the morning they stayed on a fairly well used path that was wide enough to be a road. After about an hour they turned off onto a smaller, less worn trail that was a little rougher riding but still not difficult. Sometime around noon Kai was thinking they had to be nearing the edge of Elvenhome when their guide said, "Once we're through Pixieland it's only a short way to the highway. That marks the west boundary of Elvenhome. Kent City and the orphanage are about two miles travel from there."

"You won't be coming with us?"

The young aelfe rolled his eyes. "*I'm* not going out into human territory. That's all on you."

Lovely. Kai was on the verge of asking what the youngling meant by Pixieland when he spotted the hovel. At first, he assumed it was some sort of equipment shed of cobbled-together bits of scrap plywood. But he had the uncomfortable feeling eyes watched them from within, through the badly joined pieces.

A few yards farther on, though, there was another, this one of mixed material—old tires, cement blocks, more wood scraps. And then another...and another...

"Hank." Kai reined his horse over to walk beside the draft horse. "What do you think we're seeing?"

"Nothing good," Hank murmured and nodded to a curtain doorway of rotted material. "It's pixies. Look."

There was a woman standing just inside the doorway. Her small frame was sparse on flesh even by pixie standards. She watched them with wary eyes, one hand on her hip. Two small faces peered out from behind her, awe and envy warring with caution on their faces.

Kai spotted a wagon with a round hoop top. A pixie man sat on the wood steps leading up to the door, his expression too was wary, and more hostile. A pixie woman leaned one hand on the wagon. She wore a pair of shorts and a gauzy scarf over her shoulders that did nothing to hide her breasts. Her wings were up, spread out as if on display, and she smiled invitingly at them.

More children, dogs and goats ran around beside the dirt road, and more shacks and wagons spread out.

Kai turned his horse's head to go speak with one of the women, but Hank shot a hand out and caught his bridle.

"Don't. Kai...let them be. We need to keep moving."

"But this is dreadful," Kai whispered at him. "The children are filthy. They're living in shacks."

Hank threw a meaningful glance at their guide. Yes, yes, of course. *He* wasn't at all shocked and kept his gaze straight ahead as they rode through. *What's happening here?*

They kept going. Kai kept looking, trying to get an idea of the size of the...encampment? Village? It was hard to say. The trees obscured a lot. He had a sense he was only seeing the surface of something larger. At the first trill, he was uncertain if it was a bird, but when it was repeated, spreading back into the woods around them, the fine hairs on the back of his neck stood on end. Their guide dropped a hand to the short sword on his saddle and picked up the pace.

While Kai couldn't decipher the trills, he knew coded communication when he heard it. He imagined the pixies telling each other disparaging things about the wealthy elves riding through. Or perhaps it was more sinister. In his experience, pixies didn't naturally tend toward violence, but they certainly *could* in the right circumstances. Pixie bands did have warriors, after all.

Feelings of imminent ambush aside, they crossed through the pixies' territory and emerged soon after into sunlight at the edge of the woods. Their guide pointed them in the right direction and vanished back into the trees without a word.

The shoulder of the road provided enough room for them to ride side-by-side, which they did in silence for several yards.

Finally, Hank cleared his throat. "You all right? You look a little gray."

"Distressed. I am distressed." Kai waved a hand back in the direction of *Pixieland* as their guide had so sneeringly called it. "What in all gods of earth was that?"

Hank gave him a sidelong look. "You've never seen a slum before?"

"Yes, of course. But I *did not expect one here*!" Kai took a breath and lowered his voice. "Within the demesne of Elvenhome. Right under Jessamine's nose. I don't understand it."

"Guess you'd have to ask her. Probably happened because of a lot of different things. It's not usually just one thing that builds a place like that."

"True enough, my brave friend, but one needn't..." Kai shivered, fighting back the visceral distress. "One needn't *leave* things that way."

Hank seemed of the verge of saying something but stopped.

"I hope you've gotten to know me well enough to speak your mind, Hank. What are you thinking?"

Hank took a breath and let it out. "I hope you don't take offense, this isn't directed at you, but...well, the pixie folk and the drow are like oil and water where I come from. And Lady Jessamine isn't the only queen in these woods. If the drow made things difficult for them...that could have led to their current state."

A few years ago, Kai might have exploded at those words. A few years ago, he wouldn't have been riding along a highway with a half-goblin accountant. Now he just sighed. "I recognize the possible truth in that. Perhaps I should bring the subject up with Lady Ksatha and gauge her reaction to pixies. I'm not certain... Well, I need more information before I can be a proper interfering pest."

They rode for another minute or two before Hank asked, "Again, I beg your pardon but...how come AURA is allowing this? I thought they had programs, education, job placements and such?"

"Yes, I'm sure AURA would help them if they knew about them." Kai almost tripped over the words. He'd done his research before making this trip, of course he had, and why hadn't he found any mention of a sizable colony of pixies living on Elvenhome land? That should have been in any of the AURA reports he'd read, but he was sure he hadn't seen any mention of it. Which begged the question, how did AURA not know?

Or if they did, why hadn't there been any intervention?

The orphanage, when they reached it, at least met expectations. A two-story building with many windows, it appeared to be a repurposed school. Probably not perfect as all old public buildings were not, but functional enough.

They left their horses at the little lean-to meant for them — so the school most likely had frequent Elvenhome visitors — and made their way up the front steps where they were met by a matronly human woman in a dark blue suit.

"Mr. Hiltas? Lady Jessamine phoned to say you'd be visiting for a tour this afternoon." She stuck out a hand in the human way. "Gail Albright. Good to meet you."

Kai took her hand briefly. "Thank you for accommodating us. This is my associate, Hank Onyx-Wainwright."

She held her hand out to Hank as well, smiling. "Welcome, Mr. Onyx-Wainwright." Apparently the elven prejudice they'd been laboring under these last few days didn't extend to their human employees, which was refreshing.

"I hope you don't mind me saying, we don't get many drow visitors here." She gave Kai an apologetic smile. "Don't worry too much if some of the kids stare. You'll be the talk of the week."

No, they probably didn't get drow visitors since it was an aelfe-sponsored institution. Perhaps if their respective queens weren't so at odds...but that would be like asking geese to get along with foxes.

"The kids are mostly in the classrooms this time of day. We can peek in, but I don't want to interrupt."

"Understood, Ms. Albright. We will be as unobtrusive as we can."

In the first classroom they came to, the teacher sat on a small chair with an open book on her lap, reading to a circle of about twenty young children, barely out of toddler stage. Every last one of them had a glossy pair of pixie wings fanning from their backs.

Their clothes were all very much the same, not quite a uniform, but plain denim pants and T-shirts made for wings. Nothing fancy, but the children looked clean, unlike their counterparts in the pixie slum.

They did stare, some with fear in their eyes. Kai told himself it hadn't anything to do with him, didn't affect him in the least. Generally, he couldn't stand to be around children. Noisy, germ-carrying chaos tornadoes. But he knew he was lying to himself, at least a bit, and a corner of his heart broke.

Ms. Albright chattered away about programs and adoption rates. They saw older children learning math, and the not-quite teenagers in quiet study groups, a few humans scattered among the pixies.

"Why do you receive so many pixie children, Ms. Albright?" Kai asked as they strolled to the infant room. "Is the orphanage specialized?"

She laughed a bit at that. "I suppose it looks that way, doesn't it? We're not specialized officially, Mr. Hiltas, but most of these kids are local. Crossover parents who don't make it or who abandon their little ones. We see a lot of it here."

Hank narrowed his eyes, but his tone was mild when he asked, "I didn't see any teachers or staff who were pixies. Are they all humans and elves?"

"We have an actively diverse hiring process," Ms. Albright said with forced cheer. "But yes, right now our teachers and staff are human and elven. Oh, we do have Mr. Feldspar. He's our goblin janitor."

Kai had to give Hank credit for the complete mastery of his facial expressions. He was sure his own face looked like he'd bitten into a lemon. His initial assessment that perhaps the predominate prejudice in Elvenhome didn't extend to the orphanage was rapidly changing. It was just more subtle here.

"Some of the classes have been let out for a recess, if you'd like to see the playground?"

Given that there didn't seem to be much more to see, they followed Ms. Albright to the back entrance of the converted school building and out a set of double doors.

A scattering of teachers kept half an eye on the kids running around playing while they chatted. The kids screeched and tumbled just like any other children. If Kai didn't think too hard on it, he could forget this was an orphanage. It seemed just like any other school playground. That was the horrible part, really. That there were enough kids here to make it seem like a regular school. The head count seemed far too high, even given that some of these kids were crossovers without parents in this world.

A pixie boy who was climbing a tall slide jumped from the top, wings blurring as he swooped down on his playmates.

"Trevor Fair-Sky, that's a detention!" one of the teachers hollered at the child. "Inside. Now."

The child in trouble, Trevor, trudged across the playground, head hung and wings plastered down as he plodded inside.

The adult response seemed extreme to Kai. Trevor — terrible name for a pixie — had simply been doing what pixie children do. Trying their wings. Practicing taking off from a high place. To punish that... But Kai held his peace. It wasn't his place to undermine the grownups here.

Ms. Albright must have read his expression because she explained, "We discourage flying because the children who don't have wings, or can't fly, either try it and get hurt or are jealous. It's not fair to them."

Which probably seemed reasonable to someone who didn't have wings and didn't understand children with them, but to Kai it still felt harsh.

As they were about to go back inside a commotion of a different sort broke out near the sidewalk.

"Give him back!" A young pixie woman screamed at one of the teachers standing near the fence. "I want him back!"

"Let's go inside, shall we?" Ms. Albright said, as if nothing at all were happening.

Hank didn't budge, his arms crossed over his chest. Kai took a spot at his shoulder, watching the scene play out at the fence.

"Alana, we've talked about this before," a tall aelfe woman with impressive arms was telling the pixie. "You keep up the racket, and we call the police."

"But he's mine! You have to give him back! Have pity." The pixie woman broke down in sobs.

"Police, Alana. Remember the last time you had to spend a night in the human jail cells?"

The pixie sobbed harder, but turned to go, dragging her feet as if someone had attached hundred-pound weights to them.

"Sad case."

Kai twitched when Ms. Albright spoke too close to his ear. "Oh?"

"She's under the delusion that some of the kids are hers. Changes every time she stops by, which kids she means. Upsets the little ones terribly." She held the door open for them. "We have a restraining order, but that only works so far."

"Yes, very sad." Kai had more to say on the matter, but not to Ms. Albright. She might run the orphanage, but ultimately she wasn't the one in charge here.

They spent a little more time listening to Ms. Albright prattle on about all the good they were doing in the community, the challenges they faced and the fundraisers they had planned, then they finally made their escape. And it did feel like an escape. While the building had been painted in light colors, the oppressive atmosphere weighed on him even after such a short time, and the thought that they could leave while the children they saw had no homes to go to was outright depressing. Kai had in no way been prepared for that many, although in retrospect, if there had only been a few, he supposed there would be no need for such a place to exist.

Hank rode beside him on the way back, stone-faced, back rigid, and Kai knew how he felt, though his own reaction was to try to curl in on himself, which he had to fight or end up in a fetal ball in the saddle.

Not a look that would inspire confidence.

The more he thought about it, the less everything they'd seen that day made any sense at all. He knew he was missing things, most likely obvious things. Yes, pixie birth rates were high. Yes, many went unaccounted for in the AURA systems because of that. They tracked crossovers but weren't always apprised of births that happened *here*. Strike that. They were rarely informed. Once crossovers found new lives, they didn't think it was something they had to do. Never mind that the federal government expected them to keep track and it was enormously aggravating…

"Kai?"

"Yes?" The word was sharper than he intended. He shot Hank an apologetic look.

"How do you think they're funding that place, really?" Hank still glared into the distance, though his voice was steady.

"I...suppose there are federal grants. Private funds from Lady Jessamine. Probably some charitable donations."

Hank raised an eyebrow at him. "Tell me you don't do your departmental budgets."

"Not...generally. No. I'm certainly *aware* of department funding. I have to be."

Hank nodded. "Right. There's a whole accounting office. Anyway, look—those were a lot of kids. It's not a small operation. Salaries, building upkeep, supplies, food, it all adds up. How does Lady Jessamine fund this and keep her celebrity lifestyle? Where did all the money come from to build her huge palace?"

"I'm sure they have income sources..." Kai trailed off. Where *did* it all come from? "Hank, when we get back, I'm going to start, ah, looking into some things. If I turn up financial records...?"

"You come tell me." Hank's grin was all tusks and teeth. "That's what I do best."

"I'm so glad you came along, have I told you that?"

"Not yet. But thanks."

Chapter Twelve

These aelfe mages did not understand what they asked. Ryld wondered if Yarrow heard him at all. For someone who seemed to speak almost telepathically with his brother, Ryld might as well have been speaking to a stone for all Yarrow listened.

"Even if I could do what you asked, I would not," Ryld said at last.

Yarrow stared at him. "Are you saying you won't try?"

"Yes. I will not try to do what you are asking. It is too dangerous."

"I understand your fear." Yarrow smiled. "It is all right, little drow. You have never faced your dark magic, but even when you lose control of it, does it not leave you untouched?"

Ryld felt the shadows around him stir and he was almost tempted to let them grow and give the patronizing aelfe what he wished. "I don't fear for myself, Yarrow. I fear for you and your brother."

Yarrow chuckled. "I'm not without my own power, Ryld. I wouldn't let any harm come to myself or Yew."

Ryld's lip twitched, and he controlled the impulse to bare his teeth at the elf. "You can contain them, perhaps. But you aren't drow. Your magic will not work on the shadows."

"Ryld, Ryld. You must trust me. Your darkness is no match for my light. Aren't you tired of struggling? Instead of holding the beasts back, learn to control them at your will. But in order to control one, you must first consciously form and release one, rather than wait for your emotions to dictate when that happens."

In theory that actually sounded sensible. Control was what he wanted. However, purposefully letting a rage and hate fueled beast capable of rending both men to pieces before help could arrive... Well, despite the whispers of his drow brethren, he wasn't mad, and that was utter madness.

Ryld took a breath. "I will do as you ask, but I have a condition. Kai Hiltas must be present, and he must say it is okay for me to try."

With an exasperated sigh, Yarrow threw up his hands. "If the drow mage could teach you, why would he have brought you to us?"

"I don't know. I would like to go now."

"Running from this will not help you, Ryld."

"Neither will letting the shadows tear you apart."

Yarrow forced a smile. "I see we will get no farther today. Go and speak to your mentor. Perhaps he can see sense."

Ryld stood and left the room. He waited until after the door had closed behind him to shut his eyes and take a few deep breaths as Hank had taught him to do.

Hank had taught him more than these two, he thought gloomily.

The shadows still flickered and skittered around him as he trudged up the stairs to the main floor. Hungry, he decided to find the kitchen. The place seemed to have people rushing about everywhere today. As he walked, he noticed the stares and the way the aelfe moved away as he neared. He was used to such behavior, but here the drow only lived a short ride from the residence. They saw them frequently, they must, so it was just him they didn't want to get close to. That was fine, he didn't want them close either.

From the corner of his eye, he saw a dark shape lash out from him toward an elf's leg and the way he skittered back. Well, perhaps he couldn't blame them entirely for wanting to keep their distance. He was more agitated than he wanted to admit. Hank and Kai would be back soon. Perhaps he should just wait until they returned to eat. He stood in indecision. Being hungry did not help calm him.

"Ryld?" He turned with a feeling of relief to see Hank and Kai coming up the stairs from the stable courtyard. "You all right, hon? You're, um, leaking a little around the edges."

"I am unhurt. But hungry. Perhaps the shadows are hungry too, though I've never seen them eat."

"Mother Goddess forbid," Kai muttered. "You two go on up to your suite. I will hunt down an appropriate staff member and have dinner sent up for all of us. It's been...a day."

Ryld paused and nodded. "It has been a day. Yes. Yarrow asks for things he would regret."

The barest hint of a grin tugged at Kai's mouth. "Does he now? Perhaps he should be given the opportunity to regret." Then he waved one hand over the other in negation. "No, no, little brother. Forget I said that. I am over-tired. We'll discuss the foolish things Yarrow has said when I join you upstairs."

Ryld nodded again. "You understand more than he ever will." He turned and laid a hand gently on Hank's arm as they started up the stairs. "Have you had 'a day' as well, Hank?"

"Ha, well, I shared Kai's day, so I'd say yes. It's been interesting and not all in a good way." Hank leaned in to kiss the top of Ryld's head. The shadows made way for him and did not slash toward him.

Strange. They had never been protective before Hank. Perhaps they did know something of his wishes then. Everyone else seemed to believe this had to be true. Still, they could not be trusted, and as much as he and Kai were both tempted to prove that point to Yarrow, they also both knew it was wrong.

"Tell me about your 'day'. What was interesting, and what was not good?"

Hank's voice went quiet with an odd hard edge. "Not out here. Too many ears."

What did he mean by that? Ryld knew he meant *too many people are listening*, but why? Ryld waited patiently until they had gained their suite and closed the door.

"We saw..." Hank shook his head, rubbing at his arms. "We saw a pixie slum near the edge of the forest. It was, um, not good. And we visited the orphanage, which, I dunno. It looks like a nice place? But it gave both Kai and me really bad feelings."

"If you felt bad, then there is something wrong. You had bad feelings when you met Cress too."

"Well, my instincts aren't always right every time," Hank said, sitting in one of the comfortable chairs.

Ryld sat next to him, then changed his mind and moved to sit in Hank's lap. Hank needed comfort, and touch was comforting. "You have not been wrong in your judgments since I've met you. I would trust your bad feelings."

"I think I do since Kai's alarms were going off in *his* head even louder, I think. Thing is, I'm not sure why and neither is Kai, and I'm not sure we can do much about it."

"If something is wrong, Kai will find it. If Kai finds the thing that gave you both the bad feeling, you will help fix it. Because you are good, and you do not give up easily." Ryld kissed his temple. "I am grateful you did not give up learning to understand me, even when it has been difficult."

"It wasn't any more difficult than learning anyone else's speech patterns," Hank grumbled as he hugged Ryld tight. "And I liked you from the first moment we met. Um, strike that. The first moment, I was too drunk to remember properly. The first time we had an actual conversation."

Whatever Ryld had wanted to answer flew out of his head as Kai burst through the door with his messenger bag over his shoulder and a small pack of servants at his heels.

"There, on the center table, please," he directed in his voice that Ryld associated with Kai speaking to subordinates. "Thank you. Your efficiency is much appreciated."

The servants, five of them, trooped in to place trays of food, flagons and dishes on the table before they all hurried back out again. Kai let out a breath that sounded like he might be deflating as he sank into one of the cushion piles by the long, short-legged table.

"Come eat, my dears," he said as he rummaged in his bag. "I'm going to fire up my laptop, and Ryld can tell me the extent of Yarrow's foolishness today."

Ryld slid off Hank's lap and onto one of the cushions, and Hank joined him. While he gathered his thoughts, Hank uncovered dishes and filled his glass. Ryld took a sip. "Yarrow believes in order to control the shadow beasts I must first learn to unleash them at will. I told him this was unwise. He said I was being difficult. I tried to explain that he didn't understand the beasts. He believes I am simply afraid of them and doesn't see that I'm afraid for him and Yew. That his magic might contain them, but if he failed, they would attack him and Yew. He insists. I agreed I would try if Kai was present and also agreed."

While Kai's fingers flew over his keyboard, Ryld knew he was also listening. He proved it when he quirked an eyebrow at Ryld without lifting his head. "If you could be fully aware and mindful when a shadow grows and is let loose, this would be a good step. However, I do agree with you that Yarrow is...less informed than he thinks, and that the shadows would hurt the twins. I very much doubt that he understands tuning mage fire to the shadows' energy in order to stop them. And we know a protective circle or shield will only hold against them for a moment or two."

He went silent, fingers dancing patterns on the keys that maybe only Kai understood. Then he let out a soft sigh. "I'm willing to try if you wish to, Ryld. I will be there to protect and to banish if the exercise is, hmm, less than successful."

"Kai, what are you doing exactly?" Hank filled a plate and shoved it in front of Kai. "And don't make me force you to eat. You're getting a little gray around the edges."

A crooked smile tugged at Kai's mouth. "I'm returning to my roots and doing nefarious things. Hacking. I'm hacking systems. And I'm not about to do it with the computer they supplied me with in my suite."

"Hank." Ryld's voice held an edge to it, and he grappled with the irrational spike of emotion. "Please don't feed Kai." That came out a little less spiky but still sounded tense.

"Like he'd let me." Hank took Ryld's hand and gave him a squeeze. "I was teasing him and wouldn't actually do it. But he's our friend, hon. We watch out for our friends."

"I know, here." Ryld touched his head. "The rest of me doesn't understand as well."

"It's an 'elf thing'," Kai said, still tapping away. "Feeding another person is, culturally, part of courting rituals."

"Oops. Well, I'll keep that in mind." The edges of Hank's ears had gone pink, something Ryld had discovered meant he was embarrassed or uncomfortable. "No feeding other elves."

The tension eased, and Ryld squeezed Hank's hand in conscious imitation of Hank's soothing gesture. "Thank you. This feeling is hard to control."

"Jealousy is something like your shadows." Kai finally stopped to pick up one of the little bowls of vegetable stew and take a bite. "Difficult to control. Even difficult to anticipate when it might leap out. It can be a vicious, damaging thing and nearly ended my relationship with Tenzin, even though we were already bonded."

"How did it do that?" Ryld couldn't imagine Kai having shadows like his that would attack Tenzin.

Kai glanced up at him and his forehead furrowed in concern. "Not actual shadows. Jealousy doesn't create those. But emotional ones. Tenzin thought I was having an affair with a certain young aelfe. I was keeping secrets that perhaps I shouldn't have, but it wasn't that. He...left me for a time. For a dreadful, anxious, wearying time."

Ryld's eyes widened. That it was Tenzin who had felt the jealousy and not the other way around was a shock. That he had left Kai for any time because of it was even more shocking. "It must be very powerful. Jealousy. I know Hank isn't having an affair and still it whispers lies in my heart."

"It does that." Kai glanced at his screen, tapped a bit and returned to his dinner for a moment. "But if we are aware of it and its whispering, we can keep it controlled. I have had to learn the difficult lesson that being forthright with one's love and actually, ah, telling them important things is the best way to keep it at bay."

"That seems a more reasonable response than letting the shadows eat them."

"Quite," Kai said in a dry tone. "In the spirit of communication, has Hank told you what we saw today?"

"Yes. Sad things. Maybe bad things. The bad things must be found, if they exist." Ryld nodded at Kai's laptop. "Are you hunting for the bad things?"

"I am indeed making a first foray into hunting for bad things." An unholy gleam sparked in Kai's face. "One moment...almost... Ha! There we are. And Hank will be assisting me. I'm very good at hunting computer spells and traps and setting up lines of defense in code, but I'm not as well-versed in finance." He handed the laptop across the table to Hank. "You're in. Accounting software for Kent City Orphanage. Though as you'll see, there appear to be two separate databases."

"How interesting," Hank said around a bite of a red bean filled bun as he scrolled quickly through menus. "Though not surprising. Not at all."

For the next forty minutes or so, Hank clicked and scrolled and murmured while making notes and eating absently. Ryld and Kai also ate and discussed how they would attempt Yarrow's exercise and went over again everything he and Hank had seen that day.

Kai said sometimes talking helped bring details to light, and sometimes the listener saw details in the telling that made connections appear. Ryld didn't see any, other than what they had already told him, but he was happy Kai believed his thoughts might be helpful.

When they'd all progressed to eating the sweets from the trays, Hank finally looked up from his charts. "It's pretty classic. Two sets of books." He put the laptop on the table and turned it so they could all see. "This first one's the public one. Government funding, charitable contributions, Lady Jessamine's donations, all clearly marked." Hank tapped to change the screen. "This second one is the real set of books, the full picture. The extra deposits aren't on a regular schedule, but they're consistent. And sizeable. And a couple of days after, the money that came in funnels back out. I can't tell where, but how much do you want to bet it's to accounts owned by a certain Ms. Albright?"

"A fool's bet," Kai hissed, though he looked pleased. "Let's get those pulled, Hank. The deposits and dates. I may be able to trace where the money goes with a little time."

"I don't understand. Is money being stolen? From where?" Ryld asked.

"Not exactly, sweetheart." Hank pointed to a line where a large sum of money had been entered. "These deposits don't show up in the other database. Big deposits. We think the person who runs the school is doing something illegal and getting money that way."

"What is she doing that is illegal?"

"The specifics…we have no proof and we can't be certain. Yet." Kai ran his palms over his thighs in a clearly agitated way. "But we think they could be selling children."

Ryld might not understand exactly how the computer and the accounts gave them this information, but slavery was a concept he knew. Captured enemies and punishment for crimes, the drow had kept many people in servitude, his own mother included. That the buying and selling of sentient flesh was illegal in this world had been both foreign and welcome when he'd first crossed over.

"How will you stop her?"

"I don't know yet, little brother. We have only begun to investigate. But we will, by tooth or claw, we will."

* * * *

The next morning Ryld and Kai met with Yarrow and Yew while Hank stayed behind to continue looking into accounts and recording dates and figures. Ryld was torn about not having Hank with him. On the one hand, Hank definitely helped stabilize him. On the other hand, it was safer to have Hank away from him if the shadows broke loose or in this case if he managed to let them loose on purpose.

So far, he had not been successful. In a way, that surprised him. The shadows didn't obey him, but he always felt as if he were holding them back. In his view, it seemed he should be able just to…let go. When he tried, though, it was like trying to unclench a fist that had been closed his entire life. Without the emotional extremes of rage or panic, it didn't seem possible. If frustration and irritation were enough, he should have been able to do it a dozen times over with Yarrow needling him to try again, try harder, think of this, think of that. Even Kai was shooting glares at the aelfe mage.

Yew finally stepped in, saying simply, "Perhaps dropping the reins isn't enough. You must also push them through the door."

That made sense, Ryld supposed. The shadows gathered around him didn't break free until emotion drove him to the point of retreating inside his own mind. Maybe there wasn't room in there for both him and the shadows.

Ryld closed his eyes and took a breath. In through the nose, exhale through his mouth, as Hank often coaxed him to do. He tuned out Yarrow's nattering, instead focusing on the darkness behind his eyelids, the darkness that ebbed and flowed all around him, constantly shifting, growing. Gallingly, Yarrow wasn't entirely wrong when he said Ryld was afraid of the darkness. He'd been left alone in darkness often.

The thought made him shudder, dark all around, pooling and forming into shapes, armed with teeth and claws, sharp and strong. He could tear the stupid aelfe apart. Smother him with a blanket of night, fill his mouth and nose with blackness until he stopped his ceaseless prattle and breathed no more.

Somewhere far away, Yarrow was saying, "What are you doing, Hiltas?"

Kai's answer was soft and caustic. "If you're not pulling power down now, you're a bigger fool than you seem."

Ryld pushed and felt the shadow tear from him. He opened his eyes.

Chaos erupted as a sleek catlike shadow leapt at Yarrow. Black talons raked him from shoulder to ribs. Ryld's vision grew dim, graying out around the edges, his own rapid breathing loud in his ears. Too much, it had grown too large. He brought both hands up to his face, covering his mouth as he screamed and dropped down into a ball, trying to bring it back, but he already knew it was too late. He couldn't stay while blood was being spilled and listen to them scream in pain. Then everything was gone, and he was safely in the darkness.

"Get down, you pea-brained aelfe!" Kai bellowed as Yew got in his way trying belatedly and not at all effectively to shield his twin.

Give the young mage credit, Yew ducked and rolled as Kai sent a whip of fire at the shadow. One. Single. Shadow. And Yarrow couldn't even deal with that.

The shadow snarled and turned. He'd hoped it would leave Yarrow and come at him. Nearly, but not quite. It flowed about so its back claws still sank into the unfortunate aelfe and showed Kai its teeth.

In for a penny, as they say.

It wasn't safe. His first teacher would have had fits. But Kai hurled the ball of mage lightning he'd been gathering since the moment Ryld had closed his eyes. It struck the shadow's head and nearly clove it in two before the shadow began its whirlwind dissipation.

Kai winced. A bit of the mage lightning had grazed Yarrow as well, but the burn didn't look serious.

"*That* is what Ryld was trying to warn you about." Kai panted, adrenaline warring with weariness. "Damnable, stubborn, mutton-headed youngsters."

Yew had gotten to his feet and was making distressed cooing sounds over Yarrow, who was staring in shock at Kai. His expression changed at the dressing down and he turned a baleful glare on Ryld, who was still crouched as small as he could make himself on the floor. "How dare you!"

"He can't hear you," Kai said with a gusty sigh. "He let the shadow loose, lost complete track of everything, and he has no awareness of us now."

Yarrow turned his outrage on Kai. "That...that *child* is a danger to all. He shouldn't be free to walk among people if he has no control over his power."

"That *child* is barely younger than you." Kai stalked toward the twins, power sparking at his fingertips. "And you, my dear young mage, were the one who *encouraged* him to let a shadow loose. A shadow he *knows* he has no control over. A shadow he *warned* you he could not direct. He understands his limits. He tries to live within them so no one comes to harm." He stood over them now and he knew he wasn't a comforting figure. Not at all. Too bad. "Shall I tell Lady Jessamine that you are incompetent? Unable to train him?"

"I will tell her myself he is untrainable. I told her from the start it was unlikely a drow abomination could be taught anything."

Kai pulled his lips back from his teeth, far sharper than aelfe ones. He kept his voice purposefully soft, though the urge to shriek and strike out at the brat was almost more than he could contain. "Do that. I'm sure she'll be pleased to hear of your attitude toward her guests. Go have the shoulder seen to. Bleeding around drow is a colossally bad idea."

Yew's eyes somehow got even bigger. He gathered his brother up as best he could, and the two of them fled in a wavering, stumbling line out the door.

"That was mean," Kai said to himself. "Leaning into the fairytales they hear as children. Oh, well. What's done is done." He turned and crouched beside Ryld. "Oh, my little brother. I'm so sorry. But they had to learn for themselves, didn't they?"

It was some minutes before Ryld was able to respond. He looked as drained as Kai felt when he finally looked around the room, seeing only himself and Kai remained.

"Are they hurt? I thought I saw…claws. Attack."

"Hmm. You did. But the scratches aren't terribly serious." Kai had pulled his knees up and wrapped his arms around them. "Only Yarrow. Yew didn't even break a nail. I'm pleased to hear that you saw that much, though. That's new. And it was only one shadow. You kept it to that."

Ryld nodded. "I focused on the shadows, the darkness. I felt the anger and the fear come up. That is what released it. I don't know if the anger and fear create them, or if that's what they are made of. I do know, now, that there is no separation."

211

"The darkness was a tool used against you." Kai went on, even though he knew it might be futile. Again. "The fear and the anger came from how shamefully they treated you. The shadows rise from that darkness." Kai pointed to Ryld's chest. "The darkness they created there."

Ryld was either mulling that over or simply didn't want to argue. He asked, "Is Yarrow convinced now, that it's better not to let the shadows free?"

"He believes now that you are unteachable and a menace to all life on this plane." Kai tipped his head to one side. "Because he is something of an idiot."

Ryld looked resigned. "He cannot teach me, so I am unteachable. Will we be going home now?"

"I wonder if his brother would be a better teacher. He seems less full of himself, at any rate." Kai patted Ryld's foot. "I would like to stay a little longer. I'm sorry. There are things I can't in good conscience leave undone now. Children's lives may be at stake."

"Lady Jessamine will allow us to stay if Yarrow tells her of the attack?"

Kai snorted. "Lady Jessamine will not be pleased at all to hear of her mage's behavior. The rude little sod didn't even thank me for saving him."

* * * *

Kai was correct that Lady Jessamine was not pleased with Yarrow, but her kindness and gracious nature had made him forget that she was also queen here, and that meant the welfare of her people came first.

"Yarrow is demanding he leave at once, Kai. He charged in bleeding, in front of half the court, saying he's far more dangerous than we've been led to believe."

"I spoke the truth when I told you of his abilities..."

She waved a hand. "I know, and I understand. It's not Ryld's fault. I certainly don't want you to leave. I'm afraid neither Yarrow nor Yew are willing to try to teach him further. I would like to find someone perhaps more suitable, but I also need to ensure my court is safe. You see my dilemma?"

"My lady, he was goaded, no, *encouraged* to let the shadow..." Kai cut himself off, holding up both hands. "I do understand the court's concerns. Perhaps if Ryld's contact with others were minimal for now?"

"That would probably be best." She laid a hand on Kai's arm. "I am sorry, Kai. I do want what's best for Ryld and I will do all I can to help the poor soul. For now though, I think it best he remain unseen."

"Very well. The suite is quite comfortable. I may be able to persuade him to try to work a bit if I might beg paints and brushes from your artisans."

"Of course, whatever you need. And, Kai, I do know you have much work of your own that needs seeing to back in New York. Ryld is safe under my roof. If it takes months to teach him, he is welcome to stay here. Permanently, if that's what will be best."

"I'll stay with him a bit longer if I may. I promised him I wouldn't desert him and Tenzin's always saying I need more time off."

"Of course you may stay." She squeezed his arm then let go. "Take all the time you need."

"Thank you, my lady."

Kai bowed and took his leave, a faint queasy feeling going with him. He was keeping things from her just as he had from Tenzin on more than one occasion.

Perhaps that was wrong, but he had nothing to show her but conjecture. Accusing people she most likely trusted of vile things… He needed proof.

Then he could lay it all before her with a clear conscience.

Chapter Thirteen

Hank had been trying to help Ryld feel a little bit better about the disaster with his teacher. It was all the arrogant teacher's fault, but Ryld still felt terrible. Then Kai had stormed back with news about the court and Ryld being confined to his suite. There'd been some waving of arms and some unkind words about young mages on Kai's part before he'd stormed out again. He understood why Kai was so agitated, but his anger at other people had only made Ryld withdraw more into himself.

Not long after that, a knock sounded on the door. Hank opened it to a short parade of servants carrying…art supplies? They left everything just inside the door and hurried off. None of them looked up from their feet even though Ryld had retreated to the bedroom.

"Guess I'll see what we have here," Hank muttered as the door shut again.

A tilting easel that Ryld could use the way he did his draughting desk back home — Hank set that up by the big window in their parlor. Brushes, paints, bottles of ink, and quills — he moved a side table over next to the easel for those. Paper of different sizes and textures — second side table.

"Ryld?" He stuck his head in the bedroom where Ryld was lying on his back, staring at the ceiling. "They brought some things for you to make patterns, if you want."

Ryld slowly got up, but Hank could tell he was only making the effort for his sake. They had been through so much together since Hank had become his companion, but not in all that time had he seen Ryld look so defeated. Even so, Ryld went to the area Hank had set up and sat in the chair, running his fingers over some of the items.

"Thank you. For doing this." He gestured to the supplies.

"You're welcome."

Ryld selected a feather quill. Instead of using it he twirled it between his fingers then brushed the edge over his cheek. He set it aside and chose a piece of paper and brush. While he worked, Hank used Kai's laptop to do some research.

Both databases had already been backed up to Kai's server in Research back at AURA, so even if someone got nervous, they wouldn't be able to erase the incriminating entries. Hank had earmarked every suspicious deposit and every equally suspicious withdrawal and had coded their copies to show the discrepancies — all the places where the databases didn't match. There were errors here and there, small ones, but ones that he felt confident would be born out in attempts to balance the bank statements.

Not much more he could do there, so he looked into the orphanage itself. No news articles jumped out at him, just the usual charity function this and fundraiser that in the local sources. A short police blotter mention concerning a *disturbance* and a *pixie individual*, no names given. The building had once, yes, been Kent City Elementary, left vacant for several years when the population declined, and the elementary and middle schools had been combined into one building. Purchased by Pacific Redfern and Co., a real estate developer, slated for demolition with plans for mixed-use development...

Then the demolition didn't happen. The next sale on the parcel number was to the Goodworks Foundation. Whoever they were. Frustratingly, Hank found no information on them at all. Charitable trusts didn't always have a big online presence but...something.

The next year, the orphanage opened.

Just all a little too convenient.

He was just about to start digging into information about Ms. Albright when Kai swept back in.

"You could knock," Hank said without glancing up from the screen.

"Ah. Yes. I should." Kai had the decency to look embarrassed. "I had a thought."

"Just one?"

"Terribly funny. I think the pixies might have information for us."

Hank put the laptop down. "You're going back out there, aren't you? Even though the place didn't feel safe at all."

Kai sniffed in that half-offended way. "If you're concerned, you could come with me. Perhaps they would be more comfortable speaking with you."

"Maybe." Hank stepped over to the window and kissed the top of Ryld's head. "Would you be all right if we took a trip over there?"

Ryld stopped what he was doing and looked up. "The place you are going is not safe?"

"Pixieland. We were there before." Hank chewed on his lip with his tusk. "There was a…tension there. A watchfulness. I'm not sure it's unsafe, but I wouldn't send Kai in there alone."

Ryld nodded. He seemed to consider Hank's words a moment then lifted the paper he'd been working on, handing it to Hank. "Take this with you. For luck."

The pattern on the paper was colorful, done in a loose whimsical fashion. Each color overlapped slightly with another, forming rows of fairy wings on a soft blue background.

"It's beautiful. Thank you, sweetheart." Hank leaned down for a proper kiss and it occurred to him that some part of Ryld's thoughts had been with the pixies, too. That made him more certain that Kai was right, and this was the next logical step.

He folded the paper carefully and put it in his shirt pocket. "We'll be back in a few hours."

He knew Ryld heard him. The non-answer happened when he didn't think an answer was necessary and he'd already turned his attention back to his patterns.

When they reached the stable yard, Kai went into what Hank thought of as *boss mode*, clipping out orders at the stable hands, snapping at them when they stood and stared. Poor things didn't often have to deal with exacting bundles of drow mage often, that was obvious.

The end result was that they were mounted and off into the woods in under ten minutes, Kai back on the sleek, black mare, and Hank on his lumbering but willing draft horse.

"We don't need a guide?" Hank asked as they passed under the tree line.

"I remember the way." Kai gave him a meaningful look as they rode side by side. "It seemed obvious to me that pixie-aelfe relations aren't the best here. Our chances of having anyone speak to us are increased, I'd venture, without some arrogant young aelfe buck along."

"Good point. Just don't get us lost."

Kai huffed in annoyance. "My sense of direction is — Oh. You seem to be teasing me."

Hank shot him a quick grin. "I'd say we know each other well enough by now, don't you think? You don't even knock when you come into our room."

"Yes. Ah. I do apologize again." The tips of Kai's ears darkened in embarrassment. "I realized belatedly that I might be interrupting...something."

In some ways, Kai and Ryld were more similar than they realized, especially in their ability to hyper-focus and lose track of the rest of the world. Though Hank had to chuckle at that *something*.

They rode mostly in silence, both of them on the lookout for anything out of place in this mostly idyllic wood. Good as his word, Kai got them to that first pixie hut where he stopped his horse.

"We should leave the horses," Kai suggested softly.

"Is that a good idea?"

Kai gave an uncomfortable shrug. "Perhaps not entirely. But horses are both a symbol of wealth and a tool for intimidation. We need to walk in."

"All right. Backtrack a bit?"

They left the horses in a little glade off the road and walked back to the edge of Pixieland. An oppressive sense of dread hung over the whole venture, and Hank hoped mostly that they didn't end up having to hurt anyone if things went wrong.

They passed that first hut, then the second without incident. As they reached the larger gathering of huts and caravans, though, more pixie faces peeked out of doors. More threadbare curtains twitched. The trilling calls in the trees started up as they had the first time.

Then Kai did an odd thing. He strode to the center of the encampment, right in the middle of the road, and sat down.

Hank felt awkward standing there alone. The pixies were about the same size as Ryld, on average. Maybe a little smaller. It made him feel like he was looming even though he wasn't near anyone. He debated joining Kai, then decided it was probably best one of them stayed on their feet and took a couple steps to the right where he could lean on the side of a shack and keep an eye on things. He didn't have to wait long.

A pixie man came striding out into the road and stopped in front of Kai. His iridescent wings were standing upright and stiff, like his posture. He wore his long red hair pulled back from his forehead, the rest flowing loose around his shoulders. Hank had seen plenty of pixies before but hadn't spent any significant time with them up close. They all had a certain sharpness to their features, high, sculpted cheekbones and large eyes. A beautiful people, really. Even when visibly angry.

"What's your business here, elf?" the pixie man in front of Kai demanded.

Kai turned his hands so they were palm up, a gesture that indicated both a lack of threat and a desire to meet. "I am not from here. From Elvenhome." He nodded toward Hank. "My friend and I come from AURA, on the other side of the continent. We would like to speak to anyone who has grievance. Some of the things we have seen on our visit have left us more than disturbed."

The man snorted. "What does a drow know of our troubles? The aelfe come for the women and gambling. The drow come for sport. The goblins come to take our children. They all go back to their places, and so should you. *Pixieland* is no place for your kind in the light of day."

"I have no interest in buying or taking sex, as the case may be." Kai remained calm, his voice soft. "No interest in gambling or in *sport*, whatever dreadful thing that means. I see you and your people living too close. Too many in this small territory. I see you living desperately, struggling to feed your children enough. I have been to the orphanage and have seen far too many pixie children kept by stringent human rules. I have watched as they sent a pixie mother away in tears. What goes on here? Why have these things happened?"

There was a murmur and rustle in a rough circle around them as some of the pixies who had been watching from their homes came closer, watching and listening to the spectacle.

"The orphanage can go burn in a pit of tar and waste." One woman's voice rose above the murmurs.

"Liars and thieves," another added to a general round of agreement.

"They promise food and a better life, but once you sign their infernal papers you never hear from the child again."

"Tell me about these papers." Kai raised his voice just enough to be heard by the crowd. "What do they have you sign? Are all the children given willingly to them?"

Everyone started talking at the same time until a sharp whistle cut through the chatter. A man who could have been the brother or maybe father of the first one who had approached Kai, strode up and the crowd scattered, retreating into their hovels and disappearing down rough carved streets.

"You need to leave. Now," the newcomer said.

"I have offered you no harm and will continue to do so. This is not how things should be, sir. You know this. While I can't promise to make everything right, I can try to help the children. For their sakes. Please. Come speak to me." Kai patted the gravel road. "On neutral ground, the road traveled by all."

The pixie man spat on the ground and the gleam of a short dagger appeared in his hand. "The old ways are dead and gone on the other side of the benighted gash that brought us here. Get your arse up out of the dirt, you sharp-tongued fuck. You and your orc friend come with me."

Both Kai's eyebrows had climbed to his hairline, but he rose gracefully and nodded to Hank. "As you wish, sir."

Hank jogged over to join him, and they followed the rude pixie to one of the caravans, where they all climbed the steps and entered. The interior was relatively clean and hung with faded colored scarves. A scent of honey and mildew clung to everything.

"I don't suppose you have any proof you are who you say?" the man asked.

Kai reached into his pocket, slowly, and took out his AURA ID card. "I'm Kai Hiltas, director of Research in New York." He handed the card over for the pixie to examine. "This is my associate, Hank Onyx-Wainwright. We came to Pacific Elvenhome in the hopes of finding a teacher for a young drow who struggles with his magic but have found far more than we bargained for."

The pixie flicked the card back to Kai after a cursory glance. He gestured for them to sit. "We know about your visit. You were through here two days ago with an aelfe. Does *her ladyship* know you're here now?"

"She does not. For now, I'd rather keep it that way," Kai answered in that same calm voice. Hank had become so used to Kai fussing at things that the effect was a little eerie.

The pixie smirked. "So you don't entirely trust Ms. Fancypants either. That's a point in your favor, I guess. If you're telling the truth."

"I presume you mean Lady Jessamine?"

He cocked his head slightly in acknowledgment. "I'm Sean Dove-Feather. I'd say I was a council member, but we don't officially have a council here in Pixieland." He sized them up again. "Why didn't you just ask her your questions?"

Kai let out a breath, maybe one he'd been holding for a while. "Because if she doesn't know about what's truly happening at the orphanage, she would merely deny and perhaps tip our hand too soon before we have proof. If—and my human friend would call this my drow paranoia—if she, the Mother forfend, *does* know? Then we truly would allow them room to cover their tracks."

Sean eyed them. He opened a drawer and rummaged, pulling out a sheaf of papers, and handed it to Kai.

On top were printed copies of screenshots. Several pages worth showed ads aimed at pixie crossovers that were missing their community and offering to pay for relocation.

As Kai looked at these Sean said, "They call the number, someone on the other end buys them a bus ticket. Not so many now, but several years ago they would arrive by the busload. All lonely, broke, and thinking there was more for them here than they had where they were."

Kai continued lifting pages and the relocation ads gave way to different ads, these for escort services, all featuring young pixie women and men. The final few pages were forms from Kent City Orphanage.

"May I?" Kai held up his phone and the papers.

Sean shrugged, and Kai wasted no time setting the papers down and taking photographs of each sheet. He slowed when he reached the papers from the orphanage, and Hank read over his shoulder.

"This can't be legal, can it?" Hank pointed to a paragraph buried on the second page. "Signing away parental rights without social services or the courts being involved?"

Kai took a picture of just that paragraph. "I'm not an expert on child welfare, Hank. Though it doesn't look right at all to me. We'll have to run this by Legal to be certain."

"There's nothing that ties any of those things together." Sean indicated the stacks of papers. "I can tell you though, an internet search on pixies will bring back hundreds of results like those." He pointed to the ads for pixie escorts. "You want to know what's going on? Come with me."

He stepped out of the wagon and Kai and Hank followed. He took them a short distance and knocked on a door. A pixie woman opened it a crack.

"Ella, can we come in?"

She reluctantly opened the door and let them inside. Both Kai and Hank had to stoop to enter, and the ceiling nearly touched their heads. The floor was dirt, and there were only two rickety kitchen chairs, so they stood.

"Tell them about when the orphanage people came," Sean said. Ella wrung her hands, her wings flattening to her back. "It's okay, tell them."

Without looking at them, she started to speak. "They came like usual. A couple humans with goblins. We have more twin and triplet births than singles. So they came, and my boys were only a few weeks old, and they said they could take them, find them a home where they wouldn't starve, they could go to school. I asked when I could see them, and they said when they were grown a little, so they could bond with their new family. I said I'd have to think about it but...they just kept saying if I didn't sign the paper and give them up, they would say I wasn't fit to care for them, and they would get them anyway."

"Did they threaten you?" Kai asked softly. "That you would be charged with child endangerment?"

She nodded, tears pooling in her eyes.

"This is how it always happens?" Hank turned to Sean. "Any idea how many?"

"Enough that many of the women try to hide when they come. The colony here is bigger than the one I lived in before crossing over. As Ella said, most women give birth to multiples."

"And if they don't find anyone willing when they come, what happens then?" Kai's voice had grown even softer, though there was a chilly light in his eyes.

Sean sighed and gestured toward the open door. "Look around. Do you think they lack for mothers desperate to believe their children will have a better life among the humans? Some of our people have learned not to trust, but for each one like Ella, there is a neighbor who says it's all made up just to scare us and she knows so-and-so who got a postcard from the child they sent away. There've been fights over who believes what."

Hank caught Kai's eye. "It's not hard to see why. Probably lots of disinformation from Ms. Albright and her staff."

"While I agree, we can't slide into speculation," Kai admonished before he turned back to Sean. "When the aelfe bucks come, do they pay or do they act entitled to the sex workers?"

"Depends on their mood I guess. And how much honey wine they've had."

"And the young drow?" Kai asked, a definite note of dread in his voice. "What do they come here for?"

Sean shrugged. "They mostly come to bet on the fights. Or they buy dust."

Kai actually sagged with a hand on the wall. "Thank the goddesses of the deeps. Still not a thing they should do, of course."

Sean was regarding him oddly, and Hank was sure his expression matched. He was definitely going to ask Kai what he'd been afraid the answer was on the way back. "This is all important information, Mr. Dove-

Feather. Thank you for taking the time to talk to us. Was there anything else you wanted to mention?"

"Don't go stirring the pot with the elves. This is Elvenhome land, they remind us often enough. We don't need any trouble from them. That orphanage though, if they are sending pixie children to homes and boarding schools like they say, we want to know where, and why we're not allowed to see them once they're taken."

"The children must be the primary concern." Kai put a hand to his heart and gave Sean a little bow. "If everything is being done as it should be, these records are...perhaps not *easy* to obtain, but still possible. We'll do everything we can."

* * * *

The knock on the door was light, but enough to pull Ryld's attention from the paper in front of him. Not as colorful as the wings he'd given Hank, this one was a hatch work of dark and light lines made with a very fine brush and several different pigments that now stained him up to the elbows.

"Yes? Enter."

A goblin opened the door partway, leaning in without actually entering. Ryld wondered if he'd been instructed to keep his distance.

"Beg your pardon. A visitor would like to see you. He requested I inform you he is drow."

Ryld went still. He wasn't sure what to do. What would a drow want with him? And why did he want to make sure Ryld was told he was drow? Instinct told him he should refuse to see this drow...but he was also curious.

"I—I'm not supposed to leave these rooms."

"I've been told so, yes. The drow is waiting down the hall and I'll let him in and escort him out, if you want to see him."

Ryld pressed his lips together. Tiny leaf-like shadows stirred around his legs. "Okay, show him in, please."

A moment later, the drow entered and stayed by the door after the goblin closed it. His height was more usual for a drow, almost as tall as most aelfe, and his hair was bone white, but his eyes were gray, marking him as *not* usual.

"I am Dzev." He swept Ryld a formal bow, the black, bell-shaped sleeves of his shirt trailing on the carpet. "Lady Ksatha sends her greetings and asked that I speak with you."

His accent left Ryld feeling like ants were tickling over his skin and he awaited their sting. Kai had traces of an accent too, but it was only noticeable on certain words or when he was under a great deal of strain. To Ryld's ears this drow sounded much more like himself, though less stilted. It flooded him with memory and froze his blood.

Dzev stood exactly as he was, not speaking or moving. Ryld swallowed. "I'm Ryld. Why are you here?" He meant the words to be strong, sharp, but his breath wouldn't come, and he could tell they only made him seem afraid.

"Ah. Her ladyship mentioned you might fear me." Dzev took half a step in and sank to his knees. "I am sorry for that. You are here in an aelfe court to learn from aelfe mages, I have heard."

"They are idiots." Ryld shut his mouth quickly. He probably should not have said that.

Dzev didn't quite smile, but Ryld thought it was close, and he tipped his head to the side in a drow acknowledgment. "I would lie if I said I had a high opinion of aelfe mages. But perhaps we should be fair to them and admit that drow magic is most likely not, ah, familiar to them."

"My magic is not familiar to anyone. Not how to use it, I mean."

"I had wondered." Dzev settled his hands on his knees. "Your friend and champion is a powerful drow mage and yet he seeks teachers for you. This must be something he has not encountered. And yet…I see your shadows, little one."

"Kai cannot teach me because he says his magic is different than mine. He says it's the difference between turning on a tap for water and creating a cloud to make rain."

"A good analogy, I think." Dzev placed his hands flat on the floor, and Ryld nearly cried out when he pulled power into his fingers. But it was a small amount and the only thing Dzev did was to make a little horse out of fog and have it run in circles on the carpet in front of him. "Most, though not all, drow magic is pulled up from the earth. From the mother of us all. When we came to this place, drow mages also discovered a power in numbers and computers, but we still pull the power up from below. Yours lies within you. A great dam of power I sensed even as I climbed the stairs."

The words rang true. It did feel as if he held back the weight of a tremendous force within him.

"Why did you come?" Ryld asked again.

"I knew someone very like you. Before crossing. Lady Ksatha thought I might be able to help where the aelfe have failed."

"Why did you not come before?"

Now Dzev smiled. "Diplomacy. The aelfe do like to, shall we say, do things their way. Lady Jessamine would very much like to have you in her court, I'm sure. It was better to wait to see if the aelfe could help you first."

"I will not be a part of any court. Not ever."

"A shame. Lady Ksatha would have gladly offered you a place in hers. One of prestige. A special place by her side." Dzev held up a hand when Ryld started to speak. "But Kai has told her that your fear of drow runs deep, in painful, jagged canyons. It saddens me that you were treated so shamefully, but I will not push. These things take time. I offer myself as a teacher, a more appropriate one than any aelfe, and the offer will stand no matter what you say to me today."

"I won't go to the drow."

"Understandable. If you agree, I will meet you wherever you wish. It is better to be outside than confined to a stuffy room anyway."

"I will…think about it."

"That is all I can ask. Send to me at the drow court if you wish to meet." Dzev tucked his toes under and rose in one fluid motion. "An honor to meet you regardless, Ryld. Be well."

With that, he leaned over to knock on the door. The goblin servant opened it, Dzev went through, and the door closed behind them, leaving Ryld to stare at the place the mage had knelt on the carpet. A court mage, *kneeling* on the carpet, just so he wouldn't scare Ryld.

He had a lot to ponder while he waited for Hank and Kai to return. The making of patterns usually soothed and focused him, but even that could not hold his attention long. He began to pace, one room to the next and back again. The time for a midday meal came and went but he was not hungry. Could this drow mage really teach him anything? Could he know more than Kai? It didn't seem possible. Kai was very powerful. But every time he thought back on the meeting he came to the same words. A great dam of power. He could feel the pressure pushing on him as he thought the words. And what of the other things he said? That Lady Jessamine would very much like him to join her court. Why? Why would she want that? Everyone he'd passed in the halls either eyed him warily or stared with barely concealed hostility. The aelfe held no love for the drow, and even here where the old wars and generations of conflicts were supposed to be left behind, there was still a deep mistrust. Her people did not want him here, why would she?

All these questions going around and around. He could barely contain himself when hours later the door finally opened, and Hank and Kai came through.

"I met a drow mage. Did you see there is a guard on the door? He's pretending not to be, but that is his purpose. You don't look well. Are you hurt?"

"We're fine." Hank gave his arm a squeeze. "That was, um, a lot. And we've heard things we wish we hadn't."

Kai still stood near the door, sniffing the air. "Mage, yes. He worked magic here. Ryld, are *you* well? Did he try to take you?"

"Take me? No. He made a horse run. Why would Lady Jessamine want me to stay in her court?"

"A…horse." Kai's brows furrowed in confusion. "Perhaps you could begin from the drow mage coming to your door and tell us what occurred. In the order of occurrence."

"The goblin guard came first. He said a drow wished to see me. I almost sent him away, but I wanted to know why he had come. He...said things." Ryld struggled to recall exactly what. "Earth magic, dams of power, he would teach me if I wanted, he made a horse to show me how he drew power, but his was very little compared to when you draw power." Ryld sniffed in a very close approximation of one of Kai's expressions. "His eyes were gray. He went away when I said I would think about meeting him again. He wanted to laugh when I said the aelfe mages were idiots." Ryld paused. "That might not all be in order."

"I'm sure it was fairly close," Kai said in a distracted fashion. "A court mage. A diplomat."

"Yes! He said diplomacy kept him from coming before now."

"What is she playing at? Did he say that Lady Ksatha also would like you to join her court?"

Ryld nodded, his head turning to watch Kai pace.

"Telling you Lady Jessamine wants you for hers. Showing you... Ach. Drow politics. This is why I left Elvenhome in the first place." Kai threw himself down onto the sofa to scowl at his boots. "His eyes were gray. I wonder if it was a ploy or if this one truly has seen something like your shadows before."

"He said he had known one like me before the crossing. Kai Hiltas, why would Lady Jessamine want me to stay when all of her people want me to go?"

"She has offered to let you stay as long as you need." Kai made a fluttering gesture. "She knows her court would rather you left, but she feels you would be safer here than in the city. That would be entirely up to you, of course. But I don't think she realizes that a familiar environment would be safer for you. Her court can't contain you." He stopped muttering and glanced up at Ryld. "Have you really never seen me draw a trickle of power? Has it always been during great need?"

Ryld shifted from foot to foot. There was something important that seemed just out of his grasp, but Kai didn't seem concerned the same way he was. Perhaps he misunderstood. It was not uncommon for him to get something wrong when he first met a person.

"What good is a trickle against an avalanche coming?"

Kai cocked his head to the side. "None at all. You said the mage who visited only pulled a small bit of power. To make a horse. A little magic amusement. This doesn't mean that he's incapable of pulling down enormous amounts when he needs to. I doubt Lady Ksatha would send anything but a powerful mage to meet with you."

"He knelt. Here." Ryld pointed to the place Dzev had made the little horse. "Because I was afraid of him."

"*Did* he?" Kai said softly. "Interesting indeed. For a court drow to kneel...it's an acknowledgment of power. Of someone with greater status. He may have said it was because you were frightened, and perhaps in part it was, but I have to wonder."

Ryld turned his attention to Hank, who had been quietly listening while he looked at Ryld's work. "Do you think I should learn from this mage?"

"I think if he wants to teach you, he can come to New York." Hank gave him a smile, maybe because his words had been a little sharp. "But if he knows something, I bet he'd be a better teacher than Yarrow."

"I don't know if he knows how to teach me. But you are right. Perhaps it is safer to return to New York."

Hank crossed the floor to gather Ryld into his arms. "We'll go back soon, sweetheart. I think we're closing in on what's happening at the orphanage."

"Did you learn what you needed to find?"

"Some of it, I think. We have some things that AURA legal needs to see and some good leads on how the orphanage operates." Hank tipped Ryld's face up for a kiss.

"Speaking of which." Kai reached for his laptop, sat cross-legged on the couch and immediately became absorbed in typing. "I would tell you two to get a room, but this is your room. And you're..." Kai made a sour face. "Rather cute together."

Chapter Fourteen

Hank came out of the bedroom the next morning, humming to himself. Amazing how having someone he lo — really *liked* sleeping next to him improved his mood in the morning. He stopped and backed up when he spotted the lump on the couch.

A drow-shaped lump buried under one of the soft blankets that had been scattered around the front room.

"Kai?"

An unintelligible noise came from the blanket nest, followed by soft cursing in drow. Kai's head emerged, and he looked around blearily before flopping back down. "I fell asleep on your cursed couch."

Hank did his best not to laugh, but there might have been a snicker. "Not really a morning person, are you? Should I see if I can get us some coffee?"

"My eternal gratitude," Kai muttered as he began the complicated process of untangling himself from the blankets. "The adoptions —"

"Hold off on that." Hank had already reached the door. "Until you can put words together better."

He nodded to the goblin guard on the door—obviously there to make sure Ryld didn't wander around, none of them stopped him or Kai going in and out—and made his way down to the kitchens. Coffee. Whatever they had going for breakfast. Maybe some of that nice seed bread the aelfe seemed to like...

His heart jumped hard when someone grabbed his wrist and pulled him into a hallway. He yanked away, fists up, but it was one of the goblin kitchen workers, an artisan caste goblin probably half Hank's weight.

"Um, good morning?" Hank let his arms relax, though he stayed wary. The goblin's eyes darted everywhere, and his hands wrung together anxiously.

"You...elder brother, you and your drow friend, you're looking into the orphanage, right?"

Hank leaned against the wall and folded his arms over his chest. "Why would you say that?"

"Feldspar works there. He's my wife's cousin. And he told her that he saw you there. And one of my half-brother's cousins is friendly with a pixie and she said you'd been in Pixieland, asking things."

The rambling explanation made Hank oddly homesick. This was how goblin communities worked—these complex webs of communication and obligation through kinship and acquaintance.

"All right, yes. Things seemed off there," Hank admitted. "What about it?"

The kitchen goblin winced and ducked his head. "I can't do it anymore. They're just kids."

"What are you talking about?"

"The orphanage kids!" The goblin spoke in a whisper, but it might as well have been an anguished scream. "I'm just the driver, okay? That's all I do. But the kids are crying, and the fairies are crying, and there's a pickup tonight, and it's just *wrong,* and I *can't.*"

Oh goddesses. Somewhere in the back of his mind, Hank had been afraid of something like this. But he'd been hoping it was just a pay-for-adoption scheme. "Slowly, little brother. What fairies?"

"The ones from the glade. The ones they sell."

"How would you even catch fairies? Why doesn't their little queen come looking for them?"

Tears were in the goblin's eyes now. "I don't catch the fairies. Some of the others, they do it. They cover the glade in sleep smoke and then they go in and fill orders. This many blue, this many orange and on like that. The fairies go into spelled wire mesh cages so they can't 'port out. They leave changelings for the ones they take. They're just weed and mud changelings, so they look convincing for maybe a day or two and then they 'die'. So the fairies just think they got sick and passed and don't come looking."

The nausea rolling in Hank's stomach was getting worse. "Who do they sell them to?"

"We sell them to this bunch of humans. Hard people. Lots of guns. They take the pixie kids and the fairies. Pretty sure the fairies get sold as pets. I've seen the ads. The kids, they're almost always the older kids—" Here the goblin broke off and started to sob.

"Goddesses," Hank spat out. "I have the picture. Why do you *do* this?"

The goblin sniffled and wiped at his eyes. "The money's good. I have kids to feed. Herself doesn't pay enough to feed a family of fleas. But they don't let you stop. There's…threats." He grabbed Hank's sleeve in a desperate grip. "But you're from AURA. You can make it stop."

"We can try. You said there's a pickup tonight?" Hank removed the goblin's hand as gently as he could.

"Yes. After moonset. The door on the north side of the orphanage."

"All right. For now, you're going to come down to the kitchens with me and pretend like I snagged you in the hall to get us breakfast. Plenty of coffee, please. Then tonight, you're going to make sure there's a wagon and horses waiting for us in the second glade on the path that goes toward Pixieland. You have all that?"

"Yes. Yes." The little goblin nodded frantically, as if his answer might not be enough. "Just, please. No more kids being sold out of that awful place."

Hank patted his shoulder, though part of him wanted to punch the little guy in the face. Remorse was all well and good, but he could've tried to do something before this, threats or no threats.

By the time Hank returned to the suite with a breakfast cart, piled high with food, coffee and tea, he'd managed to calm down enough that he wouldn't yell at Kai trying to explain things. He set everything out on the table, kissed a sleepy Ryld good morning and turned to Kai, who looked less like an undead drow now.

"You first," Hank said in a tone that wasn't quite snapping. "What did you find hacking into everything and everywhere last night?"

Kai squinted at him but didn't ask yet. "Mostly what we suspected. That there *are* adoptions registered from Kent City Orphanage, but not enough to account for how many children apparently go through there." He sipped at his coffee and raised an eyebrow at Hank. "Now you. You left glowing like sunshine and have returned as a thunderstorm."

Hank went through what the kitchen worker had told him and finished with, "And maybe I was acting crazy because I was so mad. Was it a stupid idea? Should we just call it in?"

Kai stared out the window a moment, then shook his head. "No. I don't think we should. Not yet. If we send AURA officers stomping in with their loud, heavy boots, we might catch the little fish, but the big ones will have warning and will scatter. Best we do this quietly tonight. Secure the children who are at risk and then tell the authorities."

"What would you like me to do?" Ryld asked.

"I have two things I would like you to do, please," Kai said. "The first is to send word to the drow mage who visited you and meet with him in the fairy glade. You might not be allowed to roam the court freely, but you're not a prisoner and I'm sure Lady Jessamine will allow you to do what you came here to do a suitable safe distance away. See if there is anything else you might learn there by listening to the fairies. Your presence should also deter anyone who might be thinking of raiding the nests. Second, I would like you to stay here tonight. If you do not see or hear from us by dawn, you will need to go to Lady Jessamine and inform her. We may need her help and ask her to send reinforcements to the orphanage. I don't anticipate that will be necessary, but it's good to have someone who is watching out for us in reserve."

Ryld nodded and picked up a piece of toast. "I will do these things."

* * * *

"So far, your little informant has been true to his word." Kai approached the wagon that had been left for them, making a cursory inspection to be certain the wood wasn't rotten and that the wheels were sound.

Hank heaved a small sigh. "He didn't seem smart enough to be acting. Certainly was dumb enough to get caught up in all of this."

"Well, he was intelligent enough to pick you to tell. We can thank the goddesses for small favors."

Kai wondered if the choice of horses had been purposeful or just what the goblin could get them. Two large beasts, both dark-colored, had been hitched to the wagon. The third horse was the black mare Kai had been assigned before. He felt he knew her well by now.

"I'm good with the wagon." Hank nodded to the driver's seat. "Drove plenty back home."

"I'm relieved to hear that." Kai mounted without another thought. "I'm *able* to drive a team but haven't in a terribly long time."

Hank chuckled and it was good to hear him in a less thunderous mood. He climbed up, took up the reins and clicked his tongue to start the team off at a fast walk.

Kai distracted himself from the worry of what lay ahead with another worry on his mind. Ryld, and more specifically the drow, Dzev, that Ryld had met with earlier. Ryld had come back from that meeting just after dark, and unlike the sessions with Yarrow and Yew, which left him frustrated and near despair, Ryld had returned calm, almost serene, thoughtful. Hank noted the difference and said so aloud, to which Ryld replied that he *liked* Dzev.

Childish, to be somehow jealous that Ryld could stand the company of another drow. Perhaps not entirely reasonable, to be suspicious of someone who was trying to help. But Dzev was *drow*. There had to be ulterior motives beyond a desire to help. Drow hard-wiring nearly demanded it.

They reached Pixieland in good time and perhaps it was the set determination on Hank's face, or perhaps someone's cousin had told someone's friend who had told someone's wife, but the pixies let them pass without a word or a single warning trill in the trees.

The road into the town was pitch black and quiet, not a vehicle in sight. Which was a good thing. Riding along a highway was dangerous enough at night. As they found a secure place on the edge of town to leave the horses, all Kai's senses were on alert. The darkness was not really a hindrance for him, all the usual sounds of insects and tiny noises of a sleeping populous seemed normal. Still, as they neared the orphanage something tingled along his skin, and he signaled for Hank to stop.

Hank did more than that, he stopped, looked and pulled back. Kai followed, and Hank whispered, "You felt it?"

"I felt something," Kai whispered back.

"It's goblin magic. Like a blanket over the area that blocks out sounds and makes it harder to see."

"Lovely." Kai shifted his awareness a bit and felt at the edges of the magic. "Not a large area. Are you affected by it?"

"If I go further, it will be like I put sunglasses on at night and stuffed some cotton in my ears. I can still function — it just makes it more difficult."

"Good to know." Kai tapped at the magic a little longer, finding the weave of it, the density of it. Finally, he took Hank's hand. "Stay close."

He couldn't do much to lift the muting blanket and if he tried, that would tell the goblin casting the spell that someone was nearby. What he could provide was a bubble to move with them so their senses wouldn't be muffled to a human level. How humans navigated their way through the world sometimes was a mystery.

Kai could make out the soft rumble of an engine running up ahead somewhere. It had to be behind the building because the only vehicles in the street were silent, and the parking lot was too far away. Still leading Hank, he slipped around the north side, opposite the playground, where there was no fence to impede them.

Trusting the cover of darkness, he peeked around the edge of the bricks. A white van was parked near the double doors at the back, its engine idling. Without windows in the doors, it was the type of van used mainly by workers in some sort of trade or another. As he watched the orphanage door opened. A woman stepped out. Kai thought she looked vaguely familiar. A human woman, perhaps one of the teachers he'd seen during their tour. She walked up first to the driver side window and spoke with the driver—though Kai couldn't make it out—then walked to the van and opened the rear doors.

Another woman came from inside the building, this one carrying something covered with a dark cloth. She set it in the of the van, then they both returned inside.

"What do you see?" Hank whispered.

"They've started loading." Kai pulled him closer to speak in his ear. "Two teachers, I think. One human, one aelfe. I don't see him, but I can feel the shape of the goblin casting the spell. Warrior caste, I think. Back and to the left of the van."

"Do we...?"

"No, wait. They haven't brought any children out. No false alarms."

"I'll go after the goblin."

Kai heaved an exasperated breath. "Hank, you can't see him."

"No." Hank grinned. "But I can smell him. Would it kill him to shower?"

Their hushed conversation was cut off by the door opening again. The human teacher led out four small pixie children. Two looked a little older, probably just into adolescence. The other two were very small.

"Are we going to meet them at the bus station...?" one of the older children asked.

"No, not until you arrive. Hush now, get in and don't cause any fuss."

Kai kept his grip on Hank's arm until the children had climbed into the van, the smallest one lifted in since the steps were too high up and the kids were wearing T-shirts over their wings.

"Shut your eyes," Kai whispered. "I'm going to dispel the darkness."

Hank did as he asked, and Kai raised his hands as he shouted the drow word for light. The words weren't important, the *intent* was, and the goblin's spell shredded under his onslaught. All three adults cried out, temporarily blinded with the lightning flash of the spell.

"Now, Hank."

Realizing they were under some sort of attack, the human teacher ran for the door. The aelfe stood her ground, slamming the doors of the van, while the goblin lifted one hand, some sort of spell gathering between his fingers, a knife clutched in his other hand. He pointed the knife toward Kai and Hank. "There!"

Hank charged him, throwing up a shield to take the brunt of whatever spell the goblin was about to hurl. Kai threw a quick, sloppy wind strike at the human teacher, quite sufficient to take her feet out from under her and tumble her down the stairs.

Unfortunately, this gave the aelfe time to throw a fireball that Kai could only partially deflect. It raked along his sleeve, and he hissed at the flare of pain along his forearm.

"So uncivilized," he snarled at her. "That was one of my better shirts."

His ball of mage lightning struck her midsection and sent her breath from her in a noisy *whoomp*. Behind her, Hank had tackled the goblin, a big one. Kai thought he might have been another palace servant, which did make sense in a goblin network sort of way.

He hesitated to intervene, both to preserve Hank's pride and because their proximity didn't give him room for a good spell strike. Hank ducked under a wild swing from the goblin's knife, picked up a loose piece of concrete from a parking barrier and smacked the goblin in the head with it.

"Well." Kai drew in a careful breath. "That could have gone worse. Are you all right?"

Hank got up, dabbing at the side of his mouth. "Fine. Caught my tusk on the way down. But fine."

The goblin was out cold but the aelfe was still moving. Kai grabbed her and hauled her up before she could crawl away.

"You have no business here," she hissed.

Kai let his eyes glow and showed his teeth. "*You* have no business selling children. Hank, check with the driver for rope or a rope substitute."

He flashed his fangs at the human woman, just to ensure she would remain cowering on the ground. Hank came back with zip ties and extension cords, most likely from the van's more everyday purpose as perhaps an electrician's or landscaper's vehicle.

With the child thieves secured, Kai opened the back of the van, his sharp teeth put away again. "Hello, children. There's been a change of plans."

It took only about twenty minutes for them to be back on the road, Hank driving the cart and Kai riding beside. In the back sat their bound prisoners, the pixie children and two empty cages. Neither he nor Hank could in good conscience keep the six fairies that had been in those cages captive a minute longer. They were all very young fairies who, as far as they had been able to ascertain, had been raised in the cages. They didn't know how to 'port so they sat on the pixie children.

Kai had photos of the van, of the children in the van and of the fairies in the cages. Anything else could wait until AURA social services and investigators caught up to this mess. Hank had left his phone with Ryld and Kai sent him a text letting him know their mission had been successful, they were unhurt and on the way back. They took a small detour once they reached the center of Pixieland. Kai held up his hand to halt in front of one of the wagons and before he dismounted a figure was pulling the door open.

"Sean? Sean Dove-Feather?"

"Kai Hiltas. What's going on here?"

He must have asked the question just to confirm because Kai already saw the gleam of a blade in his hand and he was eyeing the adults in the back of the wagon.

"Sean? What's—Oh." A pixie woman wearing a flowing robe came out behind him. Her eyes were on the kids, and she didn't wait for an answer before going right to the smallest of them. "He's pale as milk. He needs to eat immediately. Come, come with me, I have food inside."

The children, both pixie and fairy, followed her eagerly, and Kai felt a small weight lift from his heart.

"These…" Kai cursed for a bit in drow when he couldn't find words in the human language. "Have been selling your children. Tonight, we caught them at it."

Sean leapt into the back of the wagon, wings blurring. He stood on the seat over the aelfe woman with the knife at her throat and spit a few choice words of his own in his own language.

"Sean." Kai kept his warning soft. "There are witnesses. If you murder her, I would like nothing better than to lie about it, but I can't."

Hank took a more direct approach. He'd already grabbed Sean's arm before Kai finished speaking.

"You think I care? After what this bitch has done?"

"I won't let you kill her, much as I'd like to," Hank said. "She's not the one at the end of this, she's only one small piece, and we need her to get everyone in our net. Okay? Be reasonable, Sean. Those kids need your help more right now."

Sean pulled away but didn't slice her throat. He backed off. "Get them and yourselves out of here. Word is already spreading, and I can't promise you safety. You'll have to rely on being fast."

"Tally ho," Kai said in what he hoped was an ironic tone. He pulled his mare's head around and gave her a little kick to get her moving. With a snap of the reins, Hank set the horses off, the cart thundering after at its best speed.

Which…it was a delivery cart. Best speed wasn't much more than a lumbering canter. Still, they cleared Pixieland with nothing more disastrous than the disconcerting knowledge of being closely watched.

There were no more stops until they reached the aelfe court. Of course they had been seen already by the time they pulled up and most of the elves had come out or were watching with curiosity what spectacle the drow was bringing them now.

Kai searched the faces for one he knew. "Clematis." He nodded to her where she hung toward the back of the small crowd. "Please ask Lady Jessamine if she would have a few moments for us?"

She raced off, skirts flying. One didn't summon an elven queen, of course. One could request, and while Lady Jessamine might have relished pomp and ceremony, this disturbance was not something she could put off.

She came out to them with all the regal bearing and grave seriousness she could muster. "Kai Hiltas, I presume you have a very good explanation?"

"My lady, I have news of a dire nature and much to share with you. But for the moment, briefly, these three—and others—have been involved in the selling of children from the orphanage your ladyship sponsors. Pixie and fairy children both, to *human* buyers. They take the children under false pretense, then sell them on."

There were hisses of dismay from the court. No one here would be so naïve that they didn't know what that meant.

Lady Jessamine only had to make the slightest gesture and the elves hushed. "And what makes you believe this to be true?"

"We have documents, my lady. Financial and contractual evidence. The lack of adoption records. And this evening, we caught them at it, using spelled cages to transport the fairies and an unmarked van to transport poorly cared-for pixie children."

Hank reached into the back of the wagon and brought out one of the cages to emphasize the point. This time the sounds of outrage and hisses of disgust were not so easily quieted.

Lady Jessamine waited for the murmurings to die down before saying, "Very well. As a respected agent of AURA and a valued guest here at this court, I take you at your word, but would still like to see your evidence. And to speak with the prisoners." She made a few more gestures to one of the aelfe nearest to her, and he gathered two more to see to the prisoners in the back of the wagon.

"Come with me please," she said to Kai and Hank.

"Of course, my lady." Kai dismounted and waited until Hank had climbed down from the wagon to join him. "I'm prepared to share everything with you. We waited until we were certain, until we had enough evidence to share with you."

"Of course," she said softly, and Kai thought he saw a flash of anger in her eyes. Good. This was something to be angry about. "Come. We will discuss this in my receiving room."

Hank paced beside him as Kai gathered all the evidence in his mind. He would need to retrieve his laptop at some point, but what he had on his phone would do for now. His hands shook from the excitement of the chase — terrible though it had been, he couldn't help the adrenaline rush that came with a puzzle solved.

Lady Jessamine took a place on the vine-patterned loveseat in her receiving parlor and patted the cushion next to it. Kai perched there, and Hank remained standing at his right shoulder. Still playing the servant, though that was his choice.

"My dear Kai." She took his hand, something hard in her palm that she placed in his. "All the trouble you've gone through. You shouldn't have."

That hard object bit into Kai's palm, and he jerked his hand back. An emerald lay in his palm, pulsing with a sinister green-yellow light. Kai tried to remove it... and failed. It was stuck fast to his skin. "My lady... what?"

"Only what you deserve." Lady Jessamine rose from the sofa and placed her hand on Hank's chest. "Sleep."

Hank collapsed in a heap and though Kai's mind reeled in confusion, part of him snarled at himself. He'd made a terrible mistake. He reached for his magic, ready to draw power as fast as he could and again... nothing. *Nothing.* Not only was he cut off from his magic, his physical strength felt as if it were draining out the soles of his boots. She'd affixed a cursed gem to him, and he'd been blind enough to let her.

"You've... Lady Jessamine, how could you do this? Why?"

Her beautiful face had transformed with rage, her complexion an unflattering brick red. "Why else, you fool? They're just pixies and fairies. Ship ten off and they'll breed twenty more next week. This court is powerful, and wealth brings more power, the power to do what is necessary. The humans of this world are barely more than animals. They give us this pittance of land as far from civilization as they can. Someone has to teach them their place. Once I bring your *sulitek* to heel, he'll do nicely to keep the drow and the kolle in line. Conquering the humans will follow. But first, you've necessitated an accident for yourself and the orc. Could you possibly be any more inconvenient?"

It hurt. Of course it hurt. Kai had thought they were friends. He had truly believed... Ah, this world had made him careless and soft—believing people who were mortal enemies in other worlds could work together here. Fine, yes, there were some aelfe he could trust without reservation, but Val and some of his officers had earned that trust a thousand times over.

While he was angry at Jessamine, he was furious with himself. *Oh, Ryld. I am so sorry. My terrible decisions will leave you alone and in danger. Forgive me, little brother.*

Out loud, he only said, "I suppose I could be more inconvenient if I bit you."

It was the wrong thing to say, and he'd known that. He just had time to steel himself before she backhanded him across the face and knocked him from his seat. *Lovely.* He was too weak now to sit up again. Though from this vantage point, he could see Hank. *Still breathing.* Still alive always meant there was still a chance. The sharp pain of the emerald burrowing into his skin threatened to steal thoughts and sense, but he had to keep thinking to get them out of this.

Lady Jessamine spoke to someone just outside Kai's line of vision. "Take them to the north face in the Pine

Woods. If anyone asks, say they were on their way to see if that drow bitch had anything to do with what they discovered. I will handle Ryld."

Chapter Fifteen

Of all the wondrous things in this world, the little handheld computer and all the things it could do were one of the most amazing to Ryld. That he could read the message from Kai and know instantly they had succeeded in their task was a huge relief. Or, it should have been. The device did nothing to give him patience. Knowing they were safe and on their way back did not hasten their arrival.

He'd put paint to paper for a while but couldn't focus. He'd paced every inch of the rooms. Nothing made the time go any faster. When the door finally opened, he couldn't hide his disappointment that Hank and Kai did not walk through it, but instead Lady Jessamine.

"Ryld, my dear. I know you must be anxious for news of Kai and your friend. Their arrival was quite a shock, as you can imagine. Unfortunately, they had to leave again to investigate a matter of some urgency and so had no time to see you first. I do hope you understand. This whole business has been very distressing."

"Hank and Kai left? Where did they go?"

"To speak to the drow queen and gauge her involvement in the despicable happenings at the orphanage. I've sent two of my best warriors with them so there is no need for you to fear. They should return soon. In the meantime, I thought you might be tired of waiting here, and would like you to join me. We can keep each other company while we wait."

* * * *

It wasn't the first time in his life that Kai had been carried as helpless baggage in front of someone's saddle. It wasn't even the first time this had occurred involving an aelfe saddle with the added indignity of being wrapped up in a blanket to keep him still and hidden. But he had thought those days were long behind him. *Ha. They could have been if you hadn't been so blinkered.*

Liking someone caused instances of bias. He knew that. This wasn't normally an issue since he liked so few people, but damn her eyes, he had *liked* Lady Jessamine and hadn't been able to conceive of her being involved in such vile goings on. Tenzin had liked her, too, which just illustrated how good she was at keeping her mask in place.

He tried to shift his shoulders to ease the ache in his back and head. No, that made things worse. Not that there was any comfortable way to lie with one's head bumping along against a horse's side. *The north face in Pine Woods.* To arrange for some sort of accident, yes, but what sort of accident would determine whether they had any chance to escape or to call for help.

They'd taken his phone, naturally, along with the spellworking items he carried with him out of habit — the salt, the chalk, the hemlock and the little scrying mirror he'd had for years. Never mind that he couldn't reach his magic, though Kai didn't feel at all comforted that they feared him so much.

"Pardon me," he forced out in a choked rasp. Even speaking had become difficult. "Could you perhaps tell me how you're planning on doing away with us?"

In answer, the aelfe warrior in the saddle kneed him in the stomach. "Shut up, drow scum."

Ah, so we're reduced to clichés. Wonderful. At least the blanket had slipped far enough that he could see where they were headed.

The method of murder became painfully obvious when the aelfe stopped at the mouth of a small cave and examined the surrounding rock.

"Shouldn't be too hard." The green-haired warrior pointed at spots in the rock above the opening. "Couple of good fireballs here and here."

The blond one nodded. "We'll hit it together. Looks about ready to come down anyway."

Buried alive it is, then. Kai squinted in the sunlight, trying to get a good look at the cave. Depending on where they tossed him and Hank, they should be able to survive the rockslide. Then it would simply be a matter of time before they either managed to escape or died in there.

* * * *

"Sit here, yes. Now, you must tell me. You've had lessons with my mages, and I hear the drow court mage has visited with you twice now. Have you really made no progress toward learning to control yourself?"

"I—I am able to control myself, my lady. It's the shadows that are difficult to control."

Lady Jessamine laughed but Ryld had heard too much forced laughter in his life not to hear the ring of falsehood in the sound.

"The shadows are not living things separate from yourself, Ryld. I know Yarrow told you this, and you must come to believe it. The darkness that creates these beasts lives in your heart, even if you refuse to admit it to yourself."

Ryld said nothing. There was nothing to say to that without flatly disagreeing. Which he might have done with anyone else, but she was a queen and he found it difficult enough to be in her presence. It struck him how opposed her theory was to what Dzev had told him that afternoon in the fairy glade.

Dzev equated the shadows to a force of nature, just like any magic. They were neither good, nor evil, and while his mind gave them shape it was no different than the way wind and water shaped a storm. The shadows could be destructive, but not evil.

Lady Jessamine patted his hand, and Ryld jumped.

"Don't worry, we have time. You shall practice controlling the beasts every day. I predict we will do many great things together, in time."

Ryld looked up at her. "My lady, your pardon, but I don't intend to stay very long. As soon as Kai Hiltas completes his investigation we will go home soon after."

She lifted her hand and patted his head. "Don't be difficult, child. I insist you stay."

Ryld kept silent. Better to let Kai and Hank tell her they were going.

* * * *

The aelfe weren't gentle when they tossed Kai and Hank into the cave. Not that Kai had expected them to be, but he landed on the hand with the cursed jewel embedded. The thing had worked its way nearly under his skin and agony shot up his arm, whiting out his vision for a few precious seconds.

Hank lay motionless, sprawled where they had thrown him, and perhaps that was for the best. Unconscious, Hank wouldn't need to worry about Ryld or his own fate.

"What if the orc wakes up?" Green-hair asked with a frown, as if he'd heard Kai's thoughts.

"From her ladyship's sleep spell?" Blondie laughed so hard he doubled over. "He's not waking up unless someone breaks that spell and that horrid drow can't get to his magic, can he?"

They both laughed at that, ugly, mean-spirited chuckles.

Kai did manage to worm his way over to Hank and cover his head, just as the aelfe began their bombardment of the rock face. Dust and small debris rained down as they threw fireball after fireball at the cliff face. In a disheartening small space of time, the debris became chunks of rock, then huge slabs thudding down in front of the cave entrance.

Kai did his best to shield Hank as the light slowly faded and finally vanished in a great rumbling of stone. He could hear the occasional thunk of rock falling for a few moments more, then the fading sound of hoof beats as the warriors rode away.

While drow eyes were dark-adapted, even he needed a speck of light to see and there was none. No light and nothing he could do. Perhaps if a rat happened by, he might send it with a message to the drow court, though there might not be any space for even a rat to wriggle through. Other than that, he had to hope that AURA would come looking for them when he didn't check in or that someone might care enough to figure out what had happened.

"I'm sorry, Hank. You should have been safe back in New York with your Ryld. I dragged you all the way out here to die on what's worse than a fool's errand."

Kai heaved a sigh and let his head rest on Hank's chest. The curse was only getting more intense, and it was all the movement he could manage now. They probably had days before the air grew too poisoned to breathe. Not that he was giving up yet. Tenzi would expect him to find some way out of this, and he hoped fervently that there would be one, but he hated being helpless and he hated having to wait for things that might never come.

* * * *

Ryld spent an uncomfortable morning with Lady Jessamine. She grated on his nerves in the same way Yarrow had. Questioning him on things he had no answers for and pushing him to think and do as she wished. In the back of his mind was a constant worried whisper that Hank and Kai had gone into a dangerous situation, again. Waiting, again, to hear word from them was almost unbearable.

He was thinking about making an excuse. That he wanted to go lie down perhaps, since that wasn't a lie, when two elves dressed in warrior leathers strode into the sitting room. Both looked dusty and haggard, and only gave the briefest bow to their queen before spilling their news. "My lady, I'm afraid there's been a terrible accident."

Before he could say more a loud commotion drew their attention to the door and another elf burst into the room. "My queen, there's a brigade of drow on horseback coming."

Jessamine was on her feet before he finished speaking. The two elves who had come first had weapons in their hands as if they were facing the drow already.

Ryld stood too, raising his voice to be heard over the general din of people running and shouting in the hall and the messenger elf babbling about how many and how well armed the drow were.

"What accident? What happened?" Ryld demanded.

"A rock slide," the green-haired elf said. "Your companions... I'm afraid — "

"No! No — Where are they? Where's Hank?"

"The side of the mountain came down and they were caught in the fall. They're gone."

Ryld's vision dimmed and the sudden chaos in the room as more elves came running in seemed unreal, far away. Rocks. A landslide... Hank caught in the fall. No, no, it couldn't be true. Someone grabbed his arm and pulled him from the room. He didn't resist. He could barely stand. Lady Jessamine was snapping orders. It was her hand that gripped him.

Screams rose from outside the great doors of the hall, and the chilling sound of a drow battle cry. He should have been terrified, but he felt entirely numb, encased in ice. It wasn't real. None of this could be real. He must have fallen asleep and was having a terrible nightmare. Kai gone. Hank... He refused to accept they were gone.

Shafts of afternoon sunlight blinded him as he was thrust outside. Lady Jessamine shook his arm, her fingers digging into his flesh. "These vicious drow loosened the rocks that caused the landslide. They killed your friends and now they've come to take you."

He stared at her, her face a mask of rage so unlike the mask of welcome she normally wore. Rage and a desperate fear. He knew those things well. The ice started to crack around his heart, and he heard his own voice in his ears rising in a high wail of anguish.

Jessamine slapped him. "You want vengeance! Let your beasts go after these drow."

Ryld felt the darkness rushing into the place where ice had been. The brightness of the sun grew dim, shadows from every tree and rock and the warriors fighting around the hall all started to twist and jump in jerky movements, growing impossibly larger.

"Ryld!"

Ryld could no longer speak or move to answer Dzev. The drow mage yanked his horse to a halt, its hooves churning the dirt.

"Kill him!" Jessamine screamed, though to whom she was speaking Ryld wasn't sure. The drow were already outnumbered, the shadows were about to tear free. When they did, the ground would churn with blood as well as dirt.

"Your aelfe warriors were seen, Jessamine." Dzev's voice cut like a razor with his rage. "They caused the rockslide. Ryld, come to me. She tried to kill Kai and Hank."

The dam broke.

Ryld whipped his head toward Jessamine. He could only see her outline through the black lenses that bled over his eyes. She had something in her hand, reaching for him with it, and a shadow bit down on her arm just above her wrist. The bones snapped, twin *pop-pops*, and her scream of pain cut through even the dullness that stuffed Ryld's ears. More shadows rushed her, clawing and tearing. She fell away from him along with everything else. *Gone.* If Hank was gone, he wanted to be gone too.

* * * *

The pain in his arm had reached the point where the blood pounded in his ears, so Kai wasn't certain what he heard at first. Scratching? Scrabbling? Maybe there was a small mammal in here after all that he could persuade to carry a message.

But the scrabbling began to resolve into…digging? Voices outside the cave, perhaps? Had the aelfe returned to make certain?

A rock near the top of the cave arch lifted away and afternoon sun blinded him. He squinted against the glare as more rocks vanished from the pile. When the hole was large enough, a face appeared at the top of the rockslide.

"They're here, auntie!" The young face was drow, dark with white hair. Not an aelfe at all.

A face Kai recognized replaced the young drow's.

"Lady Ksatha?" he whispered.

"Good. You're not dead." The drow queen turned her head to call down. "Get the rest of these rocks moved! Hurry!"

A combination of hands and magic lifted the rocks away quickly, the sunlight becoming unbearable enough that Kai squeezed his eyes shut. He opened them again when a gentle hand landed on his arm.

"Kai Hiltas. You've managed a bit of a pickle, as the humans say." Lady Ksatha's smile was wry as she gazed down at him.

"How?" he choked out and began to cough.

"Hmm. My niece, Tsada, was the scout on this end of our holdings today. She spotted two aelfe bucks on *our* lands and followed. Good that she did, since she saw them throw you and your goblin-son friend in here and bring part of the cliff down to seal you in."

"I couldn't..." He turned his palm over to show her, and she hissed in dismay.

"That explains...everything." She smoothed the wild hair back from his forehead. "I told Tsada that a *hiltas* could never be trapped like this. But that...that is an evil thing and old. I wonder how long Jessamine has had that in her stores."

"Saving it...just for me." He managed what he hoped was a smile. "Hank is...sleep...spelled."

"Easily mended. But I think we'll let him sleep until we're somewhere more comfortable." Lady Ksatha gestured to her warriors. "Come. Get them out of here. Gently!" She raised her voice when one of the young drow was about to drag Kai out by the arm. "Gently. Please."

The journey to the drow court was a short one — since the aelfe had brought them most of the way there—and accomplished on litters rather than thrown across a saddle like a potato sack.

In the cool dark of the drow caves, Lady Ksatha brought them to one of the sleeping chambers and called mages in to remove the cursed stone from Kai's hand.

"Our Ryld," Kai told her through the pain. "We must rescue him from that *kzasht* aelfe."

"I've sent a war band to her court." She patted his shoulder. "Dzev will retrieve him."

"Ah. Thank you. For…" His throat closed over with unexpected emotion. "All of this. I should have…listened to you."

"*All* soon mended." She gave him a smile as she swept out of the room to let her mages work.

It took a full circle to remove the cursed stone, a process far more painful than Kai had anticipated, and while he was curious about the process, he managed to lose consciousness before the interesting part of nullifying the stone and working it free.

* * * *

"Ryld…"

He heard his name from the end of a long tunnel. It echoed in his head. His eyelids felt weighted down, and he ached where he wasn't numb. Finally, with all his effort, he managed to force his eyes open.

Chaos greeted him. No, not chaos. The aftermath of chaos. It was quiet, and dusk had fallen. No one was near, except Dzev.

"Hello," Dzev ventured softly. "Your eyes are blue again."

Slowly Ryld pushed himself up. He was still lying where he'd fallen just outside the court of the aelfe. The ornate double doors were open, one hanging on by a single hinge. Everywhere he looked was destruction. Broken tree limbs, uprooted plants, churned ground. Blood. No bodies, thankfully. The thought of bodies brought a sharp stab of anguish.

"Breathe. Slowly. That's it." Dzev sat cross-legged a few feet away, apparently unconcerned with the rubble and the dust in his hair. "I've just had a bat messenger. Your Hank did not perish in the rockslide. He is with her ladyship at the drow court."

"Hank is alive?" Ryld's voice sounded raw, more like a crow's voice. "He's *alive*?" The relief was almost overwhelming. "And Kai Hiltas?"

"Hank is well. And Kai...will be well again soon."

Ryld exhaled. His head was spinning, and he was sure if he tried to move he wouldn't make it more than a few inches. He was utterly drained. He looked around again at the destruction, the blood. "Is Lady Jessamine dead?"

Dzev's expression twisted in distaste. "She has survived. I would say more's the pity, but she has much to answer for."

"What happened? Where are all the people?"

"You were, ah, quite angry when Lady Jessamine insisted that Hank was dead. Some of the destruction is from our war band trying to break in to find you. The rest, I'm afraid, was you." Dzev gave him a sideways glance. "Did I mention you were *very* angry? Some of the aelfe fled into the forest. The servants, the workers, managed to scatter before any of the walls came down. We have Lady Jessamine and her mage favorites contained. As well as the leaders of her warriors.

Deaths…" Dzev held up a hand for patience. "There were two. An aelfe horse panicked, threw her rider and trampled him. Another warrior tried to shoot you before you collapsed. I, ah, I killed him."

Ryld absorbed all this information and nodded. It was still difficult to believe all the destruction around him in this once idyllic setting. "I would like to go to Hank."

"I'm certain he is impatient to see you by now." Dzev held out a hand to Ryld and turned his head to whistle. A night-black horse answered his call and came at a gallop. "Come. Starwind will take us there."

Ryld felt like his bones creaked and his muscles were about to tear. Dzev had to help him mount. "Why do I feel as if I was beaten after running a long distance?"

"You used every last bit of magic you had, little brother. It took a long time for the storm to blow itself out."

They were underway, Dzev holding Ryld securely, when Ryld asked, "What happens now?"

"AURA will come."

Ryld wondered if Tenzin might come with them, and asked belatedly, "Why did you say Kai will be well soon?"

"Lady Jessamine attached a curse to him. She would not have been able to overpower him otherwise, but she was prepared." Dzev sighed and shifted in the saddle. "Perhaps a bit too well. We have long thought she was not as bright and shining as she seemed, but I am chagrined that we were unable to foresee any of this."

It wasn't until they were nearly to the drow court that Ryld felt the fear creep in. He was going into the lair of a drow queen, willingly, feeling like a wrung-dry dishtowel. But he'd face anything to see Hank with his own eyes and know he was unhurt.

The hills into which the drow had dug their caves were forested, less barren and forbidding than the court Ryld had known. A pair of young drow guarded the entrance, but there were no giant spiders or riding lizards in sight. Maybe none of those had made the crossing with any of the drow here.

Of course they knew Dzev. They stepped aside with respectful bows as he and Ryld went past.

Perhaps he was simply too exhausted to feel panic, but that didn't explain the sudden quieting in his blood, the comfort of being not just under a roof, but also below ground, the solidity of the earth all around him.

Hank sat in a chair next to Kai's bed, and when Ryld stepped into the room, he stood.

"Hank…" Both of Ryld's hands fluttered erratically and an overwhelming pressure lifted from his heart. He didn't know why tears came, but they flowed down his cheeks as he went straight into Hank's arms.

"Sweetheart." Hank's voice hitched as he held Ryld tight. "I'm so glad you're okay. You just don't know… Thinking of you alone with that…that…person."

"Ryld…" Kai's right hand was swathed in bandages, his voice a spare ghost of a whisper. "I hear rumors of dragons."

Ryld leaned around Hank without loosening his embrace one bit. "Dragons?"

"Your shadows," Dzev answered for him. "They were quite large and did somewhat resemble dragons."

"Her mage?" Kai stopped to cough. "Dzev?"

Dzev's bow was extravagant, his forehead nearly touching the ground. He was very flexible. "I am Dzev. It is…an *enormous* honor to meet you, Kai Hiltas.

I...please don't think me ridiculous, but I have read everything about you."

"Have you?" Kai's mouth twisted into something like his normal wry smile. "Eager youngsters."

"My shadows... They didn't attack the drow, did they?" Ryld asked.

It was less a question than a request for confirmation. Everything was blurry around the edges, but he remembered consciously trying to turn his rage toward those who deserved it.

Dzev shook his head. "They did not. They attacked Lady Jessamine most, ah, enthusiastically. I was able to drive them off, and they turned most of their attention on the palace."

"Sounds like Lady J. bit off more than she could handle," Hank said with a snort. He tipped Ryld's face up so their eyes met. "Hey. Are you okay in here? With, you know, all the drow you don't know?"

"I am much better now that I see you with my own eyes. I am...okay. Right now." He reached a hand up to touch Hank's cheek. "I may never let you leave my sight again."

"Right now I feel the same. I think we'll get over it eventually." Hank gave him a hard squeeze, though, so he probably wasn't *over it* yet.

Kai hitched himself up on the pillows a little farther. "AURA's been informed? On their way?"

Dzev put a hand to his chest and bowed his head. "Teams will be 'porting in. Medical will be among the first, I'm told."

"Ah." Kai's eyes gleamed wetly. "They will be busy. If someone could inform Tenzin where I am. I've no idea where my phone ended up."

"I'm afraid I might know." Dzev put down the bag slung over his shoulder and rummaged in it. He came up with a battered phone. The glass on the top was badly cracked. "The aelfe who was trampled by his horse. He had this. It did not smell of him, so I concluded it was not his. Was it yours?"

Kai took the phone in his unbandaged hand and sighed. "Of course. I suppose it serves him right, but I would have liked to have gotten some work done."

"I will send a message to the scout at the 'port sight and they will get the message to your husband. Lady Ksatha would like to extend her hospitality, for as long as you need. Ryld, wherever you are most comfortable, you are welcome. You need rest, you are very depleted." He glanced meaningfully at Hank as he said this.

Oddly enough Ryld did not feel the urge to flee immediately now that he had Hank. Perhaps that also had to do with Kai and Dzev's presence.

"I will stay. The cave is comforting."

"Good." Hank sat down on the bed across the room and patted the blankets beside him. "I know I was asleep most of the afternoon, but spell sleep is surprisingly tiring."

"Spelled sleep is not like regular sleep," Dzev confirmed. "Your mind and body still fight, even if you are unaware. Yes, all of you, rest. I must go to Lady Ksatha, but any passing drow will get you whatever you need if you make it known."

Kai might have muttered, "*I need Tenzin,*" but Ryld couldn't be sure. Aloud, he said, "Thank you, Dzev. Everyone's been most gracious. We'll content ourselves with rest for now."

Dzev bowed himself out, and Kai heaved another put upon sigh. "My laptop most likely didn't survive, either. It's a good thing I back everything up on the servers."

Ryld yawned and shuffled over to Hank. "He will be here soon, Kai Hiltas," he said, the only assurance he could muster for his friend. Because that's what Kai had become in all of this. Mentor, friend.

He lay down on the bed next to Hank. His mind thought of a thousand things he wanted to say, to tell him, how immediate and desperate the despair had been when he believed Hank dead, how his heart had felt broken beyond anything he'd ever known…and the elation at learning he was still alive. All those things, and more, but as he laid his head down, no words would come, the weariness dragging at him.

"I can hear your brain spinning from here," Hank whispered and wrapped him up close so that Ryld would transfer his head to Hank's chest. "Just breathe with me right now. Share a heartbeat. Everything else can wait."

The last bit of tension at the thought of where he was, surrounded by unknown drow, flowed away. He did as Hank suggested. He let his breath sync, then his heart, and he was asleep.

Chapter Sixteen

"It's really not my fault this time, Tenzi." Kai clung to his husband's furry arm as they picked their way down the hill to the tents AURA had set up as a mobile command center.

Tenzin sighed and caught Kai when he stumbled. "Playing hero again *is* your fault. You could have called for backup without alerting the child thieves."

"We still thought Jessamine was the *good* queen, though. More personnel would have been in danger," Kai tried to argue and stopped at a glare from Tenzin. "I'm sorry, beloved. Truly, I am. I did think I had this under control. Up to a point, it was."

"I suppose you couldn't anticipate a curse stone." Tenzin gave up on trying to support him and scooped him up to carry him the rest of the way. "Your poor hand won't be usable for some time. The stone dug down into the bones and crushed some of them."

A wave of nausea threatened, and Kai swallowed hard. "I'm not certain I can talk about this first thing in the morning."

He didn't want to think about the hand at all. Wrapped up tight and numbed with whatever anesthetic Medical had brought with them, it only ached a bit, and if no one mentioned it, he could pretend it wasn't there.

Tenzin took him into the largest tent where half the flaps had been rolled up to let in a cross-breeze. He set Kai down on a pillow-covered lawn chaise beside a computer station, though it was obvious Kai wasn't supposed to *use* the computer since his assistant Mindy had taken *that* chair. Frustrating.

"Hey, Mr. H." She greeted him with a cheery wave. "Good to see you up. You sure you should be up?"

"*Don't* start," Kai tried out a snarl, but it sounded tired. "Is the team here?"

"Yep. All here. Vicki was super excited about 'porting. Jordie threw up. They're helping social services with sorting the pixie kid names until they get assignments from you."

Kai eased his no-longer-cursed hand into his lap, wincing. *Fine*. Perhaps it did hurt a bit. "Good. I want Sterling and Vicki to go out to the flower fairy glade. Have them explain to the queen how her fairies were being replaced with changelings, and I need them to search for spells surrounding the glade. They're most likely subtle, but there must be compulsions keeping the fairies in such a small space."

"Got it." Mindy tapped away on the computer as he spoke. "Sterling sends a roger on that."

"Please tell me he did not say *roger*."

Mindy snickered. "Just an expression, Mr. H."

"Ha. If I say I missed you, will it go to your head?" Kai waved off her laugh and continued. "Rudy and

Terrence, send them up to the orphanage to record the names of every child still there."

"Isn't that a social services issue, love?" Tenzin murmured without looking up from the oximeter he'd attached to Kai's good hand.

"Social services are swamped, and we need to get lists in place to determine which children are actually missing, which need to be returned to parents in Pixieland, and which are truly orphans." Kai closed his eyes, trying to keep all the pieces in line. "Who's in charge at the orphanage now?"

"It's that Albright woman still." Mindy set a pile of paper reports in his lap, presumably because he would be tempted to do too much if someone, Great Mother forbid, gave him a tablet. "Captain Hartgrove says he's confident that she wasn't involved in the trafficking. It doesn't sound like she was great at her job, letting kids go missing, but as he said..." She lowered her voice in a ridiculous imitation of Val. "Incompetence does not equal malicious intent."

Kai held back a laugh, barely. "Very good. I want Jordie with the enforcement officers, helping them track down who else was involved, starting with who was doing the orphanage's accounting."

"Sent and sent. Good to have you back, Mr. H."

Tenzin handed him his reading glasses, the ones he needed in the daylight when his eyes were tired — and where Tenzin had dug *those* up, Kai couldn't imagine — and Kai began slogging through the reports.

Flax was leading the officers hunting the forest for aelfe. While the majority of the court was most likely not involved in illegal activity, they *all* needed to be brought in for questioning. The kitchen staff and palace servants had come in on their own and were being most cooperative, especially Hank's little informant friend, who was singing his head off, apparently.

Information from his statement had been sent to the human police departments nationwide to assist in tracking down the human buyers, and hopefully the children from there.

Lady Jessamine was in magically blocked custody. She refused to say anything until an advocate could arrive to represent her. In a grim sort of way, Kai didn't blame her. The list of charges was longer than Tenzin was tall and included conspiracy to commit murder. *That* would put her in the human system upon conviction. Not a good place for elves, human prisons, but somehow Kai couldn't muster any sympathy.

Yarrow and Yew—likewise uncooperative so far, though in Yarrow's case, the reports put his uncommunicative state down to traumatic shock. Eyewitness accounts said the brothers had tried to banish Ryld's dragons with light spells and had nearly been eaten. Yew just glared at everyone and wouldn't speak at all.

Social services did have their hands full with Pixieland. There were ongoing negotiations with the unofficial pixie leaders about what should happen there, from relocation for those who wanted it, to better housing and employment for those who wanted to stay. Kellen and Sin had been assigned there temporarily since not having a pixie present could have been disastrous and Sin… Well, Sin was just naturally charming and had brought cases of honey for the kids suffering from malnutrition. Certainly didn't hurt.

For being on the other side of a continent from their home, everyone was remarkably well organized and there wasn't much more for Kai to do for the moment. He couldn't think of anything he was forgetting.

He looked up from the report he was reading as someone approached. Sean Dove-Feather looked every inch the pixie warrior that morning. His dark red hair was braided back from his face in two plaits, and he wore a short clout and a boiled leather vest that tied around his neck and waist, leaving his back bare for his wings. He carried a slender spear in one hand and both his wings and body were painted in a complicated design of whorls and lines in shimmering pixie dust. If Kai hadn't known better, he would have guessed an Event had just dropped him into this world.

"Well met, Kai Hiltas." He nodded at the others politely. "There is a young pix by the name of Kellen that sent me your way. He said you might know best the channels to take to have AURA redesignate Elvenhome so that elves, pixies, goblins and fairies each have an equal stake in the land here."

Ah. There it was. The thing he was forgetting.

"Good morning, Sean Dove-Feather. Pardon, please, if I don't stand. Medical will fuss." He cocked his head to the side. "I do indeed know where to begin the process. The Bureau of Land Management will need to rewrite the land use parameters and it can be done by executive order. It won't be immediate, but I will do everything in my power to get it done. Our Kellen is correct." Kai gave him a sharp-toothed smile. "I do know channels."

And people. And the ones who owe me favors.

Tenzin returned in the afternoon, still serene and patient so Medical was running smoothly. He gave Kai a quick kiss and checked his pulse. "I strongly suggest you find a stopping place in your work today, my angel. You're barely keeping your eyes open."

"Hmm. I'm nearly there." Kai glanced up at his husband over his glasses. "Does someone have the aelfe in hand? Since their court is essentially broken?"

"Val has taken it upon himself to patch them back together. They have no *tesined* of their own, so I suppose his is the most logical voice of authority." Tenzin knelt beside Kai's chaise to put them at eye level. "There are, from what I hear, three young aelfe women of good bloodlines who might be acceptable as the next queen. Though all three are frankly terrified of the prospect. I believe the court will pick Viburnum, a young mage who had been overshadowed by Yarrow and Yew. She seems sensible if not terribly confident yet, advocating for more traditional tree homes rather than lavish palaces."

"Confidence will be less important than honesty in the next few years." Kai let out a sigh. "I don't envy whoever takes up the title. Though this is a rather pretty part of the world for an elven court."

"It is, isn't it?" Tenzin's voice had a speculative note to it that made Kai sit up straighter.

"You're considering something. Tell me, beloved."

Tenzin took his hand and kissed the backs of his fingers. "It is pretty. It will be a more welcoming place again soon. And we never did get to have a honeymoon."

"Time away from the office without anyone trying to kill me?" Kai chuckled. "What a novel thought."

* * * *

It had been an interesting morning. If interesting meant exhausting. It wasn't even noon and Hank wanted to go back to bed. He'd told the whole story — from the first visit to the flower fairies to that horrifying confrontation with Lady Jessamine — to no less than seven AURA officials, some of them nicer than others.

The enforcement captain, Hartgrove, he'd been kind and hadn't badgered him or Ryld. Just wanted to put the events in order and get all the players in the right places. The human from crime scene investigations had been more confrontational and had obviously made Ryld uncomfortable. Hank had told him to come back later to finish his questions.

They were taking a break from the chaos outside in a little grotto within the drow court. A shaft went to the surface, providing light and allowing the sun to cast shimmering reflections off the water.

"Strange. Being in the aelfe court in the beautiful rooms filled with light I felt more like a prisoner there than in this place I was so afraid of," Ryld said.

"There was good reason for that even if we didn't know it." Hank bumped shoulders with Ryld. "I think your instincts were trying to tell you something the rest of us couldn't see. But yeah…we're not aelfe. It's in our nature to like caves."

Ryld nodded. "The drow here seem very different than the drow I knew before. The goblinkind too, are not the same. Do you think it's just they are a different court, or is it because they have crossed over to this world?"

"The way I understand it, we all come from different worlds and in those worlds, history and the people in them made the courts very different places." Hank scratched at his arm absently. "In my world, goblins traded with humans. They took contracts with drow. Sometimes the drow did dark things, but not…not in a conqueror's sort of way. But I've talked to other people who come from places where the drow courts were terrible places of treachery and murder. Places where aelfe warred with goblins or goblins with humans. So this court, it's not like they all came from the same place, but their queen isn't one of the brutal ones. And she says who gets to stay and who has to go. It's her influence that makes the court one way or another."

"Yes, for the aelfe too. They like to accuse the drow of arrogance, and the drow in turn accuse the aelfe of the same. Both are right, and wrong. We're more alike than we are different."

Hank smiled at that. "True. Most other races just shake their heads and say, *eh, elves.*"

Ryld smiled too. "Goblins included."

A soft cough drew their attention. Dzev.

"Pardon the intrusion, friends. The world outside is still as warm with aelfe and others, I had hoped we might have a quiet moment to talk?"

"Of course." Hank patted the rock ledge beside him. Dzev had been there when things had gone so horribly wrong. Or right. Depending on how he wanted to look at it. But Hank was beyond grateful that he'd been there for Ryld, had made certain that the deaths were few. "We needed some quiet, too."

Dzev gave them a small bow, hand over heart, before he settled himself on a stone. "As I sought you out I had many things I wished to say…and now I find I don't know where to begin." He gave a small laugh. "I don't wish to be the one to bring worry to your feet when you've had so little time to recover, but I'm also afraid we may not have much time to talk if you choose to leave soon. Ryld, little brother, after the events here and Lady Jessamine's plans to try to use you to her advantage, by whatever means, I am gravely worried others might attempt the same."

"He has a lot of people watching out for him." Hank broke off, knowing he sounded defensive. "Sorry. I don't mean to speak for you, sweetheart, but you do."

"Of course, and I meant no offense. Ryld, Lady Ksatha understands how ill-treated you were by the drow court to which you were born. She knows that her presence alone might be very upsetting to you, but she would like to meet with and talk to you, if you will allow it."

Ryld said nothing for a few long moments, then finally said, "I will try. If the shadows become restless, she must leave, or I must go. I can't promise they won't attack her."

"Understood." Dzev rose and left them.

Hank took Ryld's hand. "Are you sure?"

Ryld nodded. "A test. Logic tells me she is not the same woman who owned my mother and myself. She has offered no harm to us, in fact has helped us at every turn. Everything else inside me feels sick and wants to flee."

Hank put his arm around Ryld. "You don't have to —"

His murmured reassurance was cut short by the reappearance of Dzev with Lady Ksatha. Ryld went still under his arm, but a glance at the shadows told Hank he wasn't completely panicked.

"I'm right here, hon. You're doing good," Hank said into his hair. "You just say if it gets too much."

Dzev took a few steps closer, but Lady Ksatha stayed where she was. That alone showed Hank a vast difference between her and Lady Jessamine. She was already respectful of Ryld's boundaries and didn't push them.

"Well met, Ryld. And you, Hank," Lady Ksatha said, apparently not standing on ceremony. Hank was thankful for the informality. He wasn't sure he was up to all the subtle maneuvering and he knew for certain Ryld wasn't. She also didn't wait for a proper response from them, accepting Ryld's silence and Hank's murmured *hello*.

"I hope you have been made to feel welcome in my court. I know you are much in demand right now, so I won't keep you from your rest overlong." She paused just a moment before continuing, "I cannot apologize for the mistreatment you've received at another's hands. I can only tell you that I find it appalling. I was raised in a court where the rare few who were born with your ability are called silver-born, and they are treated with respect. One silver-born in particular became a most valued counselor to our queen, my mother. His name was Tyrk, and he was my brother."

"You say *was*, ma'am," Hank said softly. "Did something happen to him? Or is it because you're here and he's not?"

She smiled at him, although the expression didn't look happy. "That's a story best told another time. For now, I wanted you to know that not all of the drow are vicious and cruel, although you are wise not to trust until that trust is earned. I think I'll leave you now, best we move slowly. If you would like to dine with me tonight, or just have tea, you are both welcome."

Hank waited for Ryld to answer, but he apparently wasn't quite ready to. "Thank you, Lady Ksatha. We'll talk about it."

She took her leave then, and Dzev shortly after. Ryld had said not a word and so it was hard to judge his mood or his thoughts. Finally, when he did speak, he said, "I would like to stay here, for a while. Maybe a long while. But it is more important that I be where you are. Would you stay, or do you want to return to New York?"

"Well, let's talk this through first." Hank took both of Ryld's hands, turning to face him. "Why do you want to stay? I'm not saying it's a bad idea or anything. Just want to hear what you're thinking."

"Dzev has been able to teach me more about myself than anyone has in just a few talks with him. I would like to learn more. He might be willing to come to New York in time, but the court and Lady Ksatha need him here while things are so unsettled. Also, New York does not seem like a very good place for dragons."

"New York would be a really bad place for dragons, you're right." Hank looked down into the sun-dappled water for a moment, letting the foot still draped over the edge swing idly. "I love that your decisions so often have to do with what's best for others. And if you can't stay in the court itself, we could always set up somewhere in the woods. Would you miss your work while you're here? Your apartment?"

Ryld smiled. "My work is wherever I am. The patterns I make can be sent with a computer. The place I sleep is not as important to me as having you there."

"All right." Hank nodded. "And we both know I wouldn't miss *my* work, since that's you for now. Though…that brings me to something I've been kinda wrestling with the past few days. I don't think I should be taking money to be your companion anymore."

Ryld twitched and looked up at him. "You explained that no longer being my companion does not mean you want to no longer see me again." He said the words with a flat inflection, clearly trying to calm himself with the reminder. "You do not have to take money to be my companion if you don't want it. I have enough money for us both."

"Right...um. We have to talk about the concept of feeling like I'm contributing to the household, but later, maybe." Hank sighed and ran his thumbs over the backs of Ryld's hands. "I want to be with you. That's not in question. But not as...as an employee. Because..." He swallowed hard and turned his head to watch Ryld's face. "Because I love you. And being your paid companion after saying that just feels so wrong."

"I don't want you to feel wrong, Hank." Ryld squeezed his hands.

When that was all he said, Hank laughed nervously. "I thought telling you I loved you might...well, I'm not sure how I thought you would react."

Ryld looked at him. He often didn't meet his eyes, so Hank knew he was making an effort. "You show love when you do things like making sure I have eaten or setting up paper and paint for me. You say you love me without words all the time. I love you too, Hank. Very much."

"Oh well, then we don't have any choice." Hank smiled as Ryld's expression became puzzled. "I have to kiss you now. It's mandatory."

"I would like you to kiss me now, and I don't care if it's mandatory."

Hank took Ryld's face between his hands, leaned in and pressed his lips to Ryld's, always careful of the tusks. "We'll stay here until you're ready. You learning right now is the most important thing. And of course I'll stay with you. *And* no more going off with investigating drow without you."

"This makes me happy. You make me happy, Hank. My heart never wants to be without your heart."

Want to see more from these authors? Here's a taster for you to enjoy!

Endangered Fae: Finn
Angel Martinez

Excerpt

The figure crouched on the bridge shocked Diego so thoroughly he drove a hundred yards before he realized what he had seen.

A man squatted on his heels on the rail, one hand on a cable, the other clutching a ragged blanket at his throat. Threadbare cloth flapped around bare ankles. The persistent wind yanked it this way and that to show flashes of naked legs.

"Holy shit," Diego muttered, as he wrestled his ancient Toyota into the nearest side street to park. This was none of his business. Didn't he have enough problems? Even as he argued with himself, he ran, dodging traffic and ignoring angry epithets as he pelted back up the bridge against traffic. The inevitable gaper delay had slowed the flow at least, making his precarious journey easier.

People stared from the safety of their vehicles as they inched along but no one stopped to help.

Diego ignored them. His primary concern was to not startle the man into falling. He slowed his approach, ready to offer soothing words, but the man heard his footsteps. Long black hair whipped and snaked in the wind, hiding his face, though Diego caught a glimpse of bared teeth.

"Did you come after me?" the jumper snarled. "I won't go back."

"Go back where?" Diego seized the opportunity to start the man talking.

The jumper shook his head to clear the hair from his eyes and peered at Diego. Black eyes, not dark brown, but black, set in deeply shadowed sockets. "No, I suppose you don't look like one of those," he said in a softly accented, weary voice.

"One of who?" Diego edged closer to stand next to him.

"The ones who shut me in the iron cage. I changed. I escaped." His words seemed to stick in his throat and even above the traffic, Diego heard him swallow hard. "But now I'm too tired. I can't...and the river is so filthy. I think it might kill me."

At least he doesn't sound like he wants to die. "Look, if you don't want the police catching up to you, or the hospital staff, or whoever it is, this is about the worst thing you could do. You're upsetting all these people and attracting a lot of attention. They'll be here any minute." Diego reached out a hand, palm up. "Please come down. Let's get you safe and out of the wind. Then we'll see about straightening all this out."

The man regarded him through the shifting curtain of hair for a long moment. "What are you called?"

Depends who you talk to. "My name is Diego. Diego Sandoval." He lurched forward when the man swayed, his stomach plummeting to his feet, but the jumper retained his place on the rail.

The man repeated his name a few times as if trying it out, then nodded. "It's a good name. Pleasurable to say."

"And you?"

"I am called Fionnachd."

Diego tried to repeat it and won a hint of a smile from the man when he mangled the pronunciation. "Could I call you Finn?"

That got a shrug. The blanket fell back from his shoulder to reveal all too prominent bones. "You could. Some have. I don't mind."

"Climb down, Finn," Diego urged again. "I'll help you. Let's get you somewhere quiet where you can rest."

Finn took his fingers in a light grip and Diego caught a whiff of rotten orange rinds as he slid from the rail.

What the hell am I doing? He could have hepatitis or HIV or tuberculosis, or worse. He's probably crazy. Maybe even dangerous.

The intense plea in those black-on-black eyes silenced his practical objections. Lost and alone, he needed someone. Diego had never been good at walking away.

He slipped out of his trench coat, placed it around Finn's shoulders, followed it with his arm and led him away. His 'latest project', Mitch would have sneered. Not that he should care anymore what Mitch thought.

They reached the car without incident, but here, Finn balked. "They put me in one of those before."

One of...*the car?* "Well, I doubt it was as beat up as this one," Diego tried to joke, but Finn backed up a step. Diego patted the car's roof. "No lights. Not a police car. Or an ambulance."

Finn lifted his chin and sniffed the air. "You do smell kind and trustworthy. But some of the others did, too."

"They probably wanted to help you and didn't know what would upset you. Why did they arrest you? Did they say?"

Finn rubbed a hand over the side of his head, further snarling the mess of hair over the top half of his face. "Indecent exposure. I don't know what's indecent about standing on the dock watching the boats, though."

Irish. Diego was certain he'd placed the accent. "It's usually because someone's stark naked, not because they're watching boats."

"Oh."

He had no idea how much of this was a put-on. No one could be that naïve. Though someone could be that deluded. Time enough to sort it all out later. Right now, he had to get Finn off the street before he crumpled to the pavement.

"Look, this goes both ways. I don't know if I can trust you either," Diego said, as he opened the passenger door.

A Cheshire-Cat grin bloomed under the flying mass of hair. "Well said. You may be the first sensible person I've met since I woke."

Finn took the two steps to the car and let Diego help him in. He gingerly avoided touching the doorframe but finally settled back with an exhausted sigh.

Diego drove away just as sirens began to sound on the bridge.

Wanted: Demon Betrayal
Bellora Quinn &
Sadie Rose Bermingham

Excerpt

Neil set the bushel of summer squash into the panel van with the rest of the produce ready to go to market tomorrow morning and jumped down. Mr. Yaetz patted him on the back. "That's the last one. Good job, Neil. You best head home now. Don't want to get caught outside the wards after nightfall, 'specially not in that fancy car."

Neil stifled a wince and forced himself not to look around to see who might have overheard the mention of his 'fancy car'. Mr. Yaetz didn't mean anything by it, but the car was a sore point with his co-workers at the small greenhouse and urban farm lot. None of them had their own vehicle, much less a sleek convertible sports car. Explaining that it was his mother's, not his, hadn't stopped the digs about his 'slumming with the common folk' or brought him any closer to the camaraderie the rest of them shared.

"Thanks, Mr. Yaetz. I'll see you tomorrow," Neil told him and turned toward the front lot. He glanced at the horizon automatically, judging how much time he had. About forty-five minutes, maybe an hour. More than enough for the short drive home. He wasn't likely to come across any shadow beasts here on the outskirts of the city but a pack hunting farther afield was always a possibility. Of course, if he did run across shadow beasts, they would have to catch him first and the Maserati was both fast and agile.

Neil slid behind the wheel and the powerful engine purred to life. With the sun slowly sinking behind him, he swung the car out onto the road and headed for home.

As expected, Neil pulled into the driveway with plenty of daylight left and no encounters with any creatures that came out after dark. Climbing the front steps, his thoughts preoccupied with a shower and dinner, he almost missed the broken seal on his front door. He stopped cold. The warding glyph, usually a subtle shimmering gold, was inert, dull gray and cracked with lines of black. A sick knot cramped in his belly and Neil pressed his thumb down on the latch and pushed the door open but hesitated on the threshold.

"Mom?"

He listened. No answer.

Neil stepped into the foyer and slowly moved into the hall. A picture had been knocked off the wall and the broken glass from the frame glittered in the fading sunlight streaming in behind him.

"Mom?" he called again, louder.

Something crashed in the kitchen, the metallic clatter of pans hitting the tile floor. Neil ran in that direction.

His mother screamed, "Neil, get out! Get out!"

Heart hammering, he skidded into the kitchen. A black-clad, hooded man held on to his struggling mother. Another man stood next to them with a curved knife in his hand — his eyes were flat black and icy cold as they slid over him. Neil rushed them, yelling, "Get away from her!" The man with the knife lifted his free arm and flung the outstretched fingers of his empty hand at him. Neil hit the stop spell so hard it jarred him from teeth to toes, knocking him on his ass.

"Neil!" his mother shrieked.

He lifted his head in time to see the man who had floored him lift the knife and draw it down the side of her throat and across her shoulder in two professional, vicious slashes. The other man let her go as her eyes went wide and her hands flew up to clutch at the wounds. The blood didn't spray everywhere like it did in the movies. It welled up in a gush of red that soaked the front of her shirt as she choked and gasped then fell down on her knees.

"Mom! No!" Neil scrambled to his feet. The two men moved toward him in unison as his mother crumpled, face down on the floor. Her body sounded like a wet rag hitting the tiles and a shocking pool of red spread under her.

"Take him," the one holding the bloody knife said. His voice was low, emotionless and without accent, like an automaton in one of the old films they occasionally streamed when the comms satellite was functioning.

On autopilot, Neil grabbed the pendant that hung on the chain around his neck and ripped it off, throwing it on the floor. The man reached to stop him, but it was too late. The glass pendant shattered and a wall of noxious smoke rose between him and the killers. It wouldn't hold them long, a minute if he was lucky. Probably less. He turned and ran back down the hall, fleeing the house.

He stumbled down the steps and fumbled the keys from his pocket, hitting the lock button. He yanked the door open and was shaking so badly he dropped the keys on the floor.

"Fuck! Fuck!" He reached down and his fingers just touched the ring as the killers came running out of the front door. Neil grabbed the keyring and jammed the right key in the ignition. For one horrible second, he was sure it wouldn't start even though he'd just driven the car home. The engine turned over as smooth as a kitten's purr and he slammed the shifter in reverse just as the man with the blade grabbed the driver's door handle. Neil put his foot down on the pedal. The tires squealed and the car shot backward down the driveway and into the street.

Blood pounded in his ears, almost drowning out the engine sounds as he threw the car into drive and floored the gas, clutching the steering wheel hard enough to turn his knuckles white. He looked in the rear-view mirror as he sped away. They would come after him. He turned at the next intersection. Then turned again. And again. He tried to focus on what to do next but all he could see was the shock and anguish on his mother's face before she fell, and that bright pool of red spreading out under her. He looked in the mirror again but saw no sign of the men that had killed her. That didn't mean anything. They could come, he knew it. He was heading out of the city following pure instinct, but now he slowed the car for just a moment. At the next turn, he doubled back the way he'd come.

Out of the city might seem safer, but it wasn't. He had little money and the car would take him only so far. He needed resources.

He forced his fingers to relax on the steering wheel but his hands still shook. When he took a breath, it was shaky too. The red had been so stark against her blonde hair. Her eyes...had they been blank before she fell or after she hit the floor? No. No he couldn't think of that now. He raised and hand and swiped at his wet cheeks.

Bone Men. Their name whispered across Neil's mind in his father's voice, from one of his many lessons. Assassins. Twisted by the sorcery that enhanced them, marked by the lives they took. Had she been their target? Was her death retribution for something his father had done? Or…or were they there for him?

His mind raced as fast as his pulse and the car he was driving. He took another deep breath and eased his foot back off the pedal a few degrees. He needed a clear head. He needed a plan. But first he needed somewhere to hide. Instinct told him to find someone he trusted, but his training overrode that idea. He could hear his father's voice in his ear again. *Trust no one, Nielob. If they come for you, go to ground. Speak to no one you know. Hide and wait. I will find you.*

Not if he could help it. If he had his way, he'd lose both the Bone Men and his father, for good. The car would get him a good distance but he couldn't keep it. It was traceable. He'd drive into the city, find someone he could sell the car to for scrap and use the money to get a ticket to as far away as it would take him.

He couldn't take the car directly to a salvage yard without a title, too risky. He needed a fence. Months ago, while he'd been watering seedlings at work, he'd overheard Carl bragging about how his uncle was going to get a real car, one with a combustion engine. No one had believed him and Carl had gotten mad. Insisted his uncle knew a guy that dealt in contraband autos in the city. Hammersfell Road, next to the old Ackard Motors factory. There was a warehouse where they had raves. The fence organized them. Neil had no way of knowing if the bragging was just lies, but he had filed the information away anyway. His chin gave an odd quiver and the tightness in his throat squeezed hard enough to choke him. No. He couldn't give in to tears now. He couldn't afford to let out the sobs that threatened him. A safe place first. The grief tasted of bitter acid and wanted to strangle him, but he swallowed it down and kept going.

About the Authors

Angel Martinez

The unlikely black sheep of an ivory tower intellectual family, Angel Martinez has managed to make her way through life reasonably unscathed. Despite a wildly misspent youth, she snagged a degree in English Lit, married once and did it right the first time, (same husband for almost twenty-four years) gave birth to one amazing son, (now in college) and realized at some point that she could get paid for writing.

Published since 2006, Angel's cynical heart cloaks a desperate romantic. You'll find drama and humor given equal weight in her writing and don't expect sad endings. Life is sad enough.

She currently lives in Delaware in a drinking town with a college problem and writes Science Fiction and Fantasy centered around gay heroes.

Bellora Quinn

Originally hailing from Detroit Michigan, Bellora now resides on the sunny Gulf Coast of Florida where a herd of Dachshunds keeps her entertained. She got her start in writing at the dawn of the internet when she discovered PbEMs (Play by email) and found a passion for collaborative writing and steamy hot erotica. Soap Opera like blogs soon followed and eventually full novels.

The majority of her stories are in the M/M genre with urban fantasy or paranormal settings and many with a strong BDSM flavour.

Angel and Bellora love to hear from readers. You can their contact information, website details and author profile page at https://www.pride-publishing.com

PUBLISHING

Sign up for our newsletter and find out about all our romance book releases, eBook sales and promotions, sneak peeks and FREE romance books!